THE PROPOSITION

KATIE ASHLEY

Adrienne,
Thanks for loving a
douchenozzle like
Aidan! Happy ready
Loved chip
Katie
Ashley

Dedication

For the Steel Magnolias in my life: my late mother who started this writing journey with me, and for my recently departed grandmother for continuing with me down the rough and rocky path.

CHAPTER ONE

Emma Harrison stood back to admire her hard work. A brief smile of satisfaction flickered on her face. Somehow she had managed to perform an almost miraculous undertaking of transforming the dingy 4th floor conference room into an exquisite pink dream. She was especially proud of herself considering decorating and party planning weren't exactly her forte. Of course when it came to selling the image any mother-to-be would want in a baby shower, her position at one of the premiere advertising agencies in Atlanta helped a lot. Cocking her head, she noticed the *It's a Girl* banner was hanging slightly to the left. After she fixed it, her fingertips smoothed over the pale pink tablecloth adorned with refreshments and colorfully wrapped presents for the upcoming arrival.

She blew an errant strand of auburn hair out of her face and tried smoothing it back into the knot at the base of her neck. *Yes, this is exactly what I would want for my baby shower...if I ever get to have one.* A stabbing pain entered her heart before crisscrossing its way through her chest. It was a feeling she was becoming all too familiar with as her thirtieth birthday loomed around the corner, hovering over her like a dark cloud, while motherhood, along with Mr. Right, still evaded her. Being husbandless and childless was all the more painful after her parents' deaths. After losing her mother two years ago, she had sworn she would replace the love she had lost by finding a husband and having a child. Unfortunately, nothing in her life seemed to work out as well as she planned it in her head.

Struggling out of her thoughts, she flipped her watch—the one that had belonged to her late mother—over to read the time. Only fifteen minutes before the guests, mainly her coworkers, started arriving. *Okay, Em, it's time to get your game face on. The hostess of the shower can't let the green-eyed monster of jealousy consume her and cause her to go apeshit, flipping over tables and throwing gifts in a Hulk-like rage! Get a grip!*

The pep talk did little to still the churning emotions coursing through her. She gripped the table until her knuckles turned white. As the silent tears streamed down her cheeks, she quickly wiped them away. Raising her deep green eyes to the ceiling, she thought, *Please help me get through this.*

"You know, I have a nail file in my desk drawer if you want to slit your wrists. It would be a hell of a lot quicker than what you're doing now!"

Emma jumped and clutched her chest. She whirled around to see her best friend, Casey, smirking at her. She frantically swiped the remaining tears from her eyes with the back of her hand. "Jeez, Case, you scared the shit out of me!"

"Sorry. I guess you were just so lost in misery and self-loathing that you didn't hear me say your name."

Ducking her head, Emma replied, "I don't know what you're talking about. I was just checking to make sure everything looked all right before everyone gets here."

Casey rolled her eyes. "Em, what were you thinking agreeing to this? It's slow, emotional suicide."

"How could I not? Therese is the one who got me the job here. She taught me everything I know. She's gone through *three* rounds of In-Vitro Fertilization. If anyone deserves a baby shower, it's her."

"Yeah, but you didn't have to be the one to throw it. I mean, she would have totally understood—especially with everything that's happened lately with Connor."

Emma's phone buzzed on the table. She glanced at the ID and grimaced. "Speak of the devil."

"Is he still calling and texting nonstop?" Casey asked.

"Yep. Lucky me."

"Let me answer. I'll tell that asshat you're going to get a restraining order or something."

"He's harmless, Case."

"You just need to tell him to man-up, grow a pair and give you some sperm."

A giggle escaped Emma's lips. "As tempting as that would be, I'd better pass. The whole sperm/baby thing is what started this whole mess to begin with."

Casey gave a frustrated grunt. "The very fact you're considering having someone donate sperm is ridiculous." She placed her hands on Emma's shoulders. "You are way too beautiful and sweet and amazing to give up on the dating world to have a kid."

"Nice pitch there with the compliments. Have you ever thought of working in advertising?" Emma mused.

"Ha, ha, smartass. I wasn't trying to sell you anything. It's the damn truth. I don't know when you're finally going to believe it. Most of all, I want to know when the men around this city are going to get their heads out of their asses and see it too!"

Emma threw her hands up in exasperation. "Case, considering my biological clock is clanging, rather than ticking, I think it's a little late for all that."

"But you're not even thirty," Casey protested.

"I know that, but I've wanted a baby since I was twenty. I want—no I *need*—to have a family again. Losing my parents and not having brothers or sisters—" Her voice choked off with emotion.

Casey rubbed Emma's arm sympathetically. "You've still got lots of time for babies. And the husband could still come along."

Rolling her eyes, Emma said, "Might I remind you of the idiot parade I have had the misfortune to go out with in the last six months?"

"Oh, come on, they weren't that bad."

"Are we grading on an extreme curve or something? First, there was Andy the," she made air quotes with her fingers, "*practically* separated accountant whose wife tracked us down on our date and proceeded to go mental on him in the middle of the Cheesecake Factory."

"Shit, I remember him now. Didn't the cops get called?"

"Oh yes. I had to call Connor to come get me because they were both arrested for disrupting the peace!"

"So there was one bad seed in the mix," Casey argued.

"Then there was the mortician who regaled me all during dinner about the ins and outs of embalming, not to mention I think he had a pretty unhealthy attachment to some of his dearly departed clients."

Casey made a gagging noise. "Okay, I'll admit that necrophilia could turn anyone off from dating for awhile."

"*Awhile*? How about a freaking lifetime, Case?" Emma shuddered. "Thank God, it was one date, and he never touched me."

"So two bad eggs. There's a whole city of men out there, Em."

Emma swept her hands to her hips. "And I guess you're having selective amnesia about Barry, the dentist?"

Casey scrunched her face up as in pain. "Is he still in jail on those voyeurism charges?"

Emma bobbed her head. "Thankfully, the state is pretty tough on asshats who set up hidden cameras in the *men's* locker-room at the gym!"

"Well, those are the extreme cases."

"Frankly, some of the other girls in our department think I need to write a book on bad dating experiences!"

"Now wait a minute. You've gone out with some decent guys, too."

Emma sighed. "And the instant they realized I wasn't going to bed with them before the appetizer arrived, they bolted for the door. If we actually made it through dinner, then the stench of my marriage and baby desperation drove them away."

Casey grinned. "See you're going about this the wrong way. You need to give in to the idea of throwing caution to the wind and having mindless sex to conceive."

"I don't think so." Emma shook her head. "Just because Connor bailed on the idea of sperm donation, doesn't mean I'm giving up. Somehow, someway, I'm going to have a child to love."

***

Aidan Fitzgerald rubbed his blurring blue eyes. He peeked through his fingers at the clock on the computer screen. Damn, it was already after seven. Even if he wanted to finish the project, his brain was too fried. He could barely make out the words in front of him. He turned off his computer, secure in the thought that his newly elevated promotion of Vice President of marketing meant he could wait until the morning and not have someone bitch at him for slacking off.

With a groan, Aidan rose out of his chair and stretched his arms over his head. He grabbed his bag and headed to the door. As he flipped off his office lights, his stomach rumbled. There was probably nothing at the house to eat, so he'd probably need to pick up something on the way. For a brief instant, he wished there was a woman waiting on him with a home-cooked meal. He quickly shrugged the thought away. A couple of meals weren't worth the hassle of long-term relationships. In the end, he was much happier with begging dinners off one of his married sisters. At least until they launched into one of their tirades about how he couldn't be a bachelor for the rest of his life, and at thirty-two, it was time for him to settle down and have a family.

"Bullshit," he muttered under his breath at the thought. The attractive cleaning lady down the hall raised her head.

She then gave him an alluring smile. "Goodnight Mr. Fitzgerald."

"Goodnight Paula," he replied. He smacked the button for the elevator, fighting the urge to close the gap between them and strike up conversation. He raked a hand through his sandy blond hair and shook his head. Talking to Paula would most likely lead to some tryst in the storeroom closet, and as much as he would enjoy that, he was getting a little old for those kinds of hook-ups.

The elevator jolted him down to the first floor. Heated voices met Aidan the moment he stepped off, causing him to grunt in frustration. Damn, the last thing he needed after working late and being cock-teased by the cleaning lady was to come up on some domestic dispute. And from the tone of both a man and woman's voice, that's exactly what it was.

"Connor, I can't believe you cornered me here at work!" a woman hissed.

"What was I supposed to do? You won't answer my calls or emails. I had to see if you were all right."

"I told you to leave me alone, and I meant it!"

"But I love you, Em. I don't want to lose you."

At the sound of scuffling, the woman's voice raised an octave. "Stop! Don't you *dare* touch me!"

The protective side of Aidan stirred at the woman's tone, sending him barreling around the corner. "Hey! Get your damn hands off her!" he bellowed.

The couple startled at the sight of him. The woman's tear stained face flushed crimson, and she ducked her head to avoid Aidan's intense gaze. Immediately, he recognized her—Emma Harrison, 4th floor advertising, and the woman he'd tried unsuccessfully to take home from the company's Christmas Party. From the way she refused to meet his eye, he knew she recognized him as well.

Aidan turned his attention to the guy, Connor, whose eyes were wide with fear. He hastily dropped his hands from Emma's shoulders and took several steps back. Connor looked like he was ready to bolt out the nearest exit. Aidan then realized how intimidating he must appear with his fists clenched at his side, his jaw hard set. He tried relaxing his stance, but his blood still pumped so hard in his ears he couldn't.

Connor held up his hands in surrender. "I'm not sure what you think was going on, but we were just talking."

Aidan narrowed his eyes. "I think from the way she was crying and begging you to stop touching her, it was a lot more than *talking*." He started to ask Emma if she was all right, but she blew past him and escaped into the restroom. He glared at Connor.

"Look man, you've got it all wrong. I—"

"What's not to get? You obviously can't let your ex-girlfriend or ex-wife or whatever she is go, even though she can't stand for you to touch her!"

Nervous laughter erupted from Connor. He silenced it the minute Aidan cocked his eyebrows at him and took a step forward. "Trust me, you're so very, very wrong. Emma's not my ex."

"Then what's the deal?"

Connor cleared his throat. "Fine, you want the truth? Here it is. I'm gay, and Emma's been my best friend since middle school."

Aidan's mouth dropped open. "Seriously?"

"Yep."

"Huh…then I stand corrected. Sorry about that."

Connor shrugged. "It's okay. I probably would've done the same thing if I thought some asshole was hassling a woman. Well, I probably wouldn't if he was twice my size like you." He glanced past Aidan to the bathroom and grimaced. "Dammit, I hate when she's mad at me. I don't think she's ever been so angry and so hurt. I just don't know what to do to make it right, ya know?"

Aidan shifted on his feet, sensing the conversation was headed into emotional territory, which was somewhere he tried avoiding at all costs. He held one hand up. "Hey man, it's really none of my business." But the moment the words left his lips, he was sure they had fallen on deaf ears. The anguished expression on Connor's face told him he wouldn't be getting away without hearing the full, dramatic story, unless he literally tried to out run him.

With a sigh, Connor ran his hand through his dark hair. In a low voice, he said, "She's crazy about kids, and her biological clock is all in a snit to have a baby for like the last two years. Loving her the way I do, I'd promised her I'd be the father and donate to the cause."

Okay, so maybe that wasn't the story Aidan had expected. "Don't tell me. You chickened out when it came down to doing the deed?"

Connor scowled at him. "Ha, ha, asshole, real funny. For your information, it was going to be done in a clinic."

"Where's the fun in that?" Aidan mused, with a sly smile.

"Dude, gay, remember?" "Sorry." For reasons he couldn't possibly fathom, Aidan was so intrigued by the story he felt the need to prompt Connor to continue. "So what happened?"

"My partner isn't ready to have children. I promised him that Emma didn't necessarily want me involved, but he won't budge. It's been hell choosing between the man I love and my best friend."

"Why can't she just go to a sperm bank or something?"

Connor chuckled. "Emma has it in her mind there will be this horrible mix-up where her choice of a prime donor's sample was swapped with some serial killer's."

Aidan grinned. "I guess I can see her point."

A buzz went off in Connor's pocket. He dug it out and then groaned at the ID. "Shit, it's Jeff. He'll have my ass for coming here and trying to talk to Emma. I really, *really* have to go." His gaze once again went to the bathroom. "I hate to leave her though…"

"You go on. I'll see she gets to her car okay."

"Really? That would be awesome." He thrust out his hand. "It was nice meeting you…"

"Aidan. Aidan Fitzgerald."

"Connor Montgomery." After they shook hands, Connor smiled. "Thanks for all your help and for totally misreading the entire situation."

Aidan laughed. "It was a pleasure almost kicking your ass."

"Hey now," Connor replied. When his phone rang, he winced and gave a short wave before bringing it to his ear. "Babe, yeah, sorry I missed your texts. I'm on my way home now." He pushed through the glass doors and disappeared into the night.

With a shake of his head, Aidan started across the lobby to the bathroom. He rapped on the door. In a shrill voice, Emma shouted, "Go away, Connor! I have nothing else to say to you! Not to mention, you just embarrassed the hell out of me in front of one of the biggest assholes in the company!"

"Biggest asshole, huh?" he murmured under his breath. Not exactly a title he was proud of, especially coming from a woman. He was used to hearing much more flattering descriptions of himself from them. Well, at least in the beginning before he walked away. After that, things usually took a nasty turn.

"I'm not leaving this bathroom until I know you're gone!"

Aidan sighed. She was a determined one that was for sure not to mention stubborn as hell. His mind flashed back to how beautiful and sexy she'd looked at the Christmas party—how the slinky green dress she'd worn flowed over her curves making her irresistible. When he'd seen her across the room with some girlfriends, he had been determined to spend the night with her. Her shy smiles and glances up at him through her eyelashes had spurned him on to close the small space between them. Of course, by the time he'd arrived at her side, her interfering friends had already informed her of his dubious reputation as a heartbreaker and serial womanizer.

"Women," he muttered under his breath as he pushed through the bathroom door. Emma sprawled out on the tapestry settee with a wet paper towel over her eyes. On one side, her skirt was jacked halfway up her hip, giving him a fabulous view of legs and thighs. At the sound of footsteps, she gave a frustrated grunt. She stabbed the air in front of her with her index finger. "I swear if you don't leave me alone, I'm going to kick you so hard in the balls there will no longer be any question about whether you can father my children!"

Aidan chuckled. Her deep auburn hair so foretold her fiery personality—one she'd showed him at the Christmas party. All her bashfulness had evaporated in an instant when she told him in no uncertain terms that she had no desires to be one of his conquests or one night stands.

"Actually, it isn't Connor."

At the sound of a stranger's voice, Emma snatched the towel away from her eyes. Horror washed over her face at the sight of Aidan standing before her. Quickly, she jerked her skirt down and ran a hand through her disheveled hair. "I didn't expect to see you, Mr. Fitzgerald," she said, meekly.

A grin slunk across his face. "No, I imagine you were expecting to get to castrate Connor."

Emma's cheeks and neck flushed the color of her hair. "I'm sorry you had to hear that, and I'm so sorry you had to get in the middle of our argument. As embarrassing as it was—it *is*—I appreciate what you tried to do."

He shrugged. "I was happy to help."

"Well, I am grateful. And I'm sorry for ruining your evening."

Never one to forgo an opportunity, Aidan grinned. "You haven't ruined my evening. In fact, the night is still young, so why don't you let me buy you a drink?"

She twisted the paper towel in her hands before tossing it into the trashcan. "Um, that's nice of you to offer, but it's been a long day. I should probably get home."

"We could walk right across the street to O'Malley's." At her continued hesitation, he laughed. "I promise it's not an offer to try to ply you with alcohol in your weakened emotional state to get you to come home with me." Secretly, he hoped a drink or two might be able to thaw her icy veneer and give him a chance to move in for the kill.

He wasn't too surprised when shock flooded Emma's face. "Really?"

He crossed his fingers over his heart. "Scout's Honor," he lied.

The corners of her lips quirked up like she was fighting a smile. "Okay then. After the day I've had, I could sure use one."

She glanced back at the mirror. "Oh, I'm a mess. Could you give me a few minutes to freshen up?"

"Of course. I'll be right outside."

CHAPTER TWO

When the door closed behind Aidan, Emma released the breath she had been holding in a long, exaggerated whoosh. Deflated, she leaned against the bathroom counter. *Drinks with Aidan Fitzgerald, are you insane?* Every woman in the building knew his reputation of screw-em-and-leave-em, and unless you wanted your heart broken, you steered clear of him. Thoughts of their encounter at the Christmas party flashed like a lightning storm through her mind.

Being new at the company, she had her eye out for any potential single men. After catching him staring at her several times, she'd innocently questioned Casey about who he was. She had shaken her head so fast Emma was sure she was going to get whiplash. "He's sex on a stick, Em, so you need to stay the hell away from him unless you wanna get used!" she had replied.

The other ladies chimed in with very detailed descriptions of some of Aidan's infamous exploits with different women at the company. So when he came sauntering over with his bedroom eyes and swagger, she sent him on his way, tail between his legs with her hard rejection.

She dug her make-up bag out of purse. Gazing in the mirror, she reapplied some loose powder on her face. Her tear-stained eyes needed the works of new eyeliner, mascara, and eye-shadow. As a finishing touch, she rolled a tube of rose colored lipstick across her lips.

Emma surveyed her reflection and groaned. *Why are you even bothering with your face? All he cares about is what you look like from the neck down, preferably the waist!* God, of all the men in the building, it had to be Aidan that came to her rescue. Mr. Manwhore Fitzgerald himself. He was the type of man who wasn't used to ever getting rejected, so he must have a score to settle with her.

She tossed her makeup bag back in her purse. With a deep breath, she headed outside. True to his word, Aidan sat on one of the benches outside the bathroom. He shot up the moment he saw her. "Ready?"

"Sure."

They pushed through the revolving doors and stepped out onto the sidewalk. Emma's heels clicked along the pavement. The warm air from the heavy traffic rushing past them ruffled the bottom of her short skirt, and she fought to keep from having a Marilyn Monroe *Seven Year Itch* moment. "You go to O'Malley's often?" she asked, trying to make conversation.

Aidan nodded. "A couple of nights a week me and some of the guys from my department have a beer. Maybe catch the latest game." He punched the crosswalk button. "What about you?"

Emma wrinkled her nose as they started across the street. "Not really. I'm not much on the atmosphere." When he raised an eyebrow at her, she quickly said, "I mean, it's fine going with you tonight. It's just not some place my girlfriends and I like to hang out."

With his signature cocky grin, Aidan held open the door to O'Malley's for her. "Let me guess. Since you're with me, you won't have to worry about a bunch of drunken assholes hitting on you."

"Exactly. Well, maybe just one drunken asshole." She glanced up at him. "Depending on how much you drink."

Aidan's eyes widened before he laughed. "I'll try to watch myself."

A young blonde stood at the hostess stand. She beamed at the sight of Aidan and adjusted her shirt to give him a better view of her cleavage. He rewarded her efforts with a smile. "Can we get a booth, Jenny?"

"Sure, Aidan. Follow me."

As Jenny sashayed her hips in front of them, Emma rolled her eyes at Aidan to which he winked in response. Jenny sat them at a dimly lit table in the back of the bar. She handed them a menu, and then stared directly at Aidan. "See ya later!"

He gave a brief wave and then turned his attention to the menu. Feeling Emma's heated gaze, he looked back up. "What?"

"Nothing," she murmured.

"If your *nothing* is about Jenny, I told you I came here a lot."

"I didn't say anything," she countered.

"You didn't have to. The death glare you were giving me was enough." He smirked at her. "Since I know you want to ask, Jenny is not one of my conquests, and I've never seen her anywhere outside of O'Malley's. Besides, her dad owns this place, and he wouldn't hesitate to kick my ass!"

For some reason, Emma found that statement comforting. Still, she managed to keep her best poker face on and shrugged her shoulders. "It's none of my business."

He only chuckled as a waiter came up the table. "What can I get you two this evening?"

Aidan nodded at Emma. "I'll have a margarita on the rocks with no salt, please," she said.

"Heineken in a bottle."

The waiter jotted down their order on a napkin and then headed over to the bar. Emma rested her elbows onto the table and put her head in her hands. A long, exasperated sigh escaped her lips.

"Bad day, huh?"

She raised her head, and a sad smile flickered on her face. "Not one of my best. I really can't blame Connor for the worst of it either. It was already shot to hell giving Therese a baby shower."

"Your boss?" he asked, and Emma nodded. The waiter returned with their drinks. Emma took a dainty swig of her margarita while Aidan pulled a hearty gulp from his bottle. An anxious feeling came over her at his curious expression, and she feared he was about to ask a pretty loaded question.

"What was so wrong about the baby shower? Someone get shitfaced on spiked punch and not want to play one of the silly games like Guess What's in the Diaper?"

Okay, so that wasn't the question she was expecting. "How in the world do you know what goes on at baby shower?"

He grimaced. "I have four older sisters. Trust me, I've spent some time in baby shower hell."

Emma grinned. "I guess you have."

"So what happened?" he prodded.

With a shrug, she replied, "Nothing really. It was just harder than I thought it was going to be."

"Because you want a baby of your own?"

She gasped and almost knocked her margarita over. "Wait, how could you…?"

"Connor told me."

Emma widened her eyes as a warm flush danced over her cheeks and neck. "H-He did? W-What else did he say?"

Aidan took another swig before he answered. "That he was supposed to father your baby, but he backed out."

Even though she'd only had one sip of her drink, the room tilted and spun around her. She shook her head, trying to shake herself free of the nightmare turn the conversation had taken. This couldn't be happening. "I'm going to *kill* him!"

"You don't need to do that."

"Are you kidding me?" Emma's voice shot up an octave. "It was bad enough when he was texting and calling all the time. Now he's shown up at my work to harass me. But worst of all, he told *you*, of all people, the most private detail of my personal life!"

Aidan leaned forward, bumping his elbows against hers. "Me of all people…what's that supposed to mean?"

Emma ducked her head. "Nothing."

"Oh no. You're not getting off so easy."

"It's just with the type of man you are, you can't possibly understand my problems or my desires."

Aidan snorted. "Let me guess. Because of my alleged womanizing reputation, I can't fathom what it must be like for you to want to be a mother so bad you'd get your gay best friend to knock you up?"

"That's not what I meant."

"Then tell me."

Emma leaned over to where their faces were only inches apart. "Since you think you know everything, tell me if you understand this. Have you ever wanted something so bad you think you'd die if you didn't have it? That the mere thought of it keeps you up at night. You can't sleep, you can't eat, you can't drink. You are so consumed by that desire nothing else matters, and you're not sure life is worth living if you can't have it." Bitter tears stung her eyes, and she bit down on her lip to keep from sobbing right in front of him.

While Aidan remained silent, Emma shook her head and leaned back in her chair. "See? I rest my case. A man like you can't possibly understand what wanting a baby feels like for me."

"No, I get it. I really do."

She arched her auburn eyebrows at him. "I doubt that seriously."

"Maybe to a certain extent..." A slow, lascivious grin slunk across his face--one that sent warmth to her cheeks and made her squirm in her chair. "I wanted you so bad at the Christmas party I thought I'd die when you refused to come home with me."

The husky tone of his voice startled her. "Excuse me?"

He scooted his chair so close to hers that she fought the urge to back away. She gulped at his nearness. The lustful gleam flashing in his eyes made him like the Big Bad Wolf looming over her. "How much plainer can I make it? You were so damn sexy in that green dress. Your hair was down and fell in waves around your shoulders. And you kept giving me those innocent little smiles from across the room." His breath scorched against her cheek before he whispered into her ear. "I've never wanted to fuck someone so much as I wanted to you."

She shoved him away with all the strength she could muster. "God, you're such an egotistical bastard! I'm baring my soul to you about wanting a child and you tell me you want to...to..."

Aidan crossed his arms over his chest. "You're a big girl, Emma. Can't you say *fuck*?"

"You're seriously disgusting." She gripped the edges of her glass and narrowed her eyes at him. "If I didn't desperately need the rest of my margarita, I'd throw it in your arrogant face!"

He chuckled at her outrage. "Now is that any way to talk to the future father of your child?"

She snapped back in her seat like a rubber band. "E-Excuse me?"

"I'm talking about a little proposition for us both to get something we really, really want. I give a little, and you give a little."

"What do you mean?"

"I'm talking about offering up my DNA for you. Connor said you refused to go to a sperm bank because you might end up bearing Satan's spawn, so I figure I'd make a good candidate."

Emma widened her eyes as the shock waves rolled violently against her. "You can't be serious."

"About which part: me being a donor or that I'm a better choice than Satan's spawn?" he asked, with a wicked grin.

"Both…but mainly that you would want to be *my* sperm donor."

"Yeah, I'm serious."

"Do you have any idea what being a sperm donor entails?" she questioned.

He smirked at her. "I have a pretty good idea."

Emma shook her head. "How can you act so flippant about it? It's a huge commitment."

"Give me a break. We're talking about jerking off into a plastic cup, not donating an organ."

"It's a little more than that actually."

"I had some buddies do it in college. Nothing too strenuous." Aidan shrugged. "Besides, it's not like I'm agreeing to marry you and bring up the kid. It's just a little DNA shared between acquaintances. I'm sure Connor was going to sign something saying he wasn't raising the kid, right?"

"Yes, we had discussed a contract when Jeff continued not to want Connor involved."

"I bet I'm an even better candidate than Connor was."

"And how is that?"

"Everyone wants a healthy, smart, and attractive kid, right? Well, I just got a clean bill of health with my yearly company physical. My family doesn't have a history of any major diseases or mental illness. I graduated top of my class from the University of Georgia, *and* I have my MBA." He winked at Emma. "And I think it's safe to say I'd bring some mighty fine looking genes into the picture."

She eyed him suspiciously. "But what's the catch? No offense, but besides us working at the same company, I barely know you. And what I do know isn't very flattering. Regardless of how lightly you're taking it, offering a part of your essence is a huge sacrifice on someone's part. I just can't imagine you doing anything so unselfish."

Aidan swept his hand over his heart. "Damn, Emma, that really wounds me. I mean, I just put my life on the line not an hour ago when you and Connor were fighting, yet I'm still a selfish prick."

She rolled her eyes. "Just answer the question."

He grinned. "Okay, okay, you're right. My motives are not completely unselfish."

"I knew it!" she huffed.

"Here's my proposition. I offer to father your child, and you in turn, promise to conceive it with me *naturally*."

Fear radiated over her, causing to her to shudder. "Naturally? As in you and I...have sex?"

"Most women would find that a little more appealing than you just did," he mused.

She shook her head furiously. "I can't have sex with you!"

"Why?"

"I just can't."

"You're going to have to give me a reason."

Emma twisted the paper napkin in her hands like she was prone to do when she was nervous. "It's just I believe sex is something sacred and special meant to be done between two people who are deeply committed to each other and who are in love."

His brows furrowed. "And how many times have you been deeply committed to someone?"

She refused to meet his expectant gaze. "Once," she whispered.

"Holy shit." He shook his head. "That's unbelievable."

Emma snapped her gaze up to meet his. "I'm sure it's hard for you to comprehend anyone who doesn't bang everything that moves! But I don't play that game. And yes, I was twenty when I lost my virginity to a guy I'd been dating for over a year who later became my fiancée."

"I didn't realize you were divorced."

"I'm not. He got killed in a car accident six months before we were supposed to get married." Emma fought the deluge of emotions that arose from Travis's memory. Regret was there as much as grief. How many times had she tortured herself for pushing their wedding date back? At the time, she thought she was being practical and sensible. She wanted to finish college, and then she wanted him to get half-way through medical school. That's how she had met Casey. Her boyfriend, Nate, and Travis were best friends at Emory.

Aidan brought her out of her thoughts. Grimacing, he said, "Jesus, Em, I'm sorry."

"Thank you," she murmured.

"How long ago was it?"

"Four years."

He choked on the beer he had just guzzled. After he recovered from a coughing fit, he asked, "You haven't have sex in *four* years?"

"No," she whispered, running her finger along one of the deep grooves in the table's wood. She hated herself for admitting it to Aidan, but he had to understand why his proposition was so absurd. Even though her need for a baby was desperate, it wasn't desperate enough to warrant having casual sex with a notorious womanizer. Or was it…

"Fuck me," he murmured. "How do you stand it?"

Emma narrowed her eyes at his incredulous expression. "When the last four years of your life have been a living hell, sex doesn't really rank high on your list of priorities."

Aidan furrowed his brows. "What do you mean?"

She stared down at the napkin, which now lay shredded in her lap, and tried to keep her emotions in check. The last thing she wanted to do was become hysterical in front of him for the second time that evening. "After Travis, my fiancée, was killed, I just shut down for a year. I guess you could say I was like a zombie. I got up, went to work, and came home. Then just as I started to see sunlight again, my mom was diagnosed with cancer. She was my whole world, and for eighteen months, my entire life was consumed with taking care of her." Tears blurred her eyes. "And then she just slipped away."

At the sight of Aidan's stricken expression, Emma gave a nervous laugh. "I can only imagine right now you're wishing you'd never asked me out for a drink, least of all propositioned me."

"That's not what I was thinking at all."

"Oh really now?"

"If you must know, I was thinking more about how I've never met a woman like you before."

"Is there supposed to be a compliment in there?"

"Of course there is. I'm not that big of an asshole, you know." After she rolled her eyes skeptically, he took her hand in his. "You're like a paradox to me. One minute you're like this fragile flower and the next you're tough as unflinching steel."

Emma couldn't keep her mouth from gaping open. "I can't believe you just said something that deep and sensitive."

"I have my moments," he replied, with a grin.

"By all means, please try to have more of them."

Aidan's jovial expression turned serious. "I'm truly sorry about everything you've been through in the last few years. No one should have to endure so much and do it alone."

"Thank you," she murmured, as she tried not to stare at him like he had suddenly grown horns. Was it actually possible that underneath his self-centered persona there was actually a good heart? One that truly cared about all she had been through?

"And I'm also sorry about giving you such a hard time about the sex thing. It's quite refreshing to meet a woman with old-fashioned ideals."

"You're serious?"

Aidan gave Emma a sheepish grin. "Yes, I am. It's also nice to know that you're very public rejection at the Christmas party wasn't just about me but more about your personal beliefs."

"Honestly, could you be more egotistical?" Emma replied, but she couldn't help smiling at him.

"All joking aside, I can see why you want to have baby."

"Oh you can?"

He nodded. "You've had so much death and loss that you just want a little life in you." He squeezed her hand. "Right?"

Emma sucked in a raspy breath as his words reverberated through her. How was it possible for someone like Aidan to tap into the very heart of her emotions when even Casey sometimes didn't understand her deep desire for motherhood? "Yes," she murmured.

"Then let me give you that. Let me give you a baby."

She fought the urge to pinch herself at the absurdity of the situation. How had she gone from being an emotional wreck at the baby shower to having a man offering to fulfill her wildest dreams? The rational side of her mind railed against her heart. "Do you have any idea how crazy this sounds? I don't even know you! Why are you even offering up a part of yourself to me of all people?"

"I already told you why."

Emma gave a frustrated sniff. "So you can sleep with me. That's your only motivation?"

He gave her a crooked grin. "You vastly underestimate your allure and sex appeal."

"If I'm going to even begin to take you seriously, you're going to have to give me a better reason than that."

Aidan squirmed a little in his chair and cleared his throat before replying. "Well, there is another reason…"

"And?"

He scowled at her. "Okay, fine. I promised my mother when she was dying of cancer that I would have children some day. This way, I figure I can keep my promise with the least amount of commitment necessary."

Although he tried to hide it, Emma could see the pain simmering in Aidan's eyes. It was obvious how much he loved his late mother. "I'm very sorry about your mother," she murmured.

He shrugged. "It was five years ago."

"Why did she make you promise to have children? I mean, didn't she just assume you would have them one day?"

"Not really."

She gave a disgusted shake of her head. "I bet you can't even stand being around kids."

"For your information, I have nine nieces and nephews and a three month old great-nephew. If you talked to any of them, they would tell you what a good uncle I am." He took out his iPhone and scrolled through a few pictures before thrusting the screen in front of her.

"Oh," Emma murmured, as she surveyed the smiling faces. "I didn't realize you had such a big family."

"Four sisters, remember? Plus, we're Irish Catholic."

She nodded. "Aren't you a little young for a great nephew?"

He pointed to an attractive middle-aged woman. "Angela is fifteen years older than I am, and Megan wasn't actually expecting to become a mother at twenty-two."

Emma smiled at the newborn in the young girl's arms. "He's beautiful."

"In nine months, that could be you," Aidan said softly.

Emotions swelled in her chest, and she felt like she couldn't breathe. She momentarily closed her eyes, desperately trying to keep the frail thread of her sanity from snapping in two. The answer to all her problems was sitting directly across from her. All she had to do was say yes, and she could finally be a mother. It was all too much to process, and she desperately needed to get away from Aidan to think clearly.

When she finally opened her eyes again, she found Aidan staring at her. She smiled apologetically. "I've had a lot thrown at me today. I'm going to need some time to think about this."

"I understand. Take all the time you need. You know where to find me."

Emma nodded and then stood up. "Thanks for the drinks…and for listening."

He nodded. "Anytime."

And then she did something that surprised herself. She leaned over and kissed his cheek. When she pulled away, Aidan's eyes bulged. "Goodnight," she murmured before hightailing it out of the bar.

Late summer heat smacked against her face as she started into the night. Drained emotionally and physically, her legs felt wobbly, and she stumbled a little on the uneven pavement. She had just entered the dimly lit parking deck when someone grabbed her arm. Emma whirled around and used all her strength to connect with the assailant's face. Hard.

"Damn, you have a good right hook," Aidan groaned, bringing his hand to his right eye.

"Oh God, I'm so sorry! I didn't know it was you!" she apologized.

"No, it's okay. I was a dick to not call out your name first." He peeked at her through one eye. "Let me guess. You took the company up on their Female Assertiveness Training course?" She bobbed her head. "Yeah, well, they taught you well. I'm just glad you didn't go for the old SING method."

"Oh, the Solarplexus, Instep, Nose, Groin thing?"

Aidan nodded. "Nailing me in the balls wouldn't have worked very well with my offer."

Desperate to change the subject away from his manly parts, she asked, "What are you doing anyway?"

"My car is here."

"Oh, that's right," she muttered, feeling like an idiot.

"And I promised Connor I'd make sure you got to your car okay."

She tried to resist the fluttering of her heart at his act of kindness. "Thank you. That was awfully sweet of you." She pointed down the aisle. "I'm just over there."

"I can walk you." When she eyed him skeptically, he grinned. "You know, to prove chivalry isn't dead and all."

"Okay then."

Their shoes echoed off the pavement, filling the silent parking deck. "So, um, do you live nearby?" he asked.

"No, I'm about thirty minutes away in East Cobb."

"That's not too bad a drive. You know, when there isn't any traffic."

Emma ducked her head to keep from giggling at Aidan's bad attempt at small talk. She must not have hid her amusement very well because he suddenly asked, "What's so funny?"

She smiled. "Oh, I was just wondering when you might mention the weather."

"I was that bad, huh?"

"It's okay."

He grinned at her. "I guess I'm off my game because you're not like the women I usually come in contact with." When she opened her mouth to protest, he shook his head. "Trust me, Em, it's a compliment."

"Oh, I see." Emma motioned to her Accord. "Well, here I am."

"Connor would be proud I got you here safe and sound."

Emma grunted as she fished her keys out of her purse. "If he lives to see tomorrow after blabbing to you like he did. I'm surprised he hasn't taken out a billboard on I-75 saying, "Please Knock Up My Friend!""

Aidan laughed. "Go easy on him. He cares about you."

Her eyes widened in surprise at the tenderness of his tone. "I know he does." They stood awkwardly for a moment, staring into each other's eyes. "Well, thanks again for tonight and for walking me to my car."

"You're welcome." While Emma pressed the unlock button on her key fob, Aidan started walking away, but then he stopped. He turned back and shook his head. "Oh fuck it." Taking Emma totally off guard, he shoved her against the car. He wrapped his arms around her waist, jerking her flush against him. Electricity tingled through her at his touch, and his scent invaded her nostrils, making her feel lightheaded.

She squirmed in his arms. "What are you—"

He silenced her by leaning over and crushing his lips against hers. She protested by pushing her hands against his chest, but the warmth of his tongue sliding open her lips caused her to feel weak. Her arms fell limply at her sides.

Aidan's hands swept from her waist and up her back. He tangled his fingers through her long hair as his tongue plunged in her mouth, caressing and teasing Emma's. Her hands left her side to wrap around his neck, drawing him even closer to her. God, it had been so very long since someone had kissed her, and it had taken Travis a week to get up the nerve to kiss her like this. Aidan was hot and heavy right out of the gate.

Using his hips, Aidan kept her pinned against the car as he kept up his assault on her mouth. Just when she thought she couldn't breathe and might pass out, he released her lips. Staring down at her with eyes hooded and drunk with desire, Aidan smiled. "Maybe that will help you with your decision."

And then he pulled away and started off back down the aisle, leaving her hot, bothered, and alone against the car.

CHAPTER THREE

During the next day at lunch, Casey strolled through Emma's office door and tossed her wallet on the desk. "Do not under any circumstances let me near the vending machines. I have another dress fitting in a week, and it's salads and celery until then."

Emma half-heartedly chuckled. Her mind was still reeling from the previous night's events to be too involved in Casey's wedding dress diet drama. She had spent the night tossing and turning as her mind whirled with Aidan's proposition. But mainly she'd been kept awake by her lips still burning from Aidan's scorching kiss. Her body had ached with longing most of the night as well until she had finally broken down and dug her vibrator out of the nightstand drawer.

After plopping down in the chair, Casey cocked her head at Emma. "What's up with you?"

"Nothing," Emma lied.

Casey eyed her while opening up her Tupperware container. "Bullshit. You look like hell."

"Thanks. I'm going to assume that's the low carb diet stress talking, and you're not just intentionally being bitchy?"

"Ha, ha. You look like you're having a baby shower emotional hangover today," Casey replied, through a forkful of lettuce.

"No, it's nothing like that." She doodled mindlessly on her desk calendar. Although she wasn't really sure she was ready to say anything to Casey about her evening with Aidan, she would burst if she didn't tell someone. At the same time, she knew she needed her best friend's advice if she was really going to take his offer seriously. "Case?"

"Hmm?" Casey didn't look up. Instead, she stared at her salad with a disgusted expression. "You know, I'd kill for some ranch dressing right now."

"I need to tell you something."

Casey snatched her gaze from the Tupperware over to Emma. "Oh shit. I don't like your tone. What is it? You're getting fired? No, wait, *I'm* getting fired?"

Emma waved her hand dismissively. "No, no, it's nothing like that. It's just…" She drew in a deep breath. "After the baby shower, I had drinks with Aidan Fitzgerald."

"Oh Jesus you didn't! Em, I warned you about him!" Casey pinched her eyes shut. "Please tell me he didn't take advantage of your weak emotional state after the baby shower?"

"Give me a little credit," Emma huffed.

Casey's dark eyes flew open. "Then what happened?"

Emma then proceeded to tell her everything from Connor showing up and confronting her to Aidan's offer of DNA. When she got to the part of conceiving naturally, Casey shot out of her chair, sending her salad flying. "Holy shit, Em!"

"I didn't say yes."

Casey's eyes widened. "And why not?"

"Why *not*? You just freaked out two seconds ago when you thought I had hooked up with him!"

"That's different. I know you want a relationship—a *husband*, and Aidan Fitzgerald is *not* husband material. But he's sure as hell stud material." When Emma didn't respond, Casey leaned over her desk. "Why did you really turn him down?"

Emma refused to look up. "Well…you know."

"That's your answer? I can't think of a possible reason to say no! Let me break it down for you. You have the opportunity to get what you want most in this world, a *baby*, from a smart, healthy, good-looking man while combining it with potentially mind-blowing sex."

Emma flushed and shook her head. "You know my experience, or lack thereof, with men. I wouldn't even know how to begin."

"Oh, I've got a million different scenarios in mind right now on how you start," Casey replied, waggling her eyebrows.

"Ew!" Emma screeched.

Casey laughed. "Okay, okay, I won't torture you with anymore innuendos."

"Thank you."

"But," Casey said, holding up one hand, "only if you'll promise to take Aidan up on his offer."

Emma jerked her fingers through her hair in frustration. "Trust me, there's a very insistent but annoying voice in my head telling me to march up to his office this very instant and tell him yes. Like it was some weird twisted stroke of fate that made him appear when he did last night."

"Sounds like the voice of reason talking to you, and I couldn't agree with it more. He's offering to give you the experience of a lifetime, in more ways than one. I mean, if I hadn't been in love with Nate for five years, I would've considered letting Aidan make a play for me."

Emma crossed her arms over her chest. "Oh really?"

"Yes," Casey replied dreamily. "It's like I told you before, he's sex on a stick. Who wouldn't want to experience that at least once in their life?"

"So what you're saying is Nate isn't sex on a stick?"

Casey chuckled. "Nate is barely sex on a low-fat wheat-thin. But I sowed a few wild oats back in my day, so I'm totally satisfied with what I have." She bent over to grab up her abandoned container and silverware. Waving her fork at Emma, she said, "You, on the other hand, have a bag of oats needing satisfying."

Emma rolled her eyes. "Let's leave my oats out of this please."

"Come on, Em. Aren't you the least bit curious what it might be like to have sex with him?"

Heat rose in Emma's cheeks as she thought of Aidan's steamy kiss against the car. If he could get her that hot and bothered in a dingy parking lot, what could he do in the bedroom? "Of course I am. I'm about to hit my sexual prime, so I'm not totally dead in the desire area."

"Then what the hell is the problem?"

Emma pursed her lips thoughtfully. "Okay, here's a really bad analogy for you. Aidan is like the Indy 500 of Sex, and I need someone who is more—"

"Bumper cars?"

"I was going to say the slow lane, smartass."

Casey laughed. "Sorry. I couldn't help going there." She straightened up in her chair. "Go on then."

Emma twirled her pencil absentmindedly. "What I meant is that Travis and I were the same speed. Sure, I'd messed around with a few guys, had some third base action, but nothing like with him. He had only been with one other girl. We dated forever, and he was patient and took his time." She shook her head. "Aidan doesn't impress me as the patient, understanding type. He's more like the 'wham, bam, thank you ma'am' type.'"

"You won't ever know unless you try. And hell, Em, he's not a Neanderthal whose going to grab you up by the hair and drag you off to his cave." Casey paused and licked her lips. "Although that scenario has some kinky potential."

"Case, please," Emma moaned.

"Fine. Here's the bottom line. Regardless of whether you're in love with the person or not, sex is all about communicating. So just let him know what you want or don't want. He obviously wants you pretty bad if he's willing to offer up his DNA for a little roll in the hay, so I'm sure he'll be more than willing to do it your way."

Images of Aidan's fleeting kindness and concern flashed in her mind. He wasn't the total asshole she had once thought he was. "I guess so…"

Casey sighed. "Okay, Em, let's forget all about the sex pressure and about what kind of man Aidan is. Just for one moment think of nothing else but what it would feel like this time next year to hold your very own baby in your arms."

Tears stung Emma's eyes at the thought, and it took her back to what Aidan had said to her last night. A baby—that was the bottom line. Sure, Aidan was practically a stranger to her, but it would be the same thing, if not worse, if she used a sperm donor. She had the opportunity to get to know her baby's father live and in the flesh where she never would if she went to a clinic. She hadn't been left with a whole lot of options, so if she was going to have a baby, this plan made the most sense.

She drew in a ragged breath and then exhaled it noisily. Casey had managed to break down what little resolve she had left. "Once again you've proven you belong in advertising because you've just sold me on taking Aidan's proposition."

Casey squealed as she came around the side of the desk. Throwing her arms around Emma's neck, she grinned wickedly. "Oh Em, just think about the beautiful child you and Aidan are going to make together. He or she will be a hell of a heartbreaker one day!"

Emma smiled. An image flickered in her mind of a baby with her piercing green eyes and Aidan's sandy hair. She was about to make her dreams come true.

CHAPTER FOUR

A few days later when Emma glanced up, Aidan stood framed in her doorway. Cupping her hand over the phone, she motioned him in. As he swept into her office, her attention was reluctantly drawn away from his handsome features and back to the voice on the line. "Yes, I'll set that up. Thanks again." She hung up and penciled in the appointment. Once she was finished, she smiled at him. "I'm glad you could see me today."

"I'm always happy to make time for you Emma." It irked her when he smiled at the warmth tingeing her cheeks. "I'm assuming since you called me down here you're ready to take me up on my offer." He leaned in, resting his palms on her desk. His face was mere inches from hers. "I'm sure you've thought about it long and hard, weighed your options."

"Yes," she murmured, as her body was becoming all too aware of the closeness of his. She hated he had that much effect on her.

"Was it the thought of seeing me naked that finally sealed the deal?"

At his impish grin, Emma rolled her eyes. "Do you think you could muster just an ounce of maturity considering the seriousness of the situation?"

Aidan chuckled and plopped down in the chair across from her. "Fine, I'll try."

"It would be in both of our best interests to enter into this arrangement from a business standpoint. First, we need to submit to blood tests to ensure there are no chances for STD's or other health issues."

"I can assure you I'm clean, but I'll be happy to submit."

"Thank you." Emma passed a manila folder over to him. "I also had my lawyer draw this up."

He eyed it before bringing his gaze back to hers. "A contract, huh?" He leaned back in his chair and flipped the folder open. "Is this one of those contracts like in that kinky book where we outline what we're willing to do or not do during sex? Like our hard limits and safe words?"

Emma felt a wildfire of embarrassment spreading through her cheeks. "Absolutely not!"

Aidan laughed. "Glad to hear it. Just so you know, I don't go in for freaky shit like whips and chains."

"That's so good to hear! Now can you please take this seriously?" Emma huffed. She rose out of her chair and came around the side of the desk. "This contract outlines what is expected, or I suppose I should say, what is *not* expected of you in regards to what happens after you father my child." As Aidan skimmed over the first few paragraphs, she continued. "Honestly what it boils down to is protection for you. It ensures I can never try to hold you to any financial obligations, such as child support or paternity settlements."

"Section Five doesn't seem to have anything to do with finances," Aidan replied, holding out the contract.

Emma didn't have to look at the paperwork. She knew exactly what the paragraph entailed. "Section Five protects me in case you ever try to sue me for custody or try to take the child."

"You think I would do something like that?"

"Well no. It's just my attorney said—"

Aidan's eyes darkened. "This paragraph says I can never have verbal or physical contact with my child."

"I didn't think you wanted to. You said before you never really wanted children or the responsibility," she argued.

"That's true, but what if I change my mind? Say years from now, I want to see how he or she turned out? And what if the kid wanted to see me one day?"

"I don't know." She hung her head and leaned back against the desk. "When it was Connor fathering the baby, I had all the answers. We'd known and loved each other since we were twelve. His parents wanted grandchildren, so I knew he would be involved in some way, regardless of what Jeff wanted." She raised her head to meet Aidan's expectant gaze. "With you, everything's up in the air."

They stared at each other for a moment. Aidan reached in his suit pocket and took out a pen. "Fine. We'll do it your way." He started to scrawl his signature across the contract.

"Wait!" she cried.

He glanced up at her in surprise. "What is it?"

She drew in a deep breath before exhaling loudly. "If you're truly serious about seeing the baby, we can renegotiate."

"Okay. But just amend the part about being able to see the child. I don't want any part of changing diapers or middle of the night feedings, got it?"

She smiled. "I understand."

"So how do we proceed?"

"Actually, I was hoping as soon as possible—well, as soon as our test results come back. I should be ovulating then."

"Huh?"

She flushed. "It's the time when it's easiest for me to get pregnant."

"So we won't be banging 24-7?" Aidan asked with a grin.

"No. That's not how conceiving works."

"What a pity," he mused.

Emma went back around her desk to glance at her calendar. "Would a week from Monday be okay?"

"Sounds good to me."

Chewing on her lip, she hesitated before outlining for him the rest of her baby-making demands. She was embarrassed to talk about some of it in front of him.

"Spit it out, Em," Aidan ordered, his tone laced with amusement. She momentarily narrowed her eyes at him since he was all too good at reading her body language.

"Okay, so here's the deal. It's best if we have sex every other day during my fertile period. Having sex everyday can be counterproductive for conceiving. So would you be willing to meet me again on Wednesday and potentially Friday?"

"A MWF sex schedule? How efficient," he mused.

"Please be serious."

A wicked grin flashed on his face. "Fine, pencil me in. I'll be ready and erect whenever you need me."

"Thank you," she replied, with a tight smile. "Now that's taken care of, where should we meet?"

"I'm thinking you want to keep this as businesslike as possible, so it's probably best we use some neutral ground like a hotel room, rather than one of our homes."

She nodded. "That sounds good."

"Why don't I make us a reservation at the Grand Hyatt?"

Emma's mouth dropped open. "The Grand Hyatt?" she repeated.

Aidan chuckled. "I'm not a Best Western/Holiday Inn sort of guy, Em."

"Oh, no, that's fine. It's just I thought since you were helping me out and all, I would take care of the hotel fee, and several nights at the Hyatt is a little out of my budget."

Aidan shook his head. "No, I'll take care of it."

"But—"

"I think it's safe to say I make a lot more money than you, so let me take care of this." At her sharp intake of breath, he held up his hands. "Besides, you need to be saving your money to take care of the kid."

Even though she didn't like his salary reference, she realized he had a point. "Fine then. You can pay."

"Thank you."

"So Monday night at seven?" she asked.

"It's a date."

CHAPTER FIVE

At the sound of the doorbell, Emma threw on her robe and hurried down the hallway to let Casey in. She barely cracked open the door when Casey demanded, "How are you holding up?"

Emma groaned. "I'm supposed to meet Aidan in an hour, and I feel like I'm going to puke at any moment. I may need a Xanax to make it through the night!"

"I imagined as much," Casey replied as she stepped into the foyer. "Never fear. I'm here now to talk you down from the ledge and to ensure you're looking fabulous."

Emma gave Casey a quick hug. "You don't know how much this means to me."

"Don't mention it." She patted Emma's back. "Besides, you've put up with a lot of my relationship bullshit over the years. I figured I owed you!"

They strode down the hallway and into Emma's bedroom. "So what are you wearing?" Casey asked.

Emma motioned to a rather demure black dress hanging on the closet door. Casey shook her head. "No, no, no! That one is way too understated for something like tonight!"

"Honestly, Case, he knows I'm a sure thing. Why does it matter what I have on? It's not like I'll be wearing it long."

Casey rolled her eyes. "Don't be silly, Em. Men are so visual. You've got to get him raring to rip your clothes off and ravish you the moment he sees you."

"But we're having dinner first," Emma protested as Casey barreled into the closet and flicked on the light.

"Good, let him be at half-mast the entire time and wanting to eat you for dessert!"

"I seriously cannot believe you thought that, let alone said it!"

Casey gave a contemptuous snort. "Well, one of us has to think of these things."

Emma ignored her and went back to the bathroom to start on her make-up. She slid rose-colored blush across her ivory cheeks when Casey finally burst through the door. "Ooh, this one!" She thrust out a short, strapless emerald chiffon dress.

The lilac colored walls of the bathroom suddenly began to close in on Emma. She shook her head wildly at Casey. "No, I can't wear that."

"Why not? It's sexy, but not slutty, and it's his favorite color on you. Plus, it'll show off that fabulous rack of yours!"

A slow, emotional burn radiated through her chest, and for a moment, she was so overcome she couldn't speak. When she finally did, her voice was strained with emotion. "That's the dress I wore to mine and Travis's engagement party."

Casey's beaming expression momentarily faltered, but then she quickly plastered back on a smile. "You should totally wear it again. That was a happy night, and tonight is a happy one because it starts a new chapter of your life, the one where you become a mom."

Emma stared at the dress for a moment. A crystal clear image cut through her mind of her mother, clutching her heart, and smiling broadly. Her mother's voice echoed through her mind the same as it had that day in the store. *Oh Em, honey, that dress is to die for! You'll take Travis's breath away.* She closed her eyes, trying both to savor the memory and keep her emotions in check. When she was sure she wouldn't cry, she opened her eyes and smiled at Casey. "You're right. It needs some more wear and some more memories with it."

"That's the spirit!" Wrapping her arms around Emma, Casey squeezed her tight. "Damn, I'm proud to call you my best friend. You're so strong and resilient with all you've been through, and then deciding to have a baby on your own like this. You're my own little Steel Magnolia!"

Emma grinned. "Who knew it would take casual sex to get you so sentimental."

"I'm just so happy for you, and that I'll get to be an auntie."

"Godmother, remember?"

Casey wrinkled her nose. "I don't know if I want all the moral and ethical responsibility that comes with being a godmother. I'm more the naughty aunt who sneaks them into R rated movies and buys them booze when they're underage."

Emma giggled. "We're going to have to work on that mentality, especially before you become a mom!"

"Bite your tongue on that one, missy. We've got to get Nate through his internship before we even think of kids."

Emma went back to working on her make-up while Casey started in on her hair.
"What do you think? A lose knot?"

"No, Aidan likes my hair down and wavy," Emma replied as she applied some eye-shadow."

"Ah, there's my girl thinking of what Aidan wants. You'll have him eating out of the palm of your hand in no time!"

Emma rolled her eyes. "Why do I feel like Scarlett O'Hara in *Gone with the Wind* all the sudden when she bemoans why women have to act so silly to catch a husband?"

"Well, technically you're not doing all this for a husband—you just want Aidan to spring an erection…or two."

Emma's body shook with laughter, sending her eyeliner arching up her temple. "Case, dammit, look what you made me do!" she said when she finally caught her breath.

"Me? I didn't do anything but state facts."

After cleaning off her smudged eyeliner, Emma flicked her wrist over and glanced at her watch. "Shit! We have to get a move on, or I'm going to be late!

***

Emma stared down at her phone for the millionth time. "Shit, shit, *shit!*" She was now fifteen minutes late, and her original text to Aidan had gone unanswered. She feared he was going to get pissed off and just leave. After all, he didn't have to wait for women—they were usually willing and able at his slightest command. Her phone buzzed as her car eased up to the valet stand. Fumbling inside her purse, she dug it out.

One glance down at the message and her heart stilled and then restarted. "*You sure as hell better get here. Fast. Not settling for a cold shower tonight.*"

"Ma'am?" the valet asked.

With her thoughts consumed by Aidan, she didn't even realize her car door had opened and a young man now stared expectantly at her.

"Oh, I'm sorry."

Emma took the ticket from him and hurried into the hotel. Her gaze swept over the mass of strange faces in the lobby. When she didn't see Aidan, she craned her neck, searching through the crowded room.

Finally, her eyes met his, and she gave a tentative smile. He strode determinedly towards her. At his frustrated expression, she held up her hands. "Oh, Aidan, I'm so, so sorry I'm late. Traffic was a nightmare and –"

He silenced her once again by crushing his lips to hers. He kept this kiss a lot more chaste than the night in the parking deck since they were in the middle of the teeming hotel lobby. When he pulled away, Emma smacked his arm.

"You've really got to stop doing that!" she protested.

"Kissing you?"

"No, interrupting me."

"I'm sorry, but I couldn't help myself. You're like a fucking vision tonight."

She widened her eyes and then smiled. "Okay then, you're forgiven."

Aidan grinned. "Glad to hear it. Are you hungry?"

"A little," she lied. The very thought of eating made her want to throw up. Her nerves were still too out of control.

"Come on." He rested his palm against the small of her back and guided her towards the hotel restaurant. A waiter outfitted in a tux sat them at a table with a gorgeous view of the sun setting over the city. He took their drink orders and then left.

When she reached for the menu, her fingers grazed Aidan's. He glanced up and gave her his signature drop dead sexy smile. A mixture of burning longing coupled with crippling anxiety pulsed through her, and she shifted her gaze back to the menu. *Breathe, Em. You can do this.*

"What sounds good?" he asked, breaking the silence.

"Oh, I don't know," she murmured, keeping her eyes firmly on the menu. Food was the farthest thought from her mind. All she could think about was what was going to happen after dinner. What would it feel like to finally be intimate with someone else again? Most of all, she worried she could never live up to the expectations he had set for her.

Emma was never more grateful when the waiter returned with her margarita. She tipped it up and took a long, fiery gulp, sucking half the glass down. She shuddered when the alcohol hit her stomach.

By the time the waiter took their food order, she had guzzled the scorching tequila heavy drink and ordered another one.

"I guess they make a pretty mean margarita here, huh?" Aidan asked with a tight smile.

She bobbed her head enthusiastically. "Totally."

While Aidan launched into a conversation detailing his promotion to Vice President of marketing and how he was looking forward to all the traveling, Emma worked at draining her second margarita. She barely processed his ramblings about working overseas and within the country for business. Instead, she focused on slurping the liquid courage through the tiny straw. Without missing a beat, she waved the waiter over for another.

Aidan cut himself off mid-sentence and quirked his blonde eyebrows. "Are you trying to get drunk off your ass so you can endure having sex with me?"

"No, no, that's not it at all!" she cried.

He leaned in across the table. "You barely drank half of your margarita last week. Now you're downing them like a lush fresh out of rehab."

Emma drew in a deep breath, deciding it was best to be honest with him. "It's just...I'm nervous that's all."

"About us sleeping together?"

Emma nodded.

Aidan's brows creased. "Are you afraid I'm going to hurt you or make you do something you don't want to?"

"No, it's nothing like that."

"Then what is it?" he demanded.

"I'm afraid of being a disappointment."

His mouth fell open in disbelief. "How could you possibly think that?"

She shrugged. "Because you've been with a lot of women...I don't have the experience. I've only been with one man, and outside of him, I don't know what men want."

"First of all, despite what the rumor mill says my number is relatively low, Emma. It's not like I've fucked half of the city, or I'm Gene Simmons from Kiss. And second, sex is basically the same premise no matter who you're with. Different people bring different likes and desires to the table."

She toyed with the straw in her drink. "I guess I'm afraid once you've been with me, you won't want to follow through with our bargain."

"Like I'd be so turned off by the experience I'd never want to sleep with you again?"

"Yes," she murmured. When Aidan threw his head back and roared with laughter, her lip trembled slightly. "It's not funny."

His amusement quickly faded. "Oh Em, I'm sorry if I hurt your feelings. It's just I couldn't imagine you would actually believe something like that."

"Well, I did." She sighed. "I *do*."

He held up his index finger. "Let me make this abundantly clear. There is no way in hell you could ever disappoint me to where I wouldn't want you." He drew closer to her—his fiery breath singed the sensitive skin on her earlobe. "I get hard just looking at you."

Emma's cheeks flushed at his words. "I can't believe you just said that!"

Aidan grinned. "It's the truth. The moment I saw you tonight I wanted to sweep you upstairs." Taking her hand, he ducked it under the tablecloth and brought it to his lap. "See what you do to me?"

Emma's mouth ran dry at his words, and the fact he was already at half-mast just like Casey had wanted. She ran her tongue over her lips. The way he was staring at her made her body tingle from head to toe, especially between her legs. God, he was so sexy—a little too sexy for her liking. If he was able to get her so hot and bothered just sitting at the table, she couldn't imagine what it would be like in bed with him. In that moment, her anticipation won out over her nerves. "I think I'm ready to go upstairs if you are."

Aidan's eyebrows shot up in surprise. "Even without dinner?"

She bobbed her head.

"Let me guess. You're afraid you'll lose your nerve?" he asked.

With the ridiculous amount of alcohol pumping through her system, she gave him a sultry smile. "No, I'm just ready for you to fuck me." The moment the words escaped her lips, she gasped and ducked her head. "Oh my God, did I actually just say that?"

"You keep talking dirty, and I won't be able to walk upstairs without giving away my condition to the whole room." He quickly signaled the waiter for the check.

Once he had paid, Emma shot out of her chair, sending the room spinning around her. "Oh shit, I'm dizzy."

Aidan grabbed her shoulders to steady her. "Are you going to be able to walk?"

"I think so. But whether or not I ever drink again is debatable."

He chuckled as he wrapped his arm around her waist and led her out of the restaurant. Emma leaned her head against his chest, enjoying the woodsy smell of his cologne. When he started for the elevators, she glanced up and asked, "Don't we need to check-in?"

He fished the room key out of his jacket pocket and waved it at her. "All taken care of."

"Aren't you just the man with the plan," she replied, and then giggled like it was the funniest thing she had ever said. When Aidan glanced down at her in amusement, she shook her head. "Seriously, never, *ever* drinking again."

"Nah, you're pretty cute when you're tipsy," he said, punching the elevator button.

The doors opened, and they stepped inside. The car's jolt upward made Emma's legs feel rubbery, and she clung to Aidan tighter. The elevator dinged when they reached their floor. "After you," Aidan insisted when the doors opened.

"Thank you." But when she stepped out, she turned right and then left, unsure of which way to go.

"This way," Aidan instructed, taking her by the arm.

When they reached their room, Emma's gaze caught the brass nameplate on the door, and she grabbed Aidan's suit sleeve. "What are we doing here? This is a Honeymoon suite."

"Yes, I realized that when I booked it. I was told it happens to be one of the nicest ones they have." He grinned. "Besides, I thought you might be more comfortable doing what we have to do if it looked like we were married."

She blinked in disbelief. "That's so sweet. You've thought of everything, didn't you?"

"Anything to make you more comfortable."

Her heart fluttered at his words. "Thank you."

Aidan unlocked the door. "After you."

CHAPTER SIX

Emma walked into the suite and gasped. A trail of intertwining pink and red rose petals led the way from the living room into the bedroom. On the coffee table, a bottle of champagne chilled in a silver bucket next to two champagne flutes. An overflowing bowl of strawberries dipped in chocolate caused her stomach to growl. She turned her gaze and then followed the rose petals into the bedroom where rows of candles waited to be lit, and a pink wrapped package sat on the bed.

She glanced back to Aidan who was shrugging out of his suit jacket. "You did all this for me?"

"I'd like to take credit, but the staff did all the fruity candle stuff and flowers," he replied, tossing the key card on the table. At her continued bewildered expression, he chuckled. "What did you expect? A single bed and a quickie? I know this is just about procreating, but give me a little credit."

"No…but I just didn't imagine this." She smiled shyly. "For what it's worth, thank you."

"You're welcome."

"What's in the box?" she asked, motioning to the bed.

"Something for you."

"Me?"

He nodded and handed her the package. "Before you open it, let me say this. You already know you don't need to do anything but breathe to give me a raging hard-on—"

"Aidan!" she protested.

He laughed at her outrage. "Anyway, I'm kind of a lingerie man, so I thought you might humor me and wear it."

She opened the lid on the box. After whisking away the pink tissue paper, her eyes honed in on emerald green satin. Her fingers trembled as she reached inside to pull out the baby-doll nightie. The bodice had intricate green and gold beading and embroidered flowers with sheer material that would reach her thighs along with a matching thong.

"Is it okay?"

"It's beautiful," she murmured. The thought of him shopping just for her was overwhelming. Did he do that for all his conquests, or did they come with their own readymade lingerie? "Thank you."

Aidan's face broke into a wide grin. "I don't know about *it* being beautiful. It's more about how you're so fucking sexy when you're in green. Just like that green dress at the Christmas Party and the one you're wearing tonight." He tenderly brushed a strand of her auburn hair out of her face. "That color makes everything about you stand out from your hair to eyes."

"But how did you even know my size?"

"Casey helped me out with that one."

Emma rolled her eyes. "Why am I not surprised? I'll have to remember to thank her for that."

Aidan laughed. "Well, if it makes you feel any better, she swore she'd cut my balls off if I ruined this night for you."

"She didn't?" Emma squeaked.

"Oh yeah, she did."

"Between Connor and Casey, I can't believe you even want to go through with this!"

"It's okay. I work well under pressure," Aidan joked. He motioned his head to the bathroom. "Now go get your game face on and change."

Emma giggled. "Okay, then." She slipped into the bathroom and shut the door, locking it for good measure. She unzipped her dress, and it pooled into a whisper of chiffon on the floor. After exchanging her panties for the thong, she whisked off her bra and put on the nightie. There were no buttons or zippers, just a satin bow to tie in the middle to keep it in place. When she finished, she stared at her reflection in the mirror. "Oh my," she murmured. Somehow donning the nightie had morphed her into a full-on sex kitten. She could practically hear Casey's voice ringing in her ear. *Go get him, babe!*

As her hand hovered over the doorknob, she took a few reassuring breaths before opening it. Aidan had his back to her when she stepped out of the bathroom. The bedroom flickered in candlelight and soft music played from an ihome in the corner. She couldn't believe he was going to all this trouble. In her mind, she'd imagined him leading her upstairs like the Big Bad Wolf and devouring her before she could get the door closed.

She stood awkwardly in the middle of the room waiting for him to notice her. She shifted on her feet, rubbing her bare arms. Finally, she cleared her throat. When Aidan whirled around, his eyes widened. "Holy shit, Em."

Self-consciously she tugged on the baby doll's hem, trying to cover herself a little more. "How do I look?" she asked, as she slowly turned around for his approval.

He closed the space between them in two long strides. Wrapping his arms around her waist, he jerked her against him. His breath teased against her cheek as he whispered, "Sexy as hell."

"Thank you." Bolstered by his compliment, she leaned in and brought her lips to his. This time she slid her tongue into his mouth, eagerly seeking his warmth. His hands slid down from her waist to cup her buttocks. He hitched one of her legs over his hip, grinding his need into her. Emma moaned at the exquisite feeling of him through her thin panties. As he moved against her, she wanted to feel more of him—his bare skin on hers.

She tore her lips momentarily away from his. "Aren't you taking anything else off?"

"I was waiting for you to undress me."

"Oh," she murmured. Thankfully, he had already taken off his tie, so she didn't have to worry with that. Her trembling fingers reached for the buttons on his shirt. She fumbled with the first one before undoing the rest. She pulled his shirt apart and widened her eyes at his sculpted chest. Without questioning herself, she ran her hand down the center of his chest, over his washboard abs, and down to his belt buckle, causing Aidan to suck in a breath and his stomach muscles to clench. Enjoying the effect even her slightest touch had on him, she glanced up and smiled. "Nice chest. I bet you spend hours in the gym." Before he could respond, she shook her head. "Could I sound more cliché?"

He chuckled. "Nope, more like in the pool. I was an All State Swim champion back in the day."

Hmm, I bet you look good enough to eat in a Speedo, she thought.

Aidan's chest shook with laugher, and she realized with horror she had slipped up and said that thought out-loud. "Play your cards right, and I just might wear one for you."

Eager to see more of him, she hastily unhooked his buckle and jerked the belt out of the loops. After she tossed it to the ground, she glanced up at him. His heated gaze burned into her, and she felt a warmth flood her cheeks and go down her neck. She reached up to push his shirt off his arms. It slid to the floor.

Now all that was left was Aidan's pants, and for Emma that was the most intimidating—or at least what was *inside*. Once she unbuttoned his fly, her fingers fumbled on the zipper. When she pushed it down, her hand brushed against his erection. It bucked against his underwear, waiting to be freed to her touch. She leaned in against him, pressing her body flush to his, as she reached into the back of his waistband to push his pants over his buttocks. Her hands momentarily stopped to cup both of his cheeks before grabbing the material. She slid down his body in the same motion as his pants.

"No compliments for my ass?" Aidan questioned, his voice laced with amusement.

When she reached the floor, she cocked her head up at him. "*Very* nice?"

He laughed. "Thank you."

Cupping the back of his legs, she pushed her way slowly back up. Her fingernails raked over his calves and thighs. Aidan never took his eyes off of hers. Once again, she found herself cupping his buttocks as she moved her fingers to the waistband of his underwear. Just as she started to free his erection, he jerked her hand away. When she glanced up at Aidan in surprise, he shook his head. "It's going to be all about you this first time." Then he brought his lips to hers, plunging his tongue into her mouth. She wrapped her arms around his neck as he massaged her tongue with his.

Aidan kissed a warm trail from her mouth over to her ear as his hand came up to cup her bodice. "You have the most amazing pair of tits."

A nervous giggle escaped her lips.

"What?" he asked.

"You sound like a horny frat boy."

He grinned. "Do I now? And just what would you have me call them?"

"Breasts maybe?"

His fingers delved inside the bodice, cupping her warm flesh. When his thumb flicked back and forth across her nipple, she gasped. He smiled at her response. "Okay, you have the most beautiful *breasts*. Is that better?"

Emma arched into his hand. "Mmm, much better," she replied breathlessly.

"I can't wait to get my mouth on them."

She moaned as he brought his other hand to her neglected breast and started kneading them both. In a statement that surprised herself, she asked, "What's stopping you?"

"Hmm, this little bit of fabric. Do you mind if we get rid of it?"

She shook her head.

Aidan brought his fingers to the satin bow at her cleavage. Slowly, without taking his eyes off hers, he slid the ribbon loose. He gave it a slight tug before the nightie gaped open. His gaze dropped to her chest, and he licked his lips. Emma felt the heat rising between her legs, and she shifted on her feet, pressing her thighs together for relief.

Her head lolled back when his mouth closed over her nipple. He suckled it deeply before flicking and swirling his tongue across it. His hand kept stroking her other breast as his tongue worked the nipple in his mouth into a hardened pebble. She couldn't fight the cry of pleasure that escaped her lips. Her fingers automatically went to his hair, tugging and grasping at the strands as the pleasure washed over her.

Aidan licked a wet trail over to the other breast before claiming the nipple. The ache between her thighs grew, and she knew if he touched her there, he would find she was drenching in need for him.

As if he could read her mind, Aidan snaked a hand down her stomach. His fingers feathered across her belly teasingly, causing her hips to buck. He hesitated before finally dipping them between her legs. Emma panted against his lips when his fingers worked against her sensitive flesh over the fabric. Her hips arched involuntarily against his hand, rubbing herself against his fingertips.

"Think we should get rid of these, too?"

"Uh-huh," she muttered almost incoherently.

He chuckled as his fingers tugged at the waistband, sliding the underwear down over her buttocks. Just like she had done to him, his body followed the panties to the floor except he kissed and nibbled a trail down her thighs and legs. She felt at any minute her knees would buckle and give way. Thankfully, Aidan gripped the back of her thighs to keep her steady as she stepped out of her panties.

Kneeling before her, Aidan's fingers delved between her legs, seeking out her swollen clit. The moment he stroked it, she cried out and gripped his shoulders tight. His thumb continued rubbing as his fingers slid into her wet folds. They swirled against her tight walls, working her into a frenzy of desire. She bit down on her lip to keep the ecstatic cries buried in her throat from escaping. But it became useless as he continued his assault on her core and brought her closer and closer to coming. As the wave of her first orgasm crashed over her, she dug her nails into Aidan's back and thrust her pelvis hard against his hand.

Aidan rose off the floor. He kept his hands tight on her waist to steady her as she tried to get her bearings. "You're so fucking hot when you come," he murmured into her ear.

She flushed at his words, her breath still coming in uneven pants. Gently, he nudged her towards the bed and then eased her down onto her back. Pushing on her elbows, she scooted up on the mattress. Aidan loomed over her, desire burning bright in his blue eyes. Emma shuddered under his gaze. As his body covered hers, he pushed her legs wide apart. He then kissed a path from her neck, down through the valley of her breasts, and over her belly.

When his head dipped between her legs, Emma's eyes pinched shut in ecstasy. As his fingers entered her again, his tongue swirled around her clit, sucking it into his mouth. Emma fisted the sheets in both hands. "Oh Aidan!" she screamed. Immediately, her hand flew to cup her mouth. *God, what's happening to me? I've never screamed in bed before.* His fingers kept a rapid pace while he kept licking and sucking at her center.

"Oh yes! Yes, Aidan…please," she murmured, twisting the sheets tighter in her hands. Her hips kept up a manic rhythm as he plunged his fingers and tongue in and out of her. Finally, it sent her over the edge, and she climaxed violently. When she started coming back to herself, she realized one of her hands had abandoned the sheet and had twisted into Aidan's hair.

After she released him, he slid his briefs off, giving her an eye-full of his massive erection. He rose up on his knees between her legs and grinned down at her. "So what's the best baby-making position?"

What the…? Had he seriously just asked her about what position to use. "Um, well, supposedly Missionary."

"Sounds good to me." He bent over her, positioning himself between her thighs. When his cock nudged against her opening, she tensed and gripped his shoulders. Aidan kissed her tenderly on the forehead. "I'm going to take this nice and slow, okay?"

She nodded and clamped her eye-lids shut.

"No, look at me, Emma."

Obeying his command, she peeked up at him. Gently, he started easing himself inside. Emma gasped in pleasure, rather than pain, as he filled her. "Hmm," she murmured when he was finally buried deep inside.

"God, you feel amazing," he whispered into her ear.

"I could say the same about you," she replied.

He chuckled as he stayed stock still for a moment allowing her to get accustomed to his size. "Yeah, but for me, it's more about being able to feel so much. I've never been inside a woman without a condom before."

"Really?"

He bobbed his head. "Guess you're taking my non-condom virginity."

"Oh," she murmured.

Slowly, he pulled out to thrust back into her. "Oh fuck, yes, that's hot," he groaned into her ear.

Once he found a rhythm, Emma raised her hips to meet him. They moved in almost unison, their breaths coming in ragged pants.

But after several minutes, Aidan surprised her by keeping up his languorous pace. It was tender and sweet—almost like the lovemaking she used to have with Travis. An emotional ache burned through her chest, and she shuddered. She didn't like the shift of feelings she had. This was only supposed to be sex for procreation, not making love. When she gazed into Aidan's eyes, she saw the restraint in them. Taking his face in her hands, she smiled. "You don't have to hold back on me."

"It's been a long time since you had sex, and I don't want to hurt you," he replied, practically gritting his teeth from the effort.

"I'm not a virgin, so you won't hurt me." At his continued slow, almost methodical pace, Emma realized she was going to have to reach him on his terms to get him to stop. At the same time, she didn't know if she had it in her to demand what she needed to. Drawing in a deep breath, she smacked his bare ass. Hard. "Aidan Fitzgerald, you better fuck me like you mean it!"

Aidan's head jerk back like she'd slapped him. "Christ, Em, I can't believe you said that."

The usual blush tinged her cheeks, but she shook her head. "Don't treat me like some fragile flower. I want you to enjoy this."

"Fine then," he practically growled.

She squealed when he rolled them over to where she was riding him. He lay still, buried deep inside her, waiting for her to take the reigns. Tentatively, she rocked against him until she slowly started speeding up the pace. Leaning back, she rested her palms on his thighs. She rode him hard and fast, grinding against him until she found just the right spot to send her over the edge again. "Yes! Oh God!" she cried.

Aidan rose up into a sitting position. He took one of her swaying breasts in his mouth and sucked deeply while gripping her hips tight. He changed the rhythm to work her against him, pulling her almost off his cock and then slamming her back down on him. She felt him go deeper and deeper each time, and as much as she was enjoying the feeling, Aidan was grunting in pleasure against her chest.

Just when Emma thought she might come again, Aidan pushed her onto her back and brought her legs straight up against his chest to where her feet rested at his shoulders. She whimpered when he rammed himself back inside her. He smirked in satisfaction down at her, and she knew she was in for it. She had told him she wanted to be fucked, so he was going to give it to her. Hard.

As he pounded into her, his balls smacked against her ass. He groaned as the position took him deeper again. Her cries of pleasure seemed to fuel Aidan on as he thrust again and again. She felt the tension in his body and realized he was getting close. Suddenly, he spread her legs and brought them back to their original position, face to face and wrapped in each other's arms.

When Emma's last orgasm tightened her walls around Aidan's cock, he thrust one last time and then let himself go inside her. "Oh, fuck, Emma!" he cried before collapsing on top of her.

They lay entangled together, catching their breath. "Don't ever doubt yourself again," Aidan murmured into her ear.

"Really?"

He pulled back to smile at her. "Totally."

"Thanks. You were pretty amazing yourself."

"I think I already got that fact from how vocal you were." He pushed the hair out of her face. "You're certainly not shy in the bedroom, are you?"

Mortified at what she might have said or done in the heat of passion, Emma buried her face in Aidan's neck. "Oh my God," she murmured.

"Yeah, you like to say that one a lot, too. Of course, I'm a bigger fan of when you scream my name," he mused. When she continued hiding her face from him, he nudged her playfully. "Come on, Em. Don't be embarrassed. It was sexy as hell."

"Really?" she squeaked.

"Yes."

After exhaling a satisfied little sigh, she pulled away to smile shyly at him. "I guess I got carried away because I didn't know it could be like that."

"You didn't have sex like that with your fiancée?"

"Yes, but I *loved* him." At Aidan's furrowed brows, she blushed. "What I mean is I thought I'd never enjoy sex unless I was in love with the person."

"Well, I'm glad I could prove you wrong," he mused.

They lay quietly for a few minutes. Emma could tell Aidan wasn't one for post-coital cuddling, which further cemented his image as a womanizer to her. She watched as he kept staring up at the ceiling or shifting under the covers. He probably didn't sleep with most of the women he went to bed with. He cleared his throat. "Wanna join me in the shower?"

"Not yet. I'm supposed to wait before doing that."

"Why?"

She blushed. "Are you sure you really want to hear about all this?"

"Of course I am."

Emma couldn't believe that after just sleeping with Aidan she couldn't bring herself to say certain words in front of him or explain to him some aspects of successful conceiving.

He nudged her with his elbow. "Come on, Em. What is it?"

"Fine. I read that you should wait twenty or thirty minutes before using the bathroom or showering. You know, to help the sperm along and everything."

"That's it? I thought by the way you were acting it was something truly embarrassing." Aidan grinned.

"Trust me. Talking like this to you is mortifying."

"Okay, whatever. So the deal with the sperm is it's kinda like a 'you can't go swimming for thirty minutes after you eat' kinda thing?"

"I guess," she murmured.

"What else are you supposed to do?"

"Aidan," she protested.

"Come on. You can do it. You just said sperm in front of me, and I didn't run for the hills. I think I can handle it."

A giggle escaped her lips. "Well, they did say you could put a pillow under your hips. It helps tilt the cervix and uterus."

Aidan shook his head. "Okay, you got me. You said the intolerable word, uterus. I'm outta here."

She swatted him playfully as he pretended to rise out of the bed. He kissed her forehead. "Damn, you're sexy even being embarrassed."

"Yeah, right."

"Seriously, Emma, I grew up with four sisters in a small three bedroom, two bath house. I've seen and heard enough female stuff to scar any guy psychologically for years. I promise there's nothing you can possibly say that will gross me out."

She laughed. "Yeah, well, I'm an only child who took about a year before I could talk about my period in front of my boyfriend."

Aidan then took one of the extra pillows he was propping on and snaked it under the covers. He slid his hand under Emma's bottom, hoisting her hips into the air. "All right, then, it's time to help the boys out!"

She laughed and squirmed against him. "I could have done that myself."

"I'm happy to help." He wiggled the pillow underneath her but didn't remove his hand. "And I'm never going to pass up the offer to grab your ass!"

"Don't you ever stop?" Emma huffed.

"Give me another round, and you'll be begging me not to!"

"We'll have to see about that."

He gave her a wicked grin before flipping back the sheet. "Round Two begins in the shower in fifteen minutes."

"Okay," she replied.

Emma watched his gloriously naked form stride into the bathroom and turn on the water. A shiver of anticipation washed over her at the thoughts of sex with him again. Warmth filled her cheeks and crept down her neck at what she had said and done. But he had liked it, so that was all that mattered.

Time seemed to tick agonizingly slow as she waited to get up. She wondered if there would be any hot water left for her. Finally, she threw back the covers and hurried into the bathroom. Steam enveloped her when she entered, and she heard Aidan humming.

She opened the glass shower door and slipped inside. "Wow, this shower is huge," she remarked.

"Honeymoon suite, remember? They expect couples to be in here together for long periods of time."

"I suppose so," she replied.

He handed her some body wash. She squirted some onto her hand and started to lather it up when she felt Aidan's hands on her waist. When he started to pull her against him, she backed away. At his puzzled expression, she smiled sweetly. "I believe you said it was about me the first time." She reached down to grip his length. "This time it's about you."

Aidan smirked. "If you say so, ma'am."

Her hand, slick with soap, slid up and down, working him into a rock hard state. He gave a grunt of pleasure when her other hand reached between them to cup his balls, massaging them gently. "Hmm, pretty good technique for a girl who claims she doesn't have a lot of experience."

"Oh, but I've only got started, Mr. Fitzgerald."

"Christ," Aidan murmured when she sank to her knees. She ran her hands up his thighs, washing away the soap. When he was fully rinsed, she pressed his legs further apart. With her hand gripping him, she licked a trail from his navel down to his base. The water cascaded over her back as she licked his tip. She swirled her tongue around him teasingly, causing Aidan to groan. "You're killing me."

His breath hitched when she took him inside her mouth. Drawing him in and out, she kept her hand working steady as well. A faint sense of pride filled her when Aidan closed his eyes and banged his head back against the tile. His hands went to her hair, and he twisted his fingers through the long strands as she bobbed up and down on him. When she started to feel like he was coming close, Aidan gently pushed her away. "Don't want to waste it, babe," he replied, when she glanced up at him.

Aidan gripped her shoulders and pulled her up off the floor. Spinning them around, he pushed her up against the tile. He grinned at her as he hitched one of her legs over his hip and pressed himself inside of her. "You got me so worked up with that performance Round Two may be a little shorter than planned."

"That's okay," she panted. She wrapped her arms tight around his neck, pressing her breasts flush against his chest. The water suctioned them together as he began to move. After several deep thrusts caused her to cry out, Aidan glanced into her eyes. "I'm not hurting you, am I?"

"No, you're good."

"Just good?" he teased.

She grinned. "Great, wonderful, magnificent, Oh, God, Oh God!"

He laughed. "You're such a smartass." He increased his pace, eliciting moans from both of them. Just when Emma was getting close, Aidan grabbed her ass and swept her other leg off the ground, impaling her on him. She gasped with pleasure as he banged her back against the shower wall. "Squeeze me tight," he instructed. She wrapped her legs tight around him, taking him deeper when she did. "Oh God, yes," he groaned against her collarbone.

Aidan moved frantically against her. Her back burned from being smacked against the shower wall with his thrusts, but everything else felt too good to complain. Instead, she panted against his ear, crying out his name when the orgasm ripped through her. Just as she clenched around him, he came, pinning her hard against the wall. "Damn," he murmured. He turned his head to grin at her. "Yep, pretty damn good, Ms. Harrison."

She laughed. "Thank you, Mr. Fitzgerald. Think you could let me down now? I'm going to have tile burn."

His eyes widened. "Shit, I'm sorry."

"It's okay."

When she was back on her feet, her legs felt rubbery like they might not hold her. Their position wasn't actually on the "to do" list of conceiving, so she knew she needed to get back to bed. "I better go lie down."

"For the boys," he mused with a grin.

"Yes, for the boys."

After grabbing a towel, she stumbled out of the shower and wobbled into the bedroom. Drying off quickly, Emma grabbed the nightgown she had stowed in her purse and slid it over her head. A glance at the clock on the nightstand showed it was after midnight. She yawned and wondered how she was going to get up in the morning for work. Turning back the sheets, she slipped into the bed.

Aidan stepped out of the bathroom, a towel wrapped around his waist. Self-consciously, she clutched the sheet around her. "Did I wear you out?" he asked, with a grin.

A shy smile curved on her lips. "A little," she replied. She couldn't bring herself to turn away when he dropped the towel and slid on his underwear. But then her heart sank as he started to reach for his pants. "Aren't you staying?"

He turned back to her. "I hadn't planned on it really. But you can. The room's covered for the night."

"Oh," she murmured, unable to hide her disappointment.

She felt the heat of Aidan's stare before he drew in a ragged breath. The bed sagged under his weight when he sat down. "Em, you knew what kind of man I was before we got into this. I don't usually—"

"No, it's fine."

"You sure as hell don't sound or look fine about it."

"It's just you just threw me for a loop with the lingerie and champagne. It all became less business-like and more..." She shook her head. "But I get it now. It's always going to be just sex with you."

Aidan groaned and ran a hand through his wet hair. "I should have realized this would happen," he muttered.

"I'm fine, okay?" At his skeptical look, she sighed. "This is all a whacked out emotional roller coaster for me, and I'm sorry. I'm sure you hate women who get all demanding and emotional."

He grimaced. "Sometimes."

She gave him a sad smile. "I figured as much."

"Actually, it's me I hate this time for leading you on." With a frustrated grunt, he dropped his pants and started back to the bed. When his hand gripped the sheet, she jerked her head up in surprise. "What are you doing?"

"What the hell does it look like I'm doing? I'm coming to bed," he grumbled.

"But I thought—"

"I guess since you're going to be the mother of my child, I can make an exception in your case."

A strangled cry erupted from her lips. The last thing she wanted from him was pity. The moment Aidan got into bed she edged as far away from him as possible. In a huff, she twisted around in the sheets, leaving him in the cold in more ways than one.

"Em?" When she refused to answer him, he scooted across the mattress to her. "Why are you so pissed off? I'm staying, aren't I?"

Emma turned back to glare at him. "I don't want you to stay out of obligation or pity, Aidan. I want you to stay because you wanted to."

"Fuck. I didn't mean for it to come out like that. I just meant that I should stay since you were different than the others...someone special."

She momentarily softened her expression. "Really?"

"Yeah, really."

"Okay, then."

"Can I have some cover now? I'm freezing my ass off."

"Of course. I mean, we can't have anything happening to that fabulous ass of yours now can we?"

"That mouth of yours is trouble," he mused, as he slid under the covers. Surprise flooded her when he spooned up against her, and she couldn't keep the satisfied sigh from escaping her lips.

CHAPTER SEVEN

Sunlight streamed in through the open curtains, warming Emma's face. She rolled over, shielding her eyes with her arm. For a moment, she forgot she wasn't in the comforts of her own bed. And then the revelation hit her. She was in a king sized bed in the Honeymoon Suite at the Grand Hyatt.

When she turned over, she found Aidan had already left, without a goodbye. A pang of sadness crisscrossed its way through her chest, but she tried reasoning with herself that it was already almost miraculous he had stayed the night. She couldn't expect for someone like him to wake her and give her a good-bye kiss. It was way out of his realm of understanding.

She glanced over at the clock and saw it was after seven. If she wanted to make it to work on time, she knew she needed to get going. Slipping on her dress from the night before, she lamented she hadn't thought ahead of bringing something else to wear. At almost thirty, she had never experienced a walk of shame before, and now she would have one. After all, who in the world wore chiffon at seven in the morning?

Thankfully, the hallway was silent as she hurried down the floral carpeting to the elevators. When she got downstairs, only the hotel staff milled around in the lobby. She tried holding her head high as she passed them. She managed to keep her dignity until she gave the valet her ticket. He eyed her attire and rumpled hair and a knowing smile etched across his face. "One minute, ma'am."

Emma inwardly groaned and willed herself never to forget an overnight bag again.

***

She barely made it into her office before Casey stormed inside and slammed the door. "I can't believe you haven't called me!"

Holding up her hand, Emma warned, "I haven't even had coffee yet. I'd hold off on launching the Inquisition for at least thirty minutes."

"Hmm, someone's testy. Didn't you get enough sleep last night?" Casey asked, wagging her eyebrows.

"No, as a matter of fact I didn't."

Casey squealed and then flopped down in the chair. "Deets, Em! I desperately need deets!"

"Then go be a good best friend and get me some coffee," Emma moaned.

With a huff, Casey rose out of her chair. "Fine. But you better give me every single, erotic detail when I get back!"

As Casey stalked out the door, Emma sat her things down and turned on her computer. In the middle of reading her appointments for the day, her phone buzzed in her purse. She grabbed it out and scrolled through her texts. Seeing one from Aidan caused her heart to leap into her throat.

Sorry I didn't say good-bye. You looked too peaceful to wake up. Looking forward to Wednesday---A

Emma couldn't fight the goofy grin from filling her cheeks. He wasn't such a huge asshole after all. He actually cared enough to send her a text to check on her.

Quickly, her fingers flew over her keyboard. *Thanks. I did sleep well last night...well, after everything. I'm looking forward to Wednesday too.*

Casey came in the door with a steaming mug of coffee and passed it over to Emma.

As Emma blew little waves over the dark liquid, Casey's lips turned downwards into a pout. "Em, I really am hurt you didn't call me on the way home this morning. I mean, I've been dying all night and morning to hear from you! I drove Nate practically crazy last night wondering about how you were doing."

Emma shot out of her chair, sloshing coffee onto the floor. "You seriously told Nate about mine and Aidan's hookup?"

Casey rolled her yes. "Of course I did. Don't you think he'd wonder what was up when you turned up pregnant out of the blue?"

"I guess you have a point."

"I think by the end of the night, he was just as antsy to hear from you as well. I think his concern was more about making sure you were okay, and that Aidan hadn't tied you up to subject you to some kinky shit or something."

Sweeping her hand to her hip, Emma gave Casey an exasperated look. "And what did you expect? Me to text you a blow by blow account of what was happening?"

"That would have been interesting. I'm not sure how moans and groans translate in text speak."

"You're impossible," Emma muttered, gulping down some coffee. The warm liquid burned a welcoming caffeine trail down her throat and to her stomach.

"So how was it?"

A flashback of the previous night's events flickered through Emma's mind like an X-rated movie, and she couldn't help blushing. "Amazing."

"So it was everything you thought it would be with him?"

Emma nodded. "And more."

Relishing every detail, Casey leaned forward so far in her chair that she almost face-planted to the floor. "So how many times did you come?"

"Casey!" Emma cried.

"Oh come on, Em! With Nate's crazy interning hours, I have to live vicariously through you," Casey argued.

Warmth flooded into Emma's cheeks. "Okay, fine then. Four...No wait five. There was the time in the shower, too."

Casey's dark eyes widened, and she clapped her hands gleefully. "Em, that's fanfuckingtastic!!"

"Only you would clap for orgasms!"

"I can't help it! I'm just so happy for you."

A dreamy sigh escaped Emma's lips and then she told Casey some of the details that weren't so mortifying. When she got to the part about Aidan staying the night, Casey's eyebrows furrowed. "What's wrong? Didn't you think that was sweet?" Emma asked.

"Yeah, it is but…"

Emma twisted her hands frantically. "Would you just spit it out?"

"I just want you to be careful, Em. You've slept with him once, and you're already starting to invest too much emotionally."

"I am not!" Emma protested.

"Yes, you are. You wigged out when he tried to leave last night, and you're already giddy about him texting you this morning. I just don't want to see you get hurt, okay?"

Emma let her head fall back against the chair's headrest and sighed. "You're right. I am feeling too much." She blew a strand of hair out of her face and gazed over at Casey. "Why does everything have to be so damn hard on me? Women everywhere can drop their panties and have mindless sex, but no, not me. I have to get emotionally invested in a douchenozzle who is only willing to knock me up for his own pleasure!"

Casey laughed. "Don't be so hard on yourself. Even I have to admit that the douchenozzle, as you call him, does have some serious seductive game. Hell, I might've even been tempted to feel a little more with the fact he took me to dinner, gave me lingerie, and stayed the night."

"I need a new strategy. I'm going to have to keep it purely physical from now on out. I'll go in, do the deed, and get the hell out of there."

"That's my girl."

CHAPTER EIGHT

On Wednesday when Emma stepped into Aidan's office, he glanced up from his paperwork and drank in every aspect of her appearance. She knew she appeared so different than how he left her the other morning—practically naked under the sheets with her long auburn hair splayed across the pillow. Today she appeared every bit the seasoned professional woman in her pencil thin grey skirt, black frilly blouse, and heels. She'd also swept her hair into a loose knot. But even as finely dressed as she was, she might as well have been naked from the way he was staring at her.

Get in and get out quickly, and you don't get hurt she tried reminding herself. She met Aidan's hooded eyes and blushed. "Hi," she said, shyly.

"Hello. To what do I owe the pleasure of seeing you?"

Deep breath, Em. You can do this. All he can do is say no…and then potentially embarrass the hell out of you for suggesting such a thing in the middle of the day. Not to mention he could potentially file a sexual harassment charge. She glanced around. "Um, you aren't busy right at the moment, are you?"

"No, I'm in between meetings. Why?"

She chewed her lip Once again, she was unsure if she could actually approach him like this. From the moment she took her ovulation test in the bathroom, her mind screamed how crazy she was to even think of propositioning Aidan while they were at work. The entire elevator ride up, her conscious worked in overdrive to call her a brazen slut for even considering a booty call in the middle of the day.

She tuned the voices in her head out. "Well, you see, my temperature spiked a little while ago."

Aiden's brows furrowed. "You came up here to tell me you're sick?"

With a nervous laugh, Emma replied, "No, no, it's nothing like that. It's just..." She drew in a breath, trying to still her nerves. It did little to help her shaking knees. Especially since she was going to have to talk about more alleged unmentionables again. "You see I've been taking these tests to tell when I'm ovulating and when I'm most fertile. And well...it's now."

He stared at her, unblinking and barely breathing, for a moment before a smirk curved on his lips. "Oh, so you came up here for a fuck?"

Emma cringed. "Do you always have to be so crude?"

He chuckled. "I'm sorry. Would you prefer I call it an afternoon delight?" he teased, seeming to enjoy the fact she was now squirming in her heels.

"Please stop," she murmured. Testing her courage, she stepped closer to his desk. Miraculously, the legs that felt rubbery actually supported her. With him acting like such a sex crazed ass, she didn't have to worry about not feeling anything for him. This was the despicable Aidan she remembered from the Christmas party, not the one who had spooned with her the other night. She realized she needed to file away his behavior in her mind for whenever she started slipping into the emotional land mine of feeling more for him.

Drawing on more willpower caused her to inch around the side of the desk. When she met Aidan's leering gaze, she sighed. "Could you please act the way you did the other night?"

"And how was that?"

She ducked her head. "I don't know...just not like this."

"I'm sorry, Em. It's just I'm not used to being made to feel like a piece of meat in the middle of the day."

She met his amused gaze. "I'm sorry if I made you feel like that. I would much rather have waited for tonight. You can't imagine how hard this is for me. To come up here and proposition you like this is absolutely terrifying, not to mention mortifying. But as much as I hate it, I need you to help me conceive. And I need you *now*."

Aidan shifted in his chair, and Emma could tell her plea was having an effect on him. "I have to admit that you needing me like this is one hell of a turn on, Em," he mused. Motioning to the door, he instructed, "Lock it."

Emma scurried to ensure nobody would interrupt them. When she returned to his side, Aidan pressed the button on his phone. His secretary's voice came over the speaker. "Yes, Mr. Fitzgerald?"

"Marilyn, please push back my 3:00 meeting. I've had something unexpectedly come up." He winked at Emma.

"Yes sir."

"And please make sure I'm not disturbed for the next thirty minutes."

"I certainly will.

Once Emma was sure he had hung up, she shook her head. "Half an hour? Someone sure thinks highly of himself and his stamina."

Aidan laughed. "Never doubt my stamina." Rolling his chair back, he swiveled around to where his knees knocked into hers. Desire burned in his eyes as he brought his hands up and laced his fingers around the back of his head. "Okay then. I'm all yours, babe. All you have to do is take me."

Emma's eyes widened. "But aren't you…" she trailed off, her gaze flickering over to the leather couch.

He slowly shook his head back and forth. "You're the one who needs me. The ball's in your court."

Mortification and anger rocketed through her. He would make this harder on her than it had to be. "Fine," she huffed. Without taking her eyes off of his, she jerked her straight skirt up to her hips.

Aidan sucked in a breath when she flashed him a view of her lacy thigh highs. "Damn, those are sexy," he murmured.

After she slipped off her panties, Emma eased her skirt back down a little and stepped over to him. She would have loved to smack the smirk right off of his handsome face. The amused glint in his blue eyes told her he was enjoying her embarrassment way too much. With more force than she needed, she knocked his legs apart with one of her knees. She then bent over him, bringing her fingers to his belt. His erection already tented his pants. After quickly unzipping him, she started to ease down onto his lap.

"What no foreplay?" Aidan asked, his voice vibrating with humor.

She scowled at him. "This isn't about getting off. It's about getting what I want," she countered, her hand slipping into his underwear to grip him around her fingers.

"Sorry babe. But if *I* don't get off, *you* don't get what you want."

Rolling her eyes, she guided his erection between her thighs. As she slid slowly and deliciously down the length of him, Aidan groaned and brought his lips to her neck. Once he was all the way inside her, he licked a moist trail up to her ear, sucking on her earlobe. "Hmm, someone's so wet and ready for me without even a touch. I must have some effect on you, babe."

Emma ran her fingers through his hair, jerking his head up to meet her gaze. With a smile, she said, "Don't flatter yourself. It's clearly biology. It's the hormones and estrogen, not you, that's got me this…"

He gripped her hips tight, his fingers splaying into her flesh. "Say it."

She hesitated before whispering, "Wet."

Aidan growled and thrust his tongue into her mouth. Emma shifted her rhythm to ride him faster. His hands eased from her hips to the waistband of her skirt. After he untucked her shirt, his determined fingers worked their way down the row of tiny pearl buttons.

Emma bit her lip when his hand slipped inside the lacy cup of her bra to caress one of her breasts. As his thumb pinched her nipple, she couldn't help the moan that escaped her lips. She hated herself even more when Aidan smiled triumphantly up at her. He was determined she would want him for more than just procreating, and it pissed her off she had given in to him. Anger pushed her to rock harder against him, hoping to finish him off quicker.

But Aidan must have anticipated her. He gripped both sides of her buttocks firmly in his hands and then scooted to the chair edge. Emma squealed and gripped her legs around his waist to keep from falling. "Hold on," Aidan said. In one sweeping movement, he was on his feet, sending Emma's arms tight around his neck. His chuckle warmed her ear. "Ease up a bit, babe. I'd still like to breathe."

"Sorry," she whimpered.

He gently eased her down on the edge of his desk, and then brought his lips to hers. Kissing her hungrily, he pushed her onto her back. She shifted her hips and once again wrapped her legs around his waist, bringing him in even deeper. They both groaned against each other's lips at the sensation. "Fuck, Emma," he murmured as he thrust into her.

Keeping a steady pace, he tore his lips from hers to start kissing down her neck. His mouth replaced where his hand had been earlier, tonguing and sucking on her nipple. Emma closed her eyes. Her resolve not to feel anything faded as she panted and pushed herself further into his mouth. When he moved to the other breast, she knew she was close to the edge of coming. "Aidan," she panted.

He raised his head from her breast to watch her as she came. "Seeing you do that drives me crazy," he said. He thrust a few more times and then he was done. "Christ!" he cried out.

They lay motionless for a few seconds, both coming down off the shared high. Aidan raised his head and gave Emma a lazy grin. "As usual, that was pretty damn amazing."

"Yes, it was," Emma replied, her breath still coming in heaving pants.

"Any chance of your temperature spiking again today?"

"No, I don't think so."

"Damn."

She giggled. "Sorry."

Aidan kissed her before prying himself away. As he pulled up his pants, Emma slid off the desk. She readjusted her bra and then shimmied her skirt back down. "Oh, my panties!" she murmured, glancing around the floor.

"I got them," Aidan said, bending over beside the desk. He eyed the lacy black thong with the pink rosebuds before handing it over to Emma. "Too bad I didn't get to see you in just that."

"There's always next time," she quipped with a smile.

He laughed and started tucking his shirt in his pants. Emma slid up her panties and then smoothed down her hair. "Um, would you mind if I used your couch for a little while?"

"For the boys?"

She nodded.

"Of course not. I need to head on down to my meeting anyway."

"So, see you Friday night?"

Aidan winked and then smacked her ass. "See you then."

CHAPTER NINE

Two Weeks Later

Emma tried with every fiber of her being not to eye the red circled date on her desk calendar for the hundredth time. Her period was late--two days, two sleepless nights, seventeen hours, and fifty-two minutes late to be precise. Since she had always been like clock-work, her frayed nerves were working in overdrive. Sure, it was physically possible for the first time to have been a charm. But was it also possible her body was so ready to be a mother and Aidan was such a sex God they had experienced immediate success?

If the glaring circled date wasn't enough to send her over the edge, there was always today's heart encircled one. She wondered why she felt the need to mark it when there was no possible way she could ever forget its importance. It had been seared and branded on her heart and soul.

Today was the two year anniversary of her mother's death.

Just as anguished tears pricked her eyes, Casey popped her head in the door. "Come on, chick. I'm taking you to lunch."

Emma smiled. She didn't bother hiding the fact she had been crying. Casey knew the importance of the day as well. Last year, she had plied Emma with alcohol and chocolate and then spent the night, holding her in bed as she wept uncontrollably. "That's sweet of you to offer, but really, I don't mind just staying here."

"And what kind of best friend would I be if I left you here alone on today of all days?"

"The kind who recognizes how I shut-down emotionally during times of duress and withdraw from my family and friends?" Emma asked hopefully.

Casey snorted. "Nope, it's not happening. You need a bottomless margarita, some highly fattening food, and a dessert dripping in chocolate and calories. And I'm going to have the immense pleasure of supplying it."

Emma knew it was pointless to argue with Casey. Besides, she really did want to get out of the office and try to get her mind off things for a while. So she rose out of her chair and smiled. "Fine then. If you're paying, then I'm going to eat, drink, and be merry!"

"That's my girl."

As they started down on the elevator, Casey asked, "You don't mind if Nate joins us, do you?"

"Of course not. I haven't gotten to see him in forever."

"You and me both. Ugh, I think I'm going to have to start running over to the hospital on my lunch break for a quickie."

Emma rolled her eyes. "You're terrible."

When they arrived at the restaurant, Nate already had a booth waiting on them. He rose out of his seat to hug Emma. "How are you holding up, Emmie Lou?" he asked. She fought the urge to smile at hearing her granddaddy's childhood nickname on Nate's lips. It was one Travis loved to tease her with, and when Nate had overhead him, he thought it was hysterical and automatically adopted it.

Thankfully, Emma knew his question related to her mother's anniversary, not her late period. "I'm hanging in there. Some days are better than others."

He nodded and patted her back. As he resumed his seat, Casey nudged Emma to sit beside him. She knew Casey didn't want her having to sit alone. "No, no, you guys hardly get to see each other," Emma protested.

"It's better this way. I can stare into Nate's eyes sitting across from him."

"Most of all, it will keep her from molesting me under the table," Nate replied, with a wink.

Emma snickered and slid in beside him. Casey eased down across from them. After the waitress left with their drink orders, a sharp pain seized Emma's abdomen, and she gripped her menu tighter.

Casey immediately picked up on her distress. "What's the matter?"

She cut her eyes over at Nate and then back to Casey and shook her head. The last thing she wanted was to discuss womanly issues in front of him—intern or not. And even though he was more than just Casey's fiancée—he was a good and trusted friend—it still bothered her. "Oh nothing."

"Shit, you aren't cramping, are you?"

Emma felt her cheeks warming as she tried to hide behind her menu. "I said it's *nothing*."

Casey rolled her eyes. "Oh for fuck's sake, Em. Nate knows all about vaginas and ovaries, so quit acting embarrassed in front of him."

"I'm not acting embarrassed...I *am* embarrassed!" Emma replied.

Ignoring Emma, Casey looked pointedly at Nate. "You know how Em's been hitting it with Aidan to get pregnant?" He nodded. "Well, she's two days late for her period now."

Emma closed her eyes, wishing the floor would open up and swallow her whole. Nate cleared his throat, trying to ease the tension. "If you are cramping, it could be a good thing. Sometimes when the egg implants into the uterine wall, you'll experience moderate to severe pain that is similar to menstrual cramps."

Casey gave Nate a beaming grin. "Baby, you're so sexy when you spout that medical jargon."

Emma snorted as Nate leaned over the table to give Casey a lingering kiss. "You guys are seriously sickening." Once they had stopped making out, she smiled at Nate. "But thanks for the information. I'm hoping that's what it is."

"I'm hoping for you, too. You'll make a wonderful mother, Emmie Lou. God knows, you deserve some happiness," Nate replied, squeezing her hand.

"Thank you. I appreciate that." She was interrupted by her phone buzzing in her purse. She glanced at the text and smiled.

I don't know if you're still speaking to me or not, but I'm thinking of you today. No one, besides my own mother, meant as much to me as yours did. She always loved and accepted me for who I was. Not to mention she made the best damn chocolate chip cookies I've ever had! I love and miss you, Emmie Lou!

It was from Connor. He had even used her nickname. When she started to text him back, Casey cleared her throat. Emma snapped her gaze up. "Sorry, I didn't think—"

Casey motioned over Emma's shoulder. When she turned around, Connor stood with a bouquet of lilies—her mother's favorite flower. Tears filled Emma's eyes as she popped out of her seat and threw her arms around his neck. "Oh my God, I can't believe you're here!"

"I'm just glad you're hugging me, rather than slugging me."

As she pulled away, Emma giggled. "I guess I left things pretty bad between us, huh?"

"Dude, I thought I was a goner between you and that guy— oh what was his name again? The one who thought I was your boyfriend and was going to kick my ass."

Casey snickered. "His name is Aidan, but I think we can refer to him as Em's prospective Baby Daddy."

Connor's eyes widened, and he staggered back. "You got *that* guy to be your sperm donor?"

Emma shot Casey a murderous look before jerking her out of the booth. "No, not exactly." She motioned for Connor to have a seat. "I think I need to fill you in on some things."

Connor waved the waitress over before sitting down. "I'm going to need a beer…actually, go ahead and bring me the pitcher!"

CHAPTER TEN

Aidan hustled off the elevator from his last meeting of the afternoon. With his new promotion, his days were slammed from the moment he walked through the door until he clocked out. Thankfully, it was only half an hour until he could leave.

He stopped at his secretary's desk. "Any messages, Marilyn?"

She shook her head. "But there's a Ms. Harrison waiting for you in your office."

Aidan's cock twitched at the mention of Emma. The last time she'd been in his office they'd had a mind blowing quickie. He sure as hell hoped that was what she was back for. "Thank you."

He licked his lips in anticipation and pushed open his office door. Any hopes he had of getting laid were dashed the moment he saw Emma sprawled out on his couch, sobbing hysterically. His throat closed in horror, and he struggled to breathe. He'd been accustomed to scenes like these when he was growing up. With four sisters, he'd seen and heard just about everything.

But usually whenever an estrogen shit-storm rose on the horizon, he and his father got the hell out of dodge by escaping to the ballpark or pizza place. No matter how successful in business he was, there was one thing he couldn't handle: emotional females.

Emma glanced up to see him standing in the doorway. Their eyes met, and she broke down again. "Oh shit," he muttered, running his fingers through his hair. He hesitated before slowly walking over to the couch. As he stared down at her, he rocked back and forth on the heels of his feet. Finally, he took out one of his monogrammed handkerchiefs from his suit pocket and handed it to her. "Emma, what's wrong?"

"I just got my period."

He grimaced. "Um, I'm sorry. I've got some Advil over in my desk if you've got the cramps or something."

She blew her nose and glared up at him. "Don't you get it? I got my period, so I'm *not* pregnant."

"Oh," he murmured, finally understanding her major freak-out.

"And I know getting pregnant the first time was a long shot and all, but I can't help thinking what if I *can't* get pregnant? I mean, sure my gynecologist says I'm healthy and capable, but what if she's wrong?"

Aidan opened his mouth, but Emma kept barreling on, her voice raising an octave. "Or what if I just have this huge mental block that becomes a physical one where I can't conceive? What if I wasted all my fertile years and now I'm just going to be barren and alone for the rest of my life?"

She broke down again, her chest heaving from the hard sobs that racked her. Aidan stood rooted to the floor, silently debating about turning on his heels and running out the door. What the hell was he supposed to do with her like this? Reluctantly, he sank down beside her on the couch. Without him even offering, Emma threw herself at him. Her tear-soaked cheeks pressed into his neck while her body trembled against him. He momentarily froze, and she might as well been comforted by a marble statue.

He cleared his throat and tried to get his bearings. "Shh, it's okay. Don't cry," he said, patting her back. That seemed to be the encouragement Emma needed because she then tightened her arms around his neck. Since he didn't know what in the hell else to do, he just let her cry.

An eternity seemed to pass before she had worn herself out. Her breath came in frustrated pants, and her body shuddered. "Are you okay now?" he asked hesitantly.

Emma jerked away at the sound of his voice. Suddenly, a mortified expression flashed across her face. "Oh God, I'm so, so sorry! I can't believe I came up here and freaked out on you!"

"It's okay."

"No, it's not. Shit! When I saw…when I knew I wasn't pregnant, all I could think of was getting to you. I even bypassed Casey's office." She shuddered. "God, I'm so embarrassed you had to see me acting like such a psycho!" she moaned, burying her head in her hands.

Trying to lighten the mood, Aidan said, "You know, you're kinda giving me a complex here."

Emma raised her head. "What?"

"I think deep down you're most upset about the prospect of having to have sex with me again."

She giggled. "No, that's not it at all." Nudging him playfully, she asked, "Don't tell me you are actually underestimating yourself in the bedroom department?"

He grinned. "Not exactly."

"I didn't think so." She leaned over and kissed his cheek. "No, Aidan, sex with you has been the biggest surprise of all in my crazy scheme."

"A *surprise*? You're sure not one for stroking the male ego, are you?"

"Stop fishing for compliments, Mr. Fitzgerald." Emma cupped his face with her hands, trailing her thumb along the stubble on his cheek. "Besides, I thought I did a pretty good job of stroking you the last time we were together." When his eyes widened, she laughed. "And in seven to ten days when I'm fertile again, I look forward to finding myself back in the bed of such a sex god as yourself—as long as you're willing."

"Oh, I'll be willing." He took one of her hands and kissed her fingers. "I could be willing now."

She shook her head. "Seven to ten days."

He groaned. "You love to torture me, don't you?"

"I'm sorry. I promise I'll make it up to you then." Emma gave him a chaste kiss on the lips. "I really do want to thank you though. My freak-out today…it wasn't just about not being pregnant."

"It wasn't?" he asked, warily.

Drawing in a ragged breath, she said, "Today is the two year anniversary of my mom passing away. Days like these are always hard, but then realizing I wasn't pregnant…it was kind of a double blow."

He squeezed her hand. "I'm sorry. I lost my mom five years ago. Her birthday, Mother's Day, the day she died—they're a bitch."

Emma stared in awe at him, and Aidan felt surprised at himself as well. He had never imagined him sharing something so personal, but there was something about Emma that made him want to open up—to share things with her he usually wouldn't dare. "Were you close to her?" she asked softly.

Aidan shifted uncomfortably as a reel of loving memories played like a movie in his mind. "Yeah, I was. Well, I'm still close to my dad. But my mom…." A small smile curved on his lips. "She was thirty-eight when I was born. I was the long awaited son to carry on the family name, and the late-in-life baby."

"I bet she spoiled you rotten," Emma mused.

"She did. And my four sisters." He shook his head. "Jesus, it's a wonder I'm not gay growing up around all that estrogen."

Emma laughed. "No, instead you became a manwhore."

"Hey now," he replied, nudging her knee with his.

"How about a manwhore with a heart of gold?"

"That's a little better."

She smiled. "Thanks for giving me a shoulder to cry on."

"I'm glad I could help."

They sat motionless for a few seconds, staring into each other's eyes. Finally, Emma cleared her throat and stood up. "I guess I better head on home now."

When she started past him, Aidan grabbed her arm. "Why don't you come home with me tonight?" For a moment, he thought someone else was speaking. His voice sounded foreign to him, not to mention what it had suggested was a completely foreign notion to him. He rarely invited women to his home—it was always their place or a hotel room. Only long-time sexual partners crossed that barrier. But Emma was turning him into a total emotional pansy and making him break all his rules. First, he'd stayed the night with her, and now he was asking her to his house.

If he was surprised, Emma was floored. "W-What?"

"You know, so you don't have to be alone with everything that's happened today."

"Are you sure?"

He nodded. "I could throw some steaks on the grill, or I could make us some pasta or shrimp scampi."

"You cook?" she asked incredulously.

"Yes, smartass, I cook."

"I'm impressed. I had no idea you were such a triple threat. I mean, culinary skills, being master of the universe at work, and of course we can't forget your bedroom talents."

He laughed. "I'm full of surprises, babe."

She nibbled on her bottom lip, and Aidan was sure she was waging a battle with herself on whether she should take him up on his offer. "Are you sure you wouldn't mind?"

"I'm positive. We can just hang around and relax."

"That sounds heavenly."

"Meet you outside in ten?"

Emma nodded. "Want to give me directions or just follow you?"

"I can just take you and bring you back to your car."

"Oh no, that's too much trouble."

"Em, it's fine. Why don't you meet me downstairs in fifteen minutes?"

"Okay, that sounds good."

CHAPTER ELEVEN

Emma's mind raged war on herself the entire elevator ride back down to her floor. *You're breaking all your rules going to his house! Remember your 'get in, do the deed, and get out' mantra? Agreeing to let him cook for you and try to console you is sure as hell not a part of that. You're going to regret this!* She had become her own worst enemy.

"Enough!" she shouted just as the elevator doors opened. The two women waiting to get on gave her a strange look. She ducked her head and then power walked to her office. Grabbing up her purse and bag, she slammed and then locked the door.

Once she got downstairs, she paced around the lobby. Just when she thought about bailing on Aidan to preserve her own sanity, he appeared before her. "Sorry I kept you waiting."

"Um, no, it's fine."

She followed him out the side door to the parking deck. When the keyless entry in his hands flashed the lights of a coal black Mercedes convertible, she gave a low whistle. "Nice car, Mr. Fitzgerald."

Aidan chuckled. "Thank you, Miss Harrison."

"I'm impressed I get to be escorted in such style."

He shook his head. "There you go with that mouth again."

Emma tossed her bag on the floorboard and then slid across the leather seat. Besides the fact it cost twice as much as her Honda, it was impeccably clean on the inside. Not a crumb or spec of dust could be found while in her car a small village could have been fed by leftover food of grabbing breakfast or dinner on the run.

"Mind if I put the top down?"

"No, please do. It's beautiful out today."

Aidan hit a button on the console, and the roof started to retract. As they exited the parking deck, Emma dug in her purse for a clip. After sweeping her long hair back, she closed her eyes and let breeze wash over her.

"Don't tell me I'm so boring you're going to sleep on me?"

Emma giggled. "I'm sorry. I was just resting my eyes for a minute."

They weren't on the interstate long before Aidan got off on an exit. When he pulled into an older, established neighborhood, Emma turned to him in surprise. "You live here?"

He chuckled. "What's that supposed to mean?"

She shrugged. "I don't know. I guess I saw you living in a sleek and trendy apartment building with a swinging bachelor pad."

"Well, if you want the truth, I used to live in, as you say, a sleek and trendy apartment building, downtown. But then my sister, Angie, who is a real estate agent, convinced me that I needed to stop throwing money away renting and make an investment in some property. Somehow she smooth talked me into to buying in our other sister, Becky's, neighborhood." He glanced over at her and grinned. "I think it was more on the pretense of them being able to keep tabs on me, but it evens out because I get a lot of free meals." He pointed to the left at an enormous two-story colonial with a wrap around front porch. "That's Becky's."

"It's beautiful."

"Thanks," Aidan replied, making another turn. "She needs a big house to keep the monsters in."

"Monsters?"

"My three nephews."

Emma giggled. "I see."

Aidan eased into the driveway of a two-story brick house with white columns. Emma's jaw dropped at how typically un-Aidan the house appeared. All that was lacking was a white picket fence with toys strewn about, and he would look like a regular suburban husband and father.

After Emma got out of the car, she walked out of the garage and widened her eyes at the emerald green grass and multicolored flowers. "Wow, did you do all this?" she asked, motioning to the immaculately kept lawn.

Aidan snorted. "Oh God no. I can't grow anything but a little mold in my refrigerator. My dad is the one with the green thumb. Not only that, but he's retired, so it's his mission in life to do yard-work for his kids."

"That's really sweet of him." She followed Aidan up the front porch steps and into the house. He punched in the code for the alarm when it started beeping. She tried not to show her surprise as she took in the wide-open floor plan of the living room. Floor to ceiling windows bathed the room in light, and high wooden beams crisscrossed over the ceiling. Considering what she had first thought of him, she expected furniture that was functional, modern, yet cold. Nothing like the warm overstuffed chair and love seat or the antique quilt swept over a couch. "Did you have a decorator?" she asked as she trailed behind him into the kitchen.

"No, I did it all myself. Well, my sisters helped of course. They take it upon themselves to spoil me in all domestic areas." He turned around and surveyed her expression. "So you like it?"

"Like it? I *love* it. You've gone above and beyond just investing in some property. This is a home anyone would be proud of."

A slow smile spread across his face. "Thank you. Coming from someone like you, that means a lot."

"Someone like me?"

He raked his fingers through his hair, stopping to tug at the strands at the nape of his neck. "Oh you know, someone who is real—someone who appreciates a home over a house."

Emma opened her mouth to respond, but a loud thump interrupted them.

Aidan rolled his eyes. "I should probably warn you about Beau."

"You have a roommate?"

He chuckled. "Not unless you consider an eighty pound black Lab who eats me out of house and home and snores louder than a bear a roommate."

"Oh you have a dog!" Emma squealed.

He gave her an odd look. "Damn, I didn't think you'd be that excited about my old smelly Lab."

She grinned. "You don't know how much I love dogs! I've wanted to get one for so long, but my schedule has been so crazy I was afraid it would be alone too much."

"I understand. I actually take Beau to Doggy Daycare a couple days a week."

"You do?" she asked, fighting to keep the corners of her lips from turning up in a smile.

With a scowl, he replied, "Yeah, yeah, I'm a total pussy."

Emma stood up on her tiptoes to ruffle Aidan's hair playfully. "Aw, actually I think it's sweet you do that for Beau." Then she moved her hand down to his chest. "And it just goes to show what I really believed all along—you actually have a heart in there."

"I'm glad to hear I'm coming up a little in your esteem. I would hate to have our future child scarred because his mother thought his dad was a heartless, sex-fiend asshole."

Her face crumpled as she snatched her hand away from his chest. Aidan gave her a sheepish look. "I didn't mean to upset you by mentioning the baby."

"It's okay. I'm way too emotional today."

He cupped her chin and gave her a reassuring smile. "It will happen, Emma. It may be next month or next year, but you're going to get pregnant."

Tears pricked her eyes. "Thank you."

"Even if we die trying, we'll make it happen."

She laughed. "Somehow I think you would enjoy the death by sex part."

His eyes closed in exaggerated bliss. "I can't imagine a better way to go."

They were interrupted by a low, keening howl at the basement door. "Guess I better let Beau out before he has a nervous breakdown," Aidan said. He turned the knob, and Beau came lunging out. He immediately tackled Emma to her knees, but she just laughed good-naturedly. "Down Beau! No jumping!" Aidan bellowed.

"It's okay," she said, as Beau slurped his pink tongue over her cheek. "He's just glad to see somebody."

"He's an obedience school flunkie," Aidan muttered.

"Aw, I'm sure he's really the bestest boy in the whole wide world! Aren't you sweetheart?" Emma said, her voice raising an octave. Beau wiggled all over at her attention, his tail thawping against Aidan's leg. He went into doggie heaven when she started scratching behind his ears, making grunting noises and finally sitting stock still.

"Okay, boy, time to go outside."

Beau refused to budge from Emma. Aidan rolled his eyes in exasperation. "Outside. Now!"

Emma kissed the top of Beau's head and then rose to her feet. "You better go on outside before you get us both in trouble," she said, pointing to the backdoor.

Beau reluctantly started across the kitchen, his claws tapping across the hardwood floors. Aidan opened the door and let him out into the backyard. He shook his head as Beau frolicked after a butterfly. "Great. He's already totally whipped by you."

"I can't help that everyone, even animals, love me," Emma joked.

Aidan turned back to her and grinned. "Someone is cocky tonight." His eyes widened at the sight of her legs. "Oh shit, I'm sorry."

Emma glanced down to see the ragged holes where Beau's claws had snagged her stockings. "It's no big deal."

"You want something to change into?"

She bobbed her head. "That would be great, thanks."

"Follow me."

Emma fell in step behind Aidan as they started down the hallway. She wasn't too thrilled at the prospect of following him into the master bedroom, so she stopped in front of a wall of pictures. "Are these all of your family?"

Aidan turned back and then nodded. "Yeah, Angie, did that for me. She got all the pictures together and then arranged them for me as a house warming present."

"She did a great job." As Aidan dipped back inside the bedroom, Emma continued gazing at the photographs. Aidan was the spitting image of his late mother. Several of the pictures were of his parents when they were younger and older. "I love this one of your parent's at their 50th Wedding Anniversary. Your mother was so beautiful," she called.

"Thanks."

"And your dad is handsome, too."

"I told you I'd bring some attractive genes to the table!"

She rolled her eyes at his cockiness. "Your dad looks like a really sweet and nice man."

Aidan poked his head out of the bedroom door. "What's that supposed to mean?"

Emma shrugged. "I don't know. I guess I had this impression of your dad being like Hugh Hefner, and you following in his footsteps."

Aidan laughed as he handed her a pair of navy sweat pants and a white t-shirt. "Trust me, my dad is the farthest thing from Hef. My parents were high school sweethearts. I'm not sure if he ever slept with anyone but Mom. She's been gone five years, and he's barely dated at all."

"That's so romantic," Emma gushed.

"Yeah, but he's lonely. If he's not hounding one of my sisters, he's calling me, guilting me to come visit. I know he'd like someone to be there with him all the time, but he just can't seem to let go of Mom. I keep telling him to move on, but he just refuses."

Emma grew exasperated at his tone. "Maybe he's not ready yet. Maybe a love as strong as theirs isn't so easy to get over as you think," she countered.

"I guess. But Jesus, he needs to lighten up on the expectations that I should always be at his beck and call."

Emma threw her hands up in exasperation, unable to hold her temper any longer. "Has he been a good father to you or not?"

"Yeah, of course he has."

"Then he shouldn't have to call you to beg you to come by. You should be the one calling him and checking to see how he's doing. Maybe paying him back for some of the sacrifices he made while you were growing up."

"I know, it's just—"

"Trust me when I say this Aidan, he won't be here forever. I did everything I could for my mother while she was alive, and sometimes guilt still consumes me. I wouldn't ever want you to be haunted by regrets."

"Damn, Em, you make me feel like a real asshole."

With her anger evaporating, she suddenly felt embarrassed for going off on him. She ducked her head. "I'm sorry. I just know you have a really good heart, that's all."

"Then if you believe in me that much, I'll do better, okay?"

She peeked up at him through her lashes and smiled. "Okay."

He cleared his throat and motioned across the hall. "You can go change in the bathroom."

"Thanks. I probably need to wash my face too after my crying tirade. I'm probably a mess."

"Would you like to take a shower while I fix dinner?"

"Are you insinuating I stink?" she asked, with a grin.

Aidan chuckled. "No, I just thought it might make you feel better. If you want, you can soak in the Jacuzzi tub."

Emma closed her eyes and sighed. "That would be fabulous."

"Come on then."

She followed him into the bedroom. With its light blue walls and white trim, it had an airy, cozy feel. She fought the urge to giggle at what she had imagined of his bedroom—silk sheets, a mirror over the bed, and black or red walls.

It was quite the opposite. An enormous four-poster bed sat in the middle of the room. The only thing that stood out to her was how neat and organized everything was. "You must pay a fortune to your cleaning lady," she mused.

"I don't have one."

"You do all this yourself?"

Yeah, I like cleaning."

After peeking in the bathroom, Emma mused, "Looks like you're kind of a neat freak, huh?"

"I might be just a little anal retentive about everything being in order."

"Hmm."

"And what's that supposed to mean?" he asked, sweeping his hands to his hips.

"Nothing."

"Let me guess. You took a few psych courses in college, and the experts say that most often obsessively clean people are trying to put order into a life of emotional chaos?"

"I didn't say that."

He snorted. "You didn't have to, Dr. Phil. Now if you're through analyzing me, I'll let you go and take your bath."

"I appreciate it."

After she closed the door behind Aidan, she turned on the water. Slipping out of her clothes, she tried stripping herself of the day's stress. Once the tub filled up, she turned on the jets. She eased down into the bubbling water and sighed with contentment. She had just laid her head back when the door burst open.

With a shriek, she rushed to cover her breasts with her hands. Aidan chuckled. "Jesus, Em, there's no need to panic. I've seen everything you've got, remember?"

Warmth rushed to her cheeks. "I know. You surprised me, that's all."

He held up her purse. "You left this in the kitchen, and I thought you might need it."

She nodded. "Thank you."

Aidan sat the purse on the vanity. "Okay, I'm really going this time, and I promise to leave you in peace."

Emma giggled and then eased back into the tub after he closed the door. She probably could have stayed in for hours, but when her fingers started pruning and wonderful aromas started wafting back to her, she figured it was time to get out.

After drying off, she pulled on Aidan's clothes and swept her hair back into a ponytail. When she grabbed her purse, her phone buzzed. She had missed a text from Casey. *Haven't seen you since lunch. Hope you're okay.*

Emma fought the desperate sobs that threatened to overtake her. With trembling fingers, she texted Casey. *Got my period. I'm at Aidan's. Call u tomorrow.*

It only took a second for Casey to reply. *So, so sorry, babe. I'm here for you. Love ya.*

Emma couldn't help feeling surprised at Casey's reaction. She had expected her to demand to know what the hell she was doing at Aidan's rather than throwing back margaritas with her. At the very least, Emma thought she would have discouraged her for spending any time with Aidan that didn't involve baby-making.

With a sigh, she stuffed her phone back in her purse and then started out of the bedroom.

CHAPTER TWELVE

When she got to the living room, she could hear Aidan humming along with the kitchen radio. She peeked around the corner and watched in amazement as he cooked. How was it possible that this Aidan could be the same cocky, self-absorbed womanizer who sometimes drove her crazy? It was like he was two people inhabiting the same body.

Aidan caught her staring, and she smiled shyly at him as she padded barefoot into the kitchen. She inhaled deeply. "Something smells wonderful."

A pleased expression grew on his face. "I decided on the scampi. I thought we could eat out on the patio if that's okay?"

She nodded. "Sounds great."

He opened the back door, and she stepped outside. Beau came galloping up to her. "Down boy! Don't even think about it!" Aidan shouted.

Beau reluctantly nudged Emma's legs. "Good boy," she replied, rewarding him with a scratch behind the ears. As she gazed around the immaculately kept patio and backyard, her eyes widened at the sight of an in-ground pool. "This is all so beautiful."

"Thank you."

He held out a chair for her, and she eased up to the table. He already had it set it for them complete with linen napkins. A glance at her full plate of scampi sent her stomach growling. When Aidan sat down, she smiled at him. "I can't thank you enough for the bath and the clothes. I feel like a new person."

"You're welcome."

After taking a bite of pasta, she glanced up to find Aidan staring at her chest. Self-consciously, she crossed her arms over her breasts, trying to hide the fact they kept straining against the material. She cleared her throat, and he quickly looked away. "Aidan Fitzgerald, are you staring at my boobs like a horny teenage boy?"

He gave her a sheepish grin. "It's kinda hard not to when they're about to bust out of the shirt."

She huffed exasperatedly. "Well, I hated to stretch it since it isn't mine, and it fits everywhere but the chest." She glanced down and shuddered. "Ugh, I so want to get a breast reduction."

"Jesus, why would you ever want to do that? Your breasts are amazing."

Emma rolled her eyes. "That's such a man thing to say. You have no idea what a real pain they are. My back kills me, not mention it's hard finding shirts to fit. Then there's the whole factor of them getting bigger when you're pregnant."

Aidan licked his lips. "They do?"

"Yes, pervert, they do."

He laughed. "Sorry, but I'm a total boob man, so that prospect really turns me on."

"A boob man as opposed to what? An ass or a thigh man?"

He nodded. "Of course, it goes without saying that both your ass and thighs are amazing, too."

She gave him a sarcastic smile. "Oh, thank you so much. Here I was worrying that they were hideous, and you'd been traumatized to have to see them. Glad I'll rest easy tonight."

"I'll overlook that sassiness considering the day you've had. Instead, I'll offer you more wine," he remarked.

She held up her glass. "Thank you. It's delicious."

As he poured, Emma glanced out over the fading sunlight shimmering across the water. "I've got to say I'm more than a little jealous of your pool."

It's actually what sold me on this place. Like I told you before, swimming was my passion growing up, and after I left home, I always wanted another pool." He took a sip of wine and then turned his intense gaze on her. "So what was your passion when you were younger?"

"Hmm, it's probably a total cliché but singing." She ran her fingers over the rim of her wine glass. "Well, I guess it still is my passion."

"Really?"

Emma was shocked by the eager expression on Aidan's face. "Yeah, my family is really big on Bluegrass and Country. I grew up singing with a band that's made up of five of my male cousins. We would play at festivals and at the bar my Uncle Gary owns." Emma laughed. "I guess you would call it a honky-tonk more than anything."

He shook his head. "Why is it almost impossible for me to picture you singing in a smoky, rough and tumble bar?"

"Oh, I didn't just sing there. I did at church, too."

Aidan grinned knowingly. "Ah, you're a church girl. That explains a lot."

She stopped swirling the pasta around on her fork and shot him a look. "What's that supposed to mean?"

"Now I know why you felt the way you did about sleeping with me—why you don't have any sexual partners in your past besides your fiancée."

"Having morality and spirituality aren't bad things," she countered.

"I didn't say they were. In fact, it's what I like most about you."

Emma snorted. "You can't be serious."

"Well, I am." He moved his hand across the table to graze his fingers against hers. "Until I met you, I never knew innocence could be so damn sexy."

Although her cheeks warmed at his compliments, she couldn't help the smirk that curved on her lips. "You really are a smooth one, aren't you?"

Aidan jerked his hand away from hers and crossed his arms over his chest. "I didn't realize I was being smooth at the moment. I was just trying to flatter you a little."

Emma chewed thoughtfully on a bite of shrimp. "I think it oozes so naturally you don't even realize you're doing it. I think you'd even manage to do it in a coma."

"Oh really?"

"Yeah, all your nurses would be fawning over you—even the male ones. You would probably end up getting really shitty care. Not to mention there would probably be a daily fist fight over who got to give your sponge bath."

Aidan threw his head back and roared with laughter. When he gazed at her, his blue eyes twinkled with amusement. "Jesus, Em, I don't think I've ever laughed with a woman as much as I have with you."

"I assume that's a compliment, right?"

"Oh yes, a big one."

Emma nibbled on the edge of her fork, trying to decide whether she had the courage to ask the question that had been plaguing her for a while. "So have you really never been in love before?"

Aidan choked on the bite of scampi he had taken. He succumbed to a coughing fit before taking a long gulp of wine. "That one came out of nowhere," he replied, in a strangled voice.

"Not really. You just want to avoid the question."

He made a frustrated noise in the back of his throat. After staring out at the glimmering water, he finally said, "Yes, I have been in love before. Are you happy now?"

"That's all I get?"

"Were you hoping for some salacious details?"

Emma grinned. "Maybe."

"Well, I think that's enough for tonight." He picked up her empty plate and started to rise out of his chair when she reached over and lightly touched his arm. Emma could see the struggle in his eyes, not to mention he kept clenching and unclenching his jaw. He appeared to internally bashing himself about whether to be honest with her.

Not wanting to cause him pain, she shook her head. "It's okay. You don't have to tell me. It was rude to ask."

"No, no, I'll give you the gory details," he replied, easing back down.

Emma's jaw dropped open. She couldn't help leaning forward, expectantly waiting to hang onto every word. Between hearing about his parents and now his love life, so many pieces of Aidan's puzzle were coming together.

"Her name was Amy, and we were fifteen. We were both on our high school's swim-teams. She was my first relationship, my first sexual experience, and…" He fidgeted in his chair. "The first girl's heart I broke."

Emma's own heart suddenly ached for a girl she didn't even know. "Why did you break-up?"

"We dated through high school and tried making it work the first semester of college, but my heart just wasn't in it anymore. More than anything, I didn't want to be tied down. So I got the wandering eye."

"She caught you cheating?"

Aidan rubbed his hands over his face. "Fuck, I can't believe I'm telling you all this."

"Please finish."

"No, I broke it off before she found out. Then three years later, I ran into her at a friend's wedding, and we started seeing each other again. Neither one of us were swimming competitively anymore, we had finished up college and were starting our careers. After another year together, the logical thing to do was…"

"Get engaged."

He grimaced. "But as much as she wanted a proposal, I just couldn't man up and do it. The thought of being tied to her the rest of my life made me physically feel choked." His body gave a slight tremor. "And then I did something really, really shitty, so she broke up with me."

"What did you do?" Emma questioned softly.

"She walked in on me having sex with another woman."

Emma's hand flew to her mouth, and she stared at Aidan in horror. "That's…so cruel."

His expression darkened. "Yeah, in case you didn't get the memo, I'm an asshole, remember?"

"But you can be so kind and considerate. The very fact I'm not at home alone, crying into a pint of Ben and Jerry's proves that. Instead, I'm sitting here eating the dinner you cooked and wearing your clothes. That's true compassion." She shook her head sadly. "Those are the reasons why it's so hard imagining you could do something so callous to someone you loved."

Aidan shrugged. "The past is the past I guess. At least she found someone else and has been happily married for the last eight years."

"You've seen her?"

"No. My mom used to at Mass with her husband and kids" Aidan grinned sheepishly. "Mom seemed to love rubbing it in my face."

"She was probably still mad at you for ruining such a good thing."

"Probably." Aidan emptied the rest of the wine bottle into his glass. "So now that you've heard my sad story, what about you?"

"You already know mine."

Aidan shook his head. "I'm not talking about being in love. I'm talking about breaking someone's heart." He propped his elbows on the glass table. "With your face and body, it isn't possible you haven't broken at least one guy's heart."

"I never said I didn't," Emma protested.

"Aha! So spill," Aidan said.

"It's certainly not as salacious as yours."

He smirked at her. "I would imagine not, Goody Two Shoes. I'm sure the fact you wouldn't sleep around broke quite a few hearts."

Emma crossed her arms over her chest. "Last time I checked, your heart is above your waist, not below it."

Aidan laughed. "Okay, okay. I get it. So what's the story?"

"Fine. Here's the Sparknotes version: his name was Steve, we were eighteen, and I was in love with his best friend."

"Ouch, that had to suck for ol' Steve."

"I never meant to hurt him, but from the time I turned sixteen, there was never anyone in the world for me but Travis."

"Did you go out with him to make Travis jealous?"

"No, at first I thought Steve would make me forget him. We were all in school and church together, but Travis acted like I was nothing more than a friend. Steve was the kind of guy who brought you flowers and called you in the morning to see how you were doing. He also respected my boundaries about sex."

"Poor Steve," Aidan joked.

Emma laughed. "Now I didn't say he wasn't getting any sexual satisfaction."

"Just not the full enchilada."

She wrinkled her nose. "If you have to put it that way, I guess so."

Aidan grinned. "So what happened?"

"Even though he should have been everything I could ever want in a boyfriend, I felt nothing. It wasn't fair to him, so I broke up with him. He was so devastated he got Travis to come and talk to me."

Emma ducked her head, fighting the dreamy smile spreading across her cheeks. "Travis came stomping in my room, red faced and furious, demanding how the hell could I break his best friend's heart. After listening to him rant and rave for about five minutes, I finally just screamed I was in love with him."

Aidan's eyes widened. "Holy shit! That took balls. What did he say?"

Emma laughed. "That he was in love with me too, but he didn't want to hurt Steve. So we waited a few months to start dating, and then we were inseparable."

"And Steve was okay with it?"

"He wasn't thrilled, but he found someone else."

Aidan stared at her for a moment and then grinned. "After unloading that heavy shit, I think we need some more wine."

"Yes, I think we do, too."

CHAPTER THIRTEEN

When Aidan didn't return within a few minutes, Emma went in search of him. She found the kitchen empty but heard raised voices coming from the hallway. She craned her head around the corner to see who Aidan was talking to. Three sandy haired boys stood in the foyer outfitted in swimming trunks and carrying pool gear. Their faces were downcast. The smallest one, who couldn't have been more than five, stomped his foot and huffed, "But Uncle Aidan, you promised we could come swimming anytime!"

"I know, Georgie, but you see—"

The tallest one shook his head. "Dude, this is so not cool."

"Look, I told you guys that you could come back tomorrow. It's just tonight isn't a good time," Aidan argued.

Emma stepped out into the hall and cleared her throat. Four pairs of eyes focused on her. "What's going on?"

"So, *she's* why we can't go swimming!" the middle boy exclaimed.

"Ooh, Uncle Aidan's got a girlfriend!" Georgie said before dissolving in giggles.

Aidan groaned in frustration. "Emma, these are the monsters I mentioned earlier: John, Percy, and Georgie."

Stepping forward, Emma waved and gave them a bright smile. "Hi guys."

"Hi," they murmured. They seemed almost mesmerized by her presence. It made Emma wonder if they'd ever seen a woman at Aidan's house before.

She cocked her head at them. "Let me guess. Any chance you guys were named after the Romanic poets?"

The tallest one rolled his eyes. "Yeah, unfortunately our parents have a major thing for boring, stuffy British dudes."

Aidan gave an exasperated grunt. "What he means to say is my sister and brother-in-law are both English professors at Georgia State." Pointing to the tallest one, he said, "The thirteen year old with the mouth is John Keats. My middle man, Percy Shelley, is eleven, and George Byron, or Georgie, is five." He turned back to her. "And guys, this is my friend, Emma Harrison."

"It's nice meeting you. Looks like you were all set to swim, huh?"

"Yeah, until Loverboy over here decided to ruin it for us," John replied, scowling at Aidan.

Jabbing his finger in the air, Aidan practically growled, "Watch your mouth."

Emma hid her amusement behind her hand. Once she recovered, she said, "In his defense, your uncle didn't know I was going to have such a bad day today and need some company. But I don't mind one bit if you guys stay and swim."

Aidan's eyebrows rose in surprise. "You don't?" he asked at the same time Georgie squealed, "Really?"

"Sure why not."

"All right!" Percy exclaimed before barreling past Emma. John and Georgie were close on his heels.

Emma laughed at their excitement while Aidan shook his head. "I can't believe you just agreed to have them stay."

"They're here to swim, so I highly doubt they'll even bother us."

"Famous last words," Aidan muttered as he ushered Emma back outside.

At the sight of Georgie about to jump in the shallow end, Aidan rushed forward and grabbed him up. "Whoa, whoa, Little Man. Don't you dare get in without your floaties."

"But floaties are for babies!" he moaned, writhing against Aidan's chest.

"I don't want to hear it." He sat Georgie down and flipped open a brown storage bin. He pulled out two Power Ranger arm floaties. He slid them up Georgie's arms. "Your mom would kick my butt if she showed up and you weren't wearing these."

Georgie glowered at Aidan before running off and jumping in the pool.

"Uncle Aidan, will you help me with my backstroke again?" Percy asked.

Aidan glanced over at Emma. "You mind?"

"Of course not. In fact, I'd love to see you in action."

He smirked before leaning over to whisper in her ear. "I'd wear that speedo I promised you, but I think it would freak the boys out."

She giggled and shoved him away. "Go get your swim trunks, cocky."

While he disappeared into the house, John swam closer to where Emma was sitting. He propped his elbows on the ledge. "So how long have you been Uncle Aidan's girlfriend?"

She fought the flush creeping across her cheeks at his directness. "He's just my friend."

He gave her a look that said he clearly thought she was bullshitting him. "Wish I had *friends* as pretty as you," he said with a grin.

Emma couldn't help giggling. "Why thank you, John. You're quite a charmer, aren't you?"

He puffed out his chest, and Emma could have sworn she was seeing Aidan at thirteen. "The girls seem to think so."

"Hmm, I think besides your hair and eyes, you may have inherited your flirting ability from your Uncle Aidan."

Aidan chose that moment to come back outside. He glanced between her and John with a curious expression. "What are you two talking about?"

"How much John looks like you." She gave Aidan a mischievous grin and winked. "And *acts* like you."

Aidan crossed his arms over his bare chest. "John, are you making the moves on my friend?"

John paled a little. "No, I was just talking to her. I mean, you never, *ever* have girls over here or bring them to Papa's."

Now it was Aidan's turn to get flustered. "Whatever." He dove into the pool and swam over to where Percy waited expectantly on him. Emma watched as Aidan gave Percy demonstrations and then feedback on his form. In between giving instructions, he would throw a gleeful Georgie in the air and let him splash down.

Emma drew in a desperate breath and tried to still the fluttering of her heart at the sight of Aidan interacting so effortlessly with his nephews. When he pulled himself out of the pool and came striding over to her, she couldn't help staring in wonder at him.

His eyebrows shot up at her expression. "What?"

"I just never imagined seeing you around kids."

"Oh yeah, I'm freakin' Ward Cleaver, aren't I?" he snorted in response.

"You don't give yourself enough credit. For some reason, you don't like to admit how much you care about them."

"Is that right?"

She nodded. "If you were so anti-children, you wouldn't have offered to let them come and swim, and you would have let Georgie in the water without his floaties. Plus, you just spent twenty minutes giving Percy swimming lessons."

Aidan furiously toweled his wet hair, a scowl forming on his face. "Em, I don't know what you're hinting around at right now, but I'm never going to be father material, okay?"

"You shouldn't feel so negative about yourself," she protested.

Before Aidan could say anything, a shriek came from the pool. Georgie was paddling over to the ladder, tears streaming down his face. Once he got out, he streaked over to Emma and Aidan.

"He held me under!" Georgie cried, pointing at John.

"It was barely a second. Stop being such a big baby," John replied.

"I-I couldn't breathe!" Georgie snubbed, grinding the tears from his eyes with his fists.

"Walk it off, Little Man. You'll be all right," Aidan said.

His response made Georgie cry harder and earned him a glare from Emma. "What?" Aidan questioned.

"Come here, sweetie," Emma offered, opening her arms. Georgie quickly scrambled into her lap and then wrapped his arms around her neck. "Shh, you're okay now." She turned her wrath on John. "I think you owe your brother an apology."

John's eyes widened as he glanced from Emma to his uncle, but Aidan only shrugged. "Um, I'm sorry, Georgie."

"You promise not to do it again?" he asked, his voice muffled against Emma's collarbone.

"Yeah, I promise."

Emma rubbed Georgie's back in wide circles. "See, everything's fine. You want to go back in the pool?"

"No," he snubbed.

Percy rolled his eyes at John who then snickered. "Yeah, if I was pressed up against that rack, I wouldn't want to leave either!" John said while Percy nodded in agreement.

Even though he said it in low voice, both Emma and Aidan heard him. While Emma fought to keep the flush from creeping across her cheeks and neck, Aidan stepped to the edge of the pool. "All right, get out this instant. If you're going to be that disrespectful to my friend, you can march your horny little asses home!" he growled.

John and Percy's eyes widened, but they didn't mouth off. Defeated, they started for the pool steps.

"Wait, Aidan, don't make them go home for that. They're just being boys," Emma argued.

He whirled around. "Are you kidding me?"

"I'm sure they feel very bad for being rude and would be willing to apologize." She stared pointedly at the boys. "Wouldn't you?"

"Yes, ma'am," Percy said.

John nodded. "I'm very, very sorry for saying something like that about you Emma."

"Thank you."

For good measure, John glanced up at Aidan. "And I'm sorry for being disrespectful to your girl—" He paused at the death glare Aidan gave him. "To your friend," he finished.

"Me too," Percy said.

Emma gazed up at Aidan and smiled. "See, problem solved."

Georgie raised his head. "What does horny mean?"

Emma couldn't help giggling at the absurdity of the situation, especially when Aidan's eyes widened, and he stared helplessly at Emma to explain. "It's not something you need to know about, and your uncle shouldn't have said it," she replied.

"Ooh, Uncle Aidan, you're in trouble," Georgie said, wagging his finger at Aidan.

Emma grinned. "Yes, Uncle Aidan is a very bad boy. We should wash his mouth out with soap, shouldn't we?"

Georgie giggled. "Yes, we should."

"Hello?" a woman's voice called from inside the house.

"Mommy!" Georgie cried, peeling himself off Emma and running to the doorway.

Emma started to stand up, but Aidan blocked her, thrusting his towel at her. When she started to protest, he grimaced and motioned to her chest. She glanced down and flushed. Comforting Georgie had soaked her white shirt, and you could see straight through to her lacy white bra. "Oh shit!" she stared wildly around the patio for an escape.

Aidan held out his hand. "Come meet Becky."

"Are you kidding? I'm not meeting your sister looking like a bimbo from a wet t-shirt contest," she hissed.

"You're not going to have much of a choice. The minute Georgie tells her there's a woman here with me, she's going to be all over you." He stepped forward and wrapped the towel around her. "Just pretend you've been swimming."

"Okay," she murmured reluctantly.

Just as Aidan predicted, Becky appeared in the doorway, holding Georgie's hand. At the sight of Emma, she power walked over to them. With her sandy hair and piercing blue eyes, Becky and Aidan could have passed for twins. She patted Aidan on the back. "Well, Little Brother, I wouldn't have let the boys come over if I knew you had company."

"This is Emma Harrison—she's a friend from work."

Emma extended her hand and gave Becky her best smile. "It's nice to meet you."

"Likewise."

As Becky continued sizing her up, Emma cleared her throat. "Your boys are absolutely adorable. I'm so glad I got to meet them."

Becky grinned. "Thank you. I only hope they were on their best behavior." She then gazed over at Aidan with a determined look on her face. "I didn't know you had such pretty work friends."

Aidan snorted at his sister's directness. "Yes, there's a high standard of beauty at the company."

Becky nudged him playfully. "Well, we won't impose on you two any longer." She motioned John and Percy out of the pool. They reluctantly dragged themselves out and started toweling off. Becky wrapped the towel tighter around Georgie. "Now what do we say to Uncle Aidan for letting us swim?"

"Thank you," they echoed in a sing-song chorus that caused Aidan and Emma to grin.

Then both John and Percy looked pointedly at Emma. "Thanks for talking Uncle

Aidan into letting us stay…both times," John said, a pink tinge on his cheeks.

Emma smiled. "You're welcome."

Becky stared from the boys to Emma, and then she gave Aidan a knowing look. "Well, you two have a lovely evening."

"Thank you."

They walked Becky and the boys to the door. Once they were gone, Aidan groaned and rubbed his eyes as he collapsed into the chair. "Jesus, I'm glad they're gone."

"Aw, I hate to see them go. They're really sweet boys."

He chuckled. "Oh yeah, I should have asked them to spend the night. I'm sure John would have loved to share a bed with you and your rack." He shook his head with disgust. "The little pervert."

"He's thirteen. What do you expect? I highly doubt you were an angel of virtue at that age," Emma countered with a smile.

"No, I was a pervert, too."

"I figured as much. I swear he looks and *acts* so much like you." She giggled. "He's another Fitzgerald player in the making."

Aidan's cell phone started ringing, and when he glanced down at it, he grimaced. "Damn, this is the India office. I have to take it. Make yourself at home, okay?"

"No problem," Emma replied, scratching Beau's ears.

As soon as Aidan left the room, Beau hopped up on the couch with her. "Wanna find a chick flick to watch with me?"

He licked her hand. She grabbed the remote on the table and started flipping channels. "Ooh," she murmured when she saw one of her favorites, *Nottinghill*, was on. She snuggled deeper into the couch, continuing to stroke Beau's shiny black fur. After awhile, her eye-lids grew heavy, and before she could stop herself, she nodded off.

***

"Yes, I look forward to seeing you next month, Mr. Benwaldi," Aidan said before hanging up. He rose out of his desk chair with a heavy sigh. In truth, he wasn't too thrilled of the prospect of leaving the country for a month, but it had been a stipulation of his new promotion. Of course, he hadn't thought to mention his imminent departure to Emma yet. He wasn't sure how she was going to take him leaving in the middle of their baby-making quest. Maybe he could convince her to fly over for a few days if the next week's try didn't take.

Wait, what the hell was he thinking? Emma wasn't his girlfriend or his wife. Asking a woman to fly across the ocean was way past his level of commitment, even if it was more for her benefit than his.

"Man, I'm the worst host ever. Sorry that took so long," he said, as he walked into the living room. He skidded to a stop at the sight of Emma asleep on the couch with Beau beside her. For a moment, he didn't know what to do. Should he wake her up and take her to get her car, or should he offer her the guest bedroom? Or should he take her to his bed? It wasn't like they hadn't slept together before.

He eyed Beau and gave a frustrated grunt. When Beau gazed drowsily up at him, Aidan wagged his finger. "You know damn well you're not allowed on the furniture."

Beau responded by yawning and then burrowing deeper to Emma's side.

Aidan bent over the couch, his hand sweeping across Emma's cheek. "Wake up, Em," he said softly.

"Hmm?" she questioned without stirring.

"You need to go to bed."

"No. Too tired," she murmured.

He rubbed her arm. "You'll sleep better in bed."

She gave a short snore in response. Aidan rolled his eyes. Of course, she would have to make this harder on him. "Okay, fine. I'll put you to bed."

He reached underneath her legs and then brought his arms around her back. With a grunt, he lifted her up off the couch.

Emma gazed up at him through hooded eyes. "Are you my Knight in Shining Armor, now?"

"Oh yeah, I'm a helluva knight," he grumbled.

"You're making me break all my rules."

"Huh?"

Her eyes closed, and he thought she'd gone back to sleep. "You make me feel too much...I'm just supposed to use you for sex like you use me."

His chest tightened at her words. Is that really what she thought of him? Even though it was usually the truth, he didn't like hearing it from her...at least not now. "Em, open your eyes and look at me."

At his command, her drowsy green eyes focused on his. "Don't you ever think I'm using you, all right? I may have always wanted to have sex with you, but I would never, ever use you."

She wrapped her arms tighter around his neck, her lips grazing his cheek. "You're a good man, Aidan Fitzgerald, even if you don't want to admit it."

"You think so?"

Her head bobbed lazily. "I never would have imagined you would take care of me like you did tonight, especially when there was no promise of sex. But you did."

Aidan rolled his eyes as he eased Emma down on his bed. "That makes me a real gentleman, huh?"

"Umm, hmm," she murmured, snuggling under the covers.

"I'm glad you think so highly of me, Em."

"Just don't break my heart," she said softly.

She was already breathing heavily when he replied, "I'm going to try my best not to."

CHAPTER FOURTEEN

Ten days after her dinner and sleepover at Aidan's, Emma forced herself to throw her rule book out the window. Daily texts, emails, and phone calls from Aidan even made Casey a believer in resurrecting his potential boyfriend material. And now the red circled date on her calendar told her it was time to start Round Two of Baby-Making.

This time Aidan insisted she come to his house. The "all business" parameters of their arrangement had been broken, so there was no point in meeting at a hotel. After running home to freshen up, she headed over to his house.

He answered the door in boxers and a t-shirt. "Sorry, I just got out of the shower."

"Yeah, I just did the same," she replied, as she followed him into the house.

He grinned at her over his shoulder. "You should've showered here, and we could have killed two birds with one stone."

Emma laughed. "I guess you're right."

"Are you hungry?"

"A little."

"I can order in some Chinese."

Emma pretended to be horrified. "You mean you didn't cook for me tonight?"

Aidan chuckled. "Sorry babe, not tonight. Work's been kicking my ass."

"The new promotion?"

He nodded. "Even though the money is fabulous, I'm starting to wish I'd said no."

After digging in one of his drawers, he pulled out a menu and handed it to Emma. "Let me know what you want to eat."

Instead of looking at the food options, Emma was puzzled about what was different about Aidan. Then she realized what it was. "Boxers? When did you start wearing those?"

He leaned back against the kitchen counter. "Well, I did a little research, and I found out that boxers are better for the balls and sperm counts."

"I see," she replied, fighting the flush that was creeping across her cheeks.

"Yeah, the article says it seems to help the swimmers with their mobility, and we want Olympic Gold this time around."

Emma's heartbeat accelerated, and she sucked in a breath. "So you started wearing boxers to help me conceive?"

"Yep. And I also read that it's better to store up sperm to make them more potent." He pushed himself off the counter and came to stand in front of her. "So I've held off on any sexual activity that might result in me wasting swimmers."

"Oh," she murmured.

"Does that surprise you?"

She nodded. "I just assumed you were seeing someone or…"

"Screwing someone?" When Emma didn't respond, Aidan swept the hair away from her face and stroked her cheek. "There's no one but you—not even my hand since I saw you last."

Her eyes widened when she got his meaning. "I guess it's been a really long ten days, huh?"

His expression became pained. "Frankly, I'm about to explode."

Emma laughed. "I'm really impressed with how serious you're taking this."

"Whenever I attempt to do something, I intend to do it well and give it all I have. And that includes knocking you up."

She smacked his arm playfully. "You're such a charmer."

Aidan laughed. "Let's see if I can't charm the panties off of you right now."

"What about the food?" she questioned.

"We'll work up an appetite," he replied.

The menu fluttered from her hands and fell to the floor. "Sounds good to me."

Staring into each other's eyes, the electricity in the room shifted. Suddenly, it seemed Aidan couldn't get her naked soon enough. He gripped the hem of dress and then pulled it up, jerking it over her head. She was glad she chose to change her underwear when his eyes roamed appreciatively over the green and gold bra and panties she was wearing. But he didn't stare for long. Instead, he gripped her waist and hoisted her up to sit on the marble countertop. His fingers unhooked her bra and whisked it away as Emma wrapped her legs around his waist.

Aidan's lips hungrily met hers as his tongue darted in and out of her mouth. His hands cupped her bare breasts, kneading them like he knew she liked. She rewarded his efforts with a moan against his lips. Aidan's hands left her breasts to grip the waistband of her thong. He stripped it off and down over her thighs.

He then spread her legs, hooking her knees over his shoulders. When his tongue darted inside her heat, Emma threw back her head. "Mmm, oh God, yes!"

"Say my name, babe," Aidan murmured against her sex.

With him continuing his teasing assault on her clit, she very quickly rewarded him with, "Yes, Aidan! Oh, yes, oh yes, Aidan!" Her shaky legs spread wider to allow him more access. She was rewarded by Aidan sliding his fingers in and out of her while his tongue lapped and teased at her folds. Her fingers gripped the edge of the countertop as she came hard and strong.

When Aidan's erection, rather than his fingers, nudged at her opening, her eyes flew open, and she jerked back. "No, not like this! Not here!"

Aidan's eyebrows shot up into his forehand. "Don't tell me you have an aversion to sex on kitchen countertops? I promise they're clean."

Emma felt her face warming. "That's not it."

He ran his fingers through his already sweat-slicked hair. "Em, you think you could cut to the chase? I mean, I'm standing here with a raging hard-on right now, and all I want is to be buried deep inside you."

"I just don't want to look back and realize my baby was conceived on a kitchen counter, okay?"

Aidan stared at her for a moment before howling with laughter. "If my memory serves me correctly, I banged you on my desk at work after you worked me over in the desk chair."

"You wouldn't go to the couch!" she argued.

"But don't you think babies have been conceived in worse places?"

Emma crossed her arms over her bare breasts in a huff. "We're not talking about other people's babies. We're talking about *mine*."

He rolled his eyes and then grinned. "Emma Harrison, you are going to be the death of me in more ways than one." When he pulled her closer to him, she started to protest, but he shook his head. "Just hold your horses, *princess*. I'll get you back to the bedroom, okay?"

She grinned. "I'll make it worth your while, I promise."

As he lifted her off the counter, she gripped her legs tight around his waist while he held her steady around her hips. "Hmm, just what are you suggesting?"

She titled her head to the right, appearing to be lost in thought. "How does after we go a round, I give a lot of oral attention to your most prized possession?"

Aidan groaned. "Worth every fucking step of hauling your sexy ass to my bed."

Emma giggled. "I figured as much."

"You're so bossy and demanding, Em. I can't believe I give into you."

"That's because you *want* to give into me. Admit it. I've softened you towards sex."

His eyes narrowed. "Are you trying to say I'm a pussy in the bedroom now?"

"Of course not, silly. I just meant I've had an effect on the way you think and act about sex, just like you've changed me. You're tender, sweet, and thoughtful instead of just being about your own pleasure. Future women will thank me."

Aidan didn't reply. Instead, he tossed her unceremoniously onto her back on the bed. She gasped in shock at his roughness. "Why Mr. Fitzgerald, how ungentlemanly of you," she teased.

He gave a sharp shake of his head. "Your little episode in the kitchen has made me wait long enough to fuck, Ms. Harrison. You can consider yourself forewarned that there will be no more Mr. Nice Guy!"

She would have been lying if his words coupled with the gleam of desire burning in his eyes didn't turn her on. He shoved her knees apart with his hands, widening her legs. His expression turned predatorily dark as he positioned himself over her. With one harsh thrust, he drove himself inside her. Impaled by him, she shuddered at his forcefulness. He smirked down at her. "Looks like your body is betraying that prim attitude of yours. Guess I've had an effect on you as well."

"I'm not the one denying it. You are," she panted.

He continued pounding into her, the smacking of their skin echoing through the room along with Aidan's almost animalistic grunts. She knew he was screwing her like this to prove a point to himself, and she wanted nothing more to prove to him he had changed.

So she brought her hands to his face, drawing his lips to hers. He momentarily stilled his thrusting when she darted her tongue into his mouth, sweetly stroking his tongue with hers. She swept her hands through his hair, tugging at the strands at the base of his neck. He groaned low in his throat.

Emma's hands feathered down Aidan's back. Instead of raking her fingernails into his flesh, she swept deliciously slow circles over his ass. Now it was his turn to shudder. She cupped his buttocks, pressing him further inside her, while raising her hips. "Slow and sweet now, please?" she asked.

His eyes flew open, and a smile curved on his lips. "When you ask that way, how can I say no?"

With one round complete along with keeping her promise of oral attention, Emma woke up snuggled into the crook of Aidan's arm. Pressing her ear against his chest, she listened to the gentle hum of his heartbeat. She had almost gone back to sleep when Aidan's voice roused her.

"Are you awake?"

"Mmm-hmm," she murmured.

"There's something I need to tell you, and I really need for you to be fully awake for this one, Em."

His words doused her with the same effect as a cup of coffee. She rose up to peer at his troubled expression. "Why do I have the feeling you're about to drop a major bomb on me?"

Aidan exhaled a ragged breath. "Because of my new promotion, I have to go to India to help start the new office branch over there."

Inwardly, relief washed over Emma. A million devastating scenarios had raced through her mind. Most of them involved him no longer wanting to see her or be a part of baby-making. "How long will you be gone?"

"This is the part you're not going to like…two weeks to a month."

Emma gasped. "But that means you might not be here next time to…" She ducked her head. "Well, you know."

Aidan rubbed his thumb across her cheek. "But I might be. I just don't know how long it'll take."

She nodded. "It's okay. I understand."

"You do?"

"It's not like you're just choosing to go on vacation or something. It's work—you have to do it. I do realize you have a life besides me and my baby-making scheme." She smiled. "Besides, it's not like I can keep you chained to the bed for my own needs."

His chest vibrated with laughter beneath her. "Oh, Em, I didn't know you could be so kinky." Propping up on his elbows, he grinned down at her. "Anytime you want to handcuff me to the bed, you just let me know. I'll happily oblige you."

Emma pulled herself up to straddle him. "I think we're doing fine just like we are."

His fingertips feathered over her thighs. "Now why doesn't your reply surprise me? If you find kitchen counters offensive for conceiving, I'm sure any notion of bondage is out."

"You told me before you didn't go in for all that."

"That's true. But for you, I'd make an exception."

Rolling her eyes, Emma leaned over, licking her tongue up his neck and along his jaw. When she was almost to his mouth, she pulled back. "Do you think you could oblige me in another round?"

Aidan grinned. "Why of course."

At that moment, Beau leapt onto the bed with Emma's underwear between his teeth. "Beau! No, give me those!" she shrieked, grabbing for his mouth. Once she swiped the panties from him, his wet nose nudged against Emma's thigh, trying to push her off Aidan's lap.

"Beau, you old cockblocker! Get down!" Aidan cried.

Emma fell over on the bed giggling. Between Aidan's comment and Beau's antics, she could barely catch her breath. Beau began licking her face, and she had to push him away. "No, boy, stop," she gasped.

"Get down!" Aidan cried, trying to grab Beau's collar.

When Beau was successfully off the bed, Emma turned to Aidan. "What's going to happen to him while you're gone?"

Aidan shrugged. "Even though he hates staying overnight, I guess I'll board him at his Doggy Daycare."

Emma glanced over the side of the bed at Beau. He proceeded to give her the saddest hound dog face he could muster. "Aw, poor baby." She turned to Aidan and smiled. "I could keep him for you."

Aidan grunted. "What the hell would possess you to want to do that?"

"Because I love him, and I hate to think of him being unhappy for two to four weeks."

"You're serious, aren't you?"

Emma nodded. "Don't you trust me with your dog?"

He laughed. "Of course I do. And if you really want to put up with his smelly ass for two to four weeks, he's yours."

She peered over the side of the bed again. "Did you hear that boy? You're going to come and stay with me while Daddy goes to India."

Beau thumped his tail appreciatively while Aidan snickered. "I can't believe you just called me Beau's Daddy."

She gave him a wicked grin as she trailed her fingers up his thigh and then took his slackened cock in her hand. "Would you rather me call you Big Daddy?"

He licked his lips in anticipation. "Oh yeah, that's good."

"Which part? Me stroking you like this or calling you Big Daddy?" she teased.

"Mmm, both," he replied.

Once she had worked him to full mast, she guided him to her already wet core. Emma grinned at Aidan. "Okay then, Big Daddy, let's try once more to make a baby."

CHAPTER FIFTEEN

Emma gnawed on her already frayed nails. Sitting on the bathroom countertop, her legs swung back and forth. Her whole body hummed with nervous energy. She drew in a frantic breath, trying to calm her out of control emotions, but nothing short of a margarita the size of a fishbowl would help at the moment.

She cut her gaze over where Casey lounged on the settee, eyeing three different pregnancy test sticks. "How long has it been?" Emma squeaked.

Casey groaned. "About five fucking seconds since the last time you asked! Jesus, Em, you're going to give me a stroke!"

"I'm sorry. It feels like an eternity since I peed on those freakin' sticks. I'm losing my mind."

Someone started in the bathroom, and Casey leapt up, bracing herself against the door. "Sorry, it's out of order. Try the one down the hall."

The person grumbled, but then backed off. Emma widened her eyes. "I can't believe you're bogarting the bathroom for my pregnancy test!"

"Do you want a strange chick taking a whizz in the middle of your big moment?"

Nervous laughter bubbled out of Emma. "No, I guess not. But we don't know if it's going to be a big moment or not."

Casey grinned. "You're a week late this time, Em. And don't forget that Aidan took extra care of his swimmers. I think the odds are in your favor this second time around!"

"As much as I want it to be, I have a feeling Aidan will be a little disappointed at no more baby-making sessions, especially since he's storing up his energy while he's out of the country."

"Who says it has to end?"

Emma's eyebrows shot up in surprise. "Because the purpose will be over then...I'll be pregnant."

"Yeah and keeping him coming back for more just might land you something you never bargained for."

"And what's that?"

Casey gave her a knowing smile. "A husband."

The room spun around her, sending Emma's head slamming back against the mirror. She brought her hand to her forehead to still the maddening spinning. "Don't say things like that to me when I'm already about to explode." When Casey didn't reply, Emma opened her eyes. "What is it?"

"They're starting to change colors!"

Emma sucked in a breath before leaning forward on the bathroom counter. "And?"

"Holy shit, one has two lines and the others say 'Yes'!"

Falling off the counter onto the tiled floor, Emma staggered over to Casey and grabbed her by the shoulders. Bewildered, she asked, "But...so does that mean...?"

Tears sparkled in Casey's eyes. "It means you're pregnant!"

"Are you sure? You didn't read the boxes wrong or something?"

"No, I'm positive, and the tests are positive!"

Emma froze as her body desperately tried processing her emotions. They ricocheted through her at warped speed causing her body to tremble. She couldn't blink, least of all draw breath. All the painful years after Travis's and her mother's deaths she had spent hoping, praying, and longing for a child converged on this one moment. It was physically and emotionally overwhelming. Pregnant…she was actually pregnant.

Casey shook her gently. "Breathe, Em, you've got to breathe."

Silent tears streamed down Emma's cheeks. Her hand tentatively went to her abdomen. "I can't believe it's actually happening."

"It feels good to be right," Casey joked, as she wiped her own tears away on the back of her hand.

Emma's elated expression started to fade. "What if the tests were wrong? I mean, what if--"

Casey shook her head. "You could buy ten more tests to humor yourself, but it's real this time."

Reaching for a tissue, Emma dabbed her eyes. "Don't you see? There's just been so much disappointment and sadness in my life that it's hard for me to grasp that something I want so much can actually happen."

"Em—"

"You don't understand what it's been like for me. So many times I've gotten my hopes up for true happiness only to have it dashed. Travis and I were planning on starting a family right away. He joked about knocking me up, so we could have Shotgun Wedding. I wanted nothing more than to have his child, and then he was gone. Then I lost my mother." Her lip trembled. "I'm scared this is all going to fall apart, Case."

"Don't be afraid." Casey drew Emma into her arms. "I'm here for you, and everything is going to be all right. It's finally *your* time, Em. You're just going to have to keep the faith and believe it."

Emma closed her eyes and let Casey's optimism wash over her. "I want to believe it. So very, very much."

Casey pulled away to give Emma a reassuring smile. "Well, you better because it's the truth. Now look in the mirror and say the words."

"Seriously Case?"

"Do it!"

"Fine." Emma stared at her pale, mascara-streaked face in the mirror. "I'm pregnant, and I'm going to be a mother."

"Damn straight! Now when are you going to tell Big Papa the good news?"

"Oh, I don't know. Even though we've talked on the phone and skyped since he's been gone, I don't want to do it that way." At the wicked expression on Casey's face, Emma crossed her arms over her chest. "I know what you're wondering, and the answer is no. We did *not* have phone sex!"

"How disappointing," Casey pouted.

Rolling her eyes, Emma said, "Anyway, to get back to the original point, I think it's best I wait until he gets home."

"And when is that exactly?"

"Sometime next week."

"Good. By then, you will have had time to see your Gyno, and you'll know without a shadow of a doubt you can tell him the good news." She held open the bathroom door. "I say we blow out of here at five and go celebrate with non-alcoholic beverages and chocolate!"

Emma grinned. "Sounds like a plan to me."

***

A week later, Emma stepped out into the waiting room of her OB/GYN's office to the expectant faces of Casey and Connor. She couldn't hide her beaming smile. "I'm really, really pregnant!"

Popping out of their chairs, they both erupted with loud cheers and gave Emma a long, excited group hug. On the way to the car, her phone buzzed in her purse. She dug it out and gasped. *At the airport. Heading home. Want to meet for drinks at O'Malley's at six?*

She quickly texted Aidan back. *Sure. Sounds good. See you then.*

At his next response, Emma skidded to an abrupt stop and stared at her phone. Both anxiety and longing gripped her at his words. *Good. I'm looking forward to kissing and licking every square inch of that fabulous body of yours tonight.*

"What's the matter, Em?" Casey asked.

"Nothing…just a text I got."

Connor snorted. "Just a text my ass! From the practically giddy expression on your face, I'm assuming it's from Big Papa Fitzgerald!" Connor joked.

Emma giggled. "Yes, it is. He's on his way home."

Peeking over her shoulder, Connor gasped. "Damn, girl, he's looking forward to licking every inch of your body? Em's gone kinky on me!"

"Would you stop!" she shrieked, jerking the phone away from his view. Her reaction sent Connor and Casey giggling like mad as they hopped into the car.

Fumbling for her car keys, she wasn't quite sure how to respond to Aidan's text. Finally, she typed a quick *See you then.* As she cranked up, she had a gnawing feeling in the pit of her stomach that telling Aidan wasn't going to be as easy as she thought.

CHAPTER SIXTEEN

As his plane skidded across the runway at Hartsfield Jackson, Aidan fought the urge to shout for joy. For him, there was truly no place like home. He tapped his foot impatiently while he waited for the plane to come to a stop. Four weeks away had felt like an eternity. Even though he wanted nothing more than to grab a couple of chili dogs from the Varsity along with a twelve pack from the liquor store, he had very important dinner plans and even bigger nighttime plans.

After deplaning, he broke into a jog from the gate, grabbing up his luggage as fast as he could. Glancing at his watch, he had forty-five minutes to make it to O'Malley's. He would've liked to have had time to freshen up, but his rumpled shirt and wrinkled dress pants were just going to have to do.

Miraculously, he stepped into O'Malley's a little before six. When Jenny saw him, her face lit up. "Hey stranger! Glad to see you're back."

He smiled. "Thanks. It's good to be home. You can't imagine how much I missed this old hole in the wall. You can't quite find the same beer or burgers over there."

Jenny laughed. "So do I need to reserve a large booth for the crew and your Welcome Home party?"

"Um, no, actually, I'm meeting someone."

"Someone or some *woman*?"

He coughed. "A woman."

Aidan couldn't help feeling surprised when Jenny's smile widened. "Is it the pretty red-head you were here with before?"

His mouth gaped open. "Wait, how did you guess that?"

She grinned. "I knew there was something between you two when you came in—something different from the other women I've seen you with."

"But we weren't even dating then." He shook his head. "We're not even dating *now*."

"Oh please." Jenny waved her hand dismissively at him and grabbed two menus. She led him to the same secluded area he had sat in with Emma before. This time she gave them the back corner booth, ensuring they would have a lot of privacy. "You guys make a really good-looking couple," she said before leaving him once again open-mouthed.

Aidan's only response to Jenny's compliments was to give a frustrated grunt. He eased down in the booth and took out his phone. After scrolling through several emails and texts, he glanced up to see Emma sweeping through the door. He sucked in a breath and tried to still the accelerating of his heartbeat. What the hell was happening to him? No woman had ever had this much of an effect on him. The time away seemed to have made her even more beautiful than he remembered, but there was something different about her—something softer, more vulnerable. It was a hell of a turn on.

When Jenny said something to Emma, she beamed and ducked her head. Without blinking, Aidan watched Emma as she followed Jenny to the table. Her dress slid over her hips, accentuating the curves he was familiar with. Her long auburn hair hung in waves, cascading over her shoulders. He gritted his teeth when he noticed some of the other male patrons ogling Emma as she passed them by. Even though he had no right, he wanted to scream at them that she belonged to him.

Her face lit up when she met his gaze. "Hey!"

As he started rising out of the booth, she rushed over and threw her arms around his neck. He opened his mouth to say hello, but her lips crushed against his. As she deepened the kiss, Aidan tried to keep his bearings by tightening his arms around Emma's waist. Damn, he had missed the feel of her lips, her tongue, and the way her body molded against his.

A low whistle behind them caused Emma to jerk back much to Aidan's dismay. Jenny grinned at them and winked. "Now who needs the guys when you can get a homecoming like that, huh?"

Emma's cheeks grew red, but she laughed. Tilting her head to the side at Aidan, she asked, "Am I enough of a Welcome Home party?"

He grinned. "At the moment, hell yes, you are."

Jenny squeezed past them to sit their silverware on the table. "I guess I'll leave you two lovebirds alone now."

"Thanks Jenny," Aidan said.

He arched his eyebrows when Emma plopped down next to him in the booth rather than sitting across from him. "Miss me that much, huh?"

Her laughter made his heart vibrate with warmth. "Yes, actually I did."

Aidan stared into her twinkling green eyes. "I missed you, too." *A hell of a lot more than I want to admit.*

"Me or the sex?" she asked.

"Both," he answered honestly.

She giggled. "I figured it would only be the sex."

"You underestimate yourself as usual." Propping his arm on the back of the booth, he turned to get a better look at her. "But I can't help myself if it sounds like I've only been missing the sex when I tell you how fucking gorgeous you look tonight."

"No, it's okay." Her cheeks flushed. "And thank you."

Aidan leaned over to nuzzle her neck, inhaling the delicate smell of her perfume. He groaned in the sweet agony. "The way your dress is hugging all your curves and your hair falling loose and wavy, just begging me to run my fingers through it, makes me want to forget dinner and take you home instead."

When she stiffened, he raised his head. "What's wrong?"

"I need to tell you something."

"Anything. Well, as long as it isn't something like you're not coming home with me tonight."

"I'm pregnant," she blurted.

The air wheezed out of him, and he felt like he had been kicked in the groin. "Okay, that's not quite what I was expecting."

"I found out a week ago, but I wanted to wait until you got back to tell you. I thought it would mean more in person."

Now he knew why she appeared so different. Pregnancy had her absolutely glowing with pure happiness. A sense of immense pride radiated through him that he had a part in making that happiness. His lips curved in a genuine smile. "That's wonderful news, Em. I'm thrilled for you."

Happy tears sparkled in her eyes. "Oh Aidan, I can never thank you enough for making this dream possible!" she cried, throwing her arms around his neck again. She squeezed him tight. "I still can't believe it happened after only two months of trying. Do you know how blessed and lucky we are? Some people have to try for months and months—even years."

"Yeah, that would have been miserable," he joked.

A girlish giggle escaped her lips. "I am sorry that we didn't get to…well, you know, have sex as much as you would have liked."

Just the mention of that word on her luscious lips made him squirm in the booth. "So am I, especially since I've practically been a monk the last few weeks."

Her eyes widened. "You mean you kept up with the boxers and no activity of any kind?"

"Well, I might have taken care of business once or twice," he replied, sheepishly. "But I abstained all last week in preparation." Now after all that work, he was going home, tail between his legs, and extremely frustrated. It was truly going to be just him and his hand that night.

Emma cupped his face in her hands. "Oh, you poor baby! You've really gone above and beyond for me through this whole thing."

When she brushed her fingers over his lips, he grabbed her hand. "Please, Em, don't. I'm way too fucking frustrated for shit like that."

A smile that was both teasing and sweet spread on her face. "I tell you what. Since you've made me the happiest woman in the world, I think I more than owe you a round or two to put a smile on your face."

For the second time that night, Aidan felt like he had been kicked in the groin. "You can't be serious."

Her brows furrowed. "Don't you want me to be serious?"

"Of course I do! I want to push your dress up over your thighs, rip off the lacy thong I imagine that you're wearing, and fuck you senseless right here in the booth."

Emma sucked in a breath and widened her eyes. "I take that as a yes."

Aidan grinned. "Hey, it's been *four* weeks babe. You're lucky I'm not dragging you into the bathroom for a quickie." When her nose wrinkled in disgust, he couldn't hold back his laughter. "Don't worry, Em. I'll control myself." Running his hand under her dress, he squeezed her thigh. "At least while we're in public."

He was surprised when she didn't smack his hand away. Instead, she merely smiled invitingly up at him. "Can we at least eat first?"

"Of course we can. You're eating for two now, right?"

Emma snorted. "Supposedly yes. But the way I've been packing it in lately, you would think I was having triplets or something."

Aidan waved the waiter over. After Emma finished rattling off all that she wanted, Aidan couldn't hide his amusement. "You're seriously going to eat all that?"

She bobbed her head as the waiter left. "It won't matter as much this time since I assume I'll be burning a lot of calories later, right?"

He chuckled. "Hell yes!"

For the rest of dinner, he behaved himself. Instead, he focused on how joyfully animated Emma became as she talked about the baby and the pregnancy. He had never seen her talk a mile a minute or smile so much. He began to wonder how her cheeks couldn't hurt. He momentarily stiffened when she mentioned that both Casey *and* Connor had accompanied her to her first doctor's appointment. "So now he's all about you having a baby as long as he didn't father it?"

Emma's fork froze in mid-air while her face crumpled. "He just wanted to come and support me since you were out of town."

"That was nice of him," Aidan said, unable to keep the sarcasm out of his tone.

"If you don't want him at the first ultrasound, I won't invite him."

Aidan didn't know why the hell it bothered him. It wasn't like he had any plans of being involved in the baby's life…or did he? For some reason, just the thought of Connor being in *his* baby's life dropped a heavy blanket of possessiveness around him. Shuddering, he tried ridding himself of the feeling. Besides Connor seemed like a genuine guy—he obviously didn't have to worry about him being competition in Emma's bed.

"Aidan, you didn't answer me?"

He met Emma's intense stare. "What?"

"I asked you again if you wanted it to just be the two of us at the first ultrasound."

Swallowing hard, he finally responded, "Um, yeah, sure."

Any doubt about his decision faded at the expression of pure, unadulterated happiness that flashed on Emma's face. Knowing he was the reason behind it warmed him straight through to his soul. It was a feeling he thought he could come to enjoy experiencing more of.

"Great," she replied, nibbling on her last French fry.

He couldn't help grinning when he surveyed her empty plate. "Would you like some dessert?"

She pursed her lips at his teasing. "No, I'm good for now, thanks."

"Then can we please get the hell out of here and go back to your house before I have a permanent case of blue balls?"

Emma giggled. "I guess so. Just be glad I have some Ben and Jerry's in the freezer, or we would be making a pit stop."

Aidan groaned as he threw a wad of bills on the table. "You love to torture me, don't you?"

Running her hand up his thigh, Emma stopped just before she touched his cock. When he sucked in a sharp breath, she merely took her hand away and picked up her drink. Swirling the straw around, she then brought it to her lips and worked it in and out of her mouth while she drank. "Hmm, that's so good."

His mouth gaped open in shock. He couldn't believe she was doing this to him. His sweet, innocent Emma, the mother of his child, was being a total cock-tease. And in some small way, he was enjoying the hell out of it.

When she finally looked at him, she burst out laughing. "I'm sorry. I couldn't help myself."

"Just make sure you keep that attitude up the rest the night," Aidan replied, nudging her out of the booth.

CHAPTER SEVENTEEN

After they left O'Malley's, Aidan followed Emma home. When she pulled in the garage, she hopped out of her car and met him in the driveway. He glanced around the yard. "Where's Beau?"

Emma laughed. "I put him in his swinging bachelor's pad down in the basement before I came to meet you. Want me to go let him out?"

He shook his head as they started up the walk-way "No, I can wait to see him until after I devour you at least once."

Emma made a tsking noise. "Poor Beau. His Daddy is always thinking of his own needs first."

Aidan laughed. "He's a dude, so he would totally understand."

"Oh really?"

"You better believe if some bitch in heat came by, he wouldn't think twice about thinking with his dick and running out on me."

"Is that what I am to you? A bitch in heat?" Emma questioned, feigning outrage.

"Of course not…well, you might've been before I got you pregnant."

Shaking her head at him, she unlocked the front door and held it open for Aidan. When she turned to close and lock it behind them, Aidan beat her to the punch. Grabbing her from behind, he took her hands and placed them flush against the wooden door. He buried his face into the side of her neck before wrapping his arms around her waist and pressing his erection against her backside. Grinding into her, he moaned, "God, Em, I want you so much it hurts."

The feel of his need against her caused warmth to flood her core. She had missed him emotionally, but the growing ache between her legs was her body's way of showing her just how much he had been missed physically.

One of his hands slid from her waist up her torso to cup her breast. When he kneaded it roughly like she usually enjoyed, she yelped in pain, rather than pleasure.

At her reaction, Aidan instantly tensed. He spun her around to face him, his brows creased with worry. "I'm sorry, Em. You used to get off when I did that."

She cupped his face in her hands, rubbing her thumbs along his jaw-line. "It's not your fault. I should have warned you that my breasts are…" She bit her lip and tried to imagine how she was going to explain this. "Well, they're really tender right now because of being pregnant." Even though she tried fighting it, she felt her face flushing in embarrassment.

"Oh, I see." When she forced herself to look at Aidan, he was staring quizzically at her breasts. After he scratched his chin, Emma asked, "What?"

"Is there, like, milk already in them or something?"

She laughed. "No, no, it's nothing like that."

Although he seemed relieved, he still wasn't touching her. Slowly, she grabbed the hem of her dress and pulled it over her head. She held Aidan's smoldering gaze as she reached behind her back and unhooked her bra. After she let it drop to the floor, she took his hands in hers and brought them to her chest. "Just be gentle, okay?" She worked his hands over her breasts, illustrating the pattern and pressure to use. "Mmm, that's good," she said.

As his fingers rolled and teased her nipples to hardened peaks, he arched his eyebrows questioningly at her. "Very good," she murmured.

While he kept up his ministrations, she reached over to loosen his tie. Once she slipped it off, she started at the buttons on his shirt. After whisking it away, she started for his belt buckle. She must not have been moving fast enough because Aidan's hands left her breasts to unzip and kick off his pants.

At the sight of his rumpled boxers—the very ones he was wearing just for her to conceive— she grinned. Taking his hand, she led him down the hall towards the bedroom. He used his free hand to caress her backside. It was like he couldn't stop touching her even for a second. When they got into the bedroom, he slid his hand from her buttocks to grip her waist, pulling her towards him. She wrapped her arms around his chest, enjoying the sensation of feeling his bare skin on her breasts.

Aidan's mouth met Emma's in a frenzied, desperate kiss as she guided them over to the bed. She brought her hands to his chest and shoved him, sending him sprawling onto the bed. Instead of lying down, he raised himself up into a sitting position. Grabbing Emma's hips, Aidan tugged her closer.

After spending a few minutes delicately licking and sucking her nipples, he kissed from the hollow of her breasts down over her stomach. His nimble fingers whisked off her panties, leaving her naked and feeling vulnerable in front of him. When he didn't begin kissing or stroking her, Emma glanced down at him. Her breath hitched at the sight of him staring at her belly.

"What's wrong?" she asked.

"Nothing," he murmured.

"You didn't expect me to already be showing, did you?"

"No, of course not. But your body is already changing in little ways. I can tell." Lightly, he grazed her abdomen with the back of his fingers. He wore an almost mesmerized expression. "So there's a part of me in there, huh?"

"Yes," she said softly.

He titled his head to the side, smiling up at her. "Damn. That's pretty amazing when you stop to think about it."

The tiny fluttering of her heart broke into a full gallop at his words. "It is."

When Aidan leaned in to feather tender kisses across her belly, Emma came undone. The gesture brought tears to her eyes.

She bit down so hard on her bottom lip to keep from sobbing that a metallic rush of blood filled her mouth. Just as she thought she might go over the emotional abyss, he flicked his tongue over her clit while his fingers sought out her core. Gasping, she brought her hand to his hair and fisted the strands. All thoughts escaped her mind except for the exquisite torment of his tongue as it licked and sucked over her sex.

It didn't take long for her to throw her head back and cry out his name as she came. As her body was still reeling, he gripped her waist and spun her around, pushing her towards the bed. Emma fought the wave of dizziness that spiraled over her that was unfortunately not the usual post orgasm kind, but instead was another aspect of pregnancy plaguing her.

With a hungry smile, Aidan pressed her down onto the mattress. But then when positioned himself over her body, he froze. He then rocked back to sit on his knees between her legs. "What's wrong?" Emma asked.

He scratched his head. "Um, I don't quite know how to say this."

Propping up on her elbows, Emma asked, "What do you mean?"

"Here's the thing. I'm kind of afraid."

Emma felt like her eyebrows were going to shoot right off her forehead. "Excuse me?"

"What I mean is, I'm afraid of doing something that will hurt the baby. Like crushing it with my body on yours or thrusting too deep or some shit like that."

"Oh, I see," she murmured. She fought the urge to laugh at the absurdity of the situation. Never in a million years would she have imagined Aidan being afraid of sex.

"Well, my doctor didn't say anything about abstaining from sex, so I think we'll be fine."

Hope flashed in Aidan's eyes. "You think?"

She could no longer hold back her laugher. "Yes, I'm positive."

"Oh, so this is funny now?"

She nodded. "If you could see the look on your face."

Scowling, he crossed his arms over his chest. "Well, excuse me, for wanting to protect our child."

Emma rose up and took Aidan's face in her hands. "I'm sorry. I shouldn't have laughed. It's just that most couples, married or unmarried, don't stop having sex when pregnancy happens." When he started to argue, she put a finger over his lips to silence him. "But I do appreciate your worry and concern. Each and every time we've been together, you've always been considerate not to do anything that would hurt me. I'm sure you'll continue doing the same thing now."

He grimaced. "It's just...I'm worried because it's been awhile for me. If I'm being totally honest, it's one of the longest periods of going without sex in my adult life, and I'm worried about getting too carried away."

"It'll be fine. Trust me, I'll let you know if something is wrong."

Aidan gave her a wary look before he nodded.

"Now why don't you make love to me? Nice and slow," she said.

Aidan blew out a puff of air. "I can try."

Emma couldn't help giggling at the determined expression on his face. "I can't believe Mr. Aidan Fitzgerald—Sex God Extraordinaire—is doubting his bedroom abilities."

At her taunting, Aidan's expressed flipped over from anxious to smoldering in barely a second. "There goes that mouth of yours again," he replied, his voice low and husky.

"Umm, hmm," Emma murmured, bringing his face to hers. She needed his warm lips on hers desperately. Sliding her tongue into his mouth, she caressed his, causing him to groan deep in the back of his throat.

Emma reached between them and took his erection in her hand. She stroked him hard and fast, causing Aidan's jaw to clench. After working his glorious length a few more moments, Aidan grunted, his hips bucking back and forth into her hand.

"Em," he murmured.

She then guided his erection to her folds. He entered her slowly, tediously, inch by inch, until she was filled with him. She realized then how much she had missed the feeling of him being inside her. When he pulled out, Emma gasped at the empty feeling. His frantic eyes met hers, and she smiled. "It's okay. Keep doing what you're doing."

"I'll try," he replied, plunging back inside of her.

Emma gripped Aidan's shoulders while widening her legs. His pace became exquisitely languorous. With each stroke, Emma raised her hips to meet him. They moved in perfect unison together, panting and drawing breaths in the same measure.

Aidan took Emma's hand and brought it between them. "Touch yourself," he instructed. Embarrassment filled her at his request. When she started to jerk her hand away, Aidan shook his head. "If you won't touch yourself, then touch me...touch *us*."

A shudder went through her at his words, and she felt herself not only relenting but feeling wildly turned on. Tentatively, she slid her hand down to where they were joined, feeling him sliding in and out of her. She ran her fingers over his cock, slick from their shared arousals. Aidan moaned in approval. "Yeah, babe. Oh fuck, that feels good." After working him over, she finally brought her hand back to her clit and started to stroke and rub it.

Closing her eyes, she let the feeling wash over her. It was almost too much—the sensation from Aidan thrusting in and out coupled with stimulating herself. It didn't take long for an orgasm to build and ripple through her. "Aidan! Oh Aidan!" she screamed.

"Oh, fuck, Em, I don't think I'm going to last much longer," Aidan said, through gritted teeth.

She brought her lips to his, kissing him hard and passionately while he shuddered and came into her. He fell against her like he usually did, covering her body with his. "Dammit to hell!" he cursed. His expression was one of horror when he met her gaze. "Christ, did I hurt you just then?"

Emma rolled her eyes. "Aidan, would you stop worrying? I'm fine."

"You sure?"

She grinned. "Maybe ready for dessert."

He snorted. "I thought what we just did was some fucking wild dessert!"

"Hmm, well, that was really, really hot, but I'm more in the mood for something cold and sweet." When he quirked his eyebrows at her, she giggled. "But what we just did was pretty sweet too!"

"Let me guess. Ben & Jerry's are calling your name, huh?"

Emma nodded.

"Then let me be a true gentleman and go get it for you."

"Ooh, post sex ice cream…how romantic!" she mused.

"There goes that mouth of yours again," Aidan replied, as he climbed out of bed and started for the kitchen.

"Good thing I'm about to fill it with ice cream, huh?"

Aidan winked at her over his shoulder. "I could think of something better to cram in your mouth."

She tossed a pillow at him for his audacity. "Go get the ice cream, and I'll think of letting you back in this bed."

"Oh, you'll let me back. In fact, I'll wager you'll be begging me."

As he started out of the bedroom, Emma couldn't help shivering in anticipation of what the rest of the night held in store.

CHAPTER EIGHTEEN

Drifting between sleep and consciousness, Emma felt something moist trailing up her bare back and over her neck. When Aidan pressed his morning erection against her backside, her eyes flew open. She turned to gaze at him over her shoulder. "Good morning to you, too. Or should I say the both of you," she said, her voice laced with amusement.

Aidan's chuckle hummed in her ear. "I'm sorry I woke you. I couldn't help getting so turned on when I woke up next to a fiery, naked goddess."

"Are you thinking by merely flattering me I'm going to let you have your way with me again?"

"I sure as hell hope so."

"Hmm, I thought I gave you your consolation sex prize last night. I don't recall this morning being a part of the deal."

"So you want to tease me and play hard to get, huh?" Aidan snaked his hand across her belly and between her legs. She sucked in a breath. "Was that a yes?" he asked, his fingers speeding up their tempo.

"It's definitely not a no," she murmured, tilting her head back against his shoulder.

Just as she felt herself building to an orgasm, the familiar morning nausea seized her. "No, no, stop!" she cried.

Aidan gazed down at her in surprise. "What's wrong?"

"I—" She clapped her hand over her mouth, willing herself not to throw up on him. She clambered over his legs and streaked into the bathroom. She barely made it before her stomach clenched. She gripped the sides of toilet seat and retched violently. Over and over, her stomach heaved. Exhausted, she sank to her knees. When she glanced up, Aidan stood framed in the doorway. He had managed to slide on his underwear, and she noticed her episode had killed his libido.

"Morning sickness?"

"Umm, hmm," she moaned.

"Can I get you anything?"

"No, I—" She heaved again. Dragging her arm across her mouth, she didn't dare look at Aidan. It was too embarrassing having him see her this way. Staring at the tile, she said, "I'm fine. Really. Go back to bed."

Without a word, Aidan left the bathroom. Emma couldn't blame him. She could only imagine this unattractive aspect to pregnancy would just be another reason to drive him away. What would he want with someone like her when he could have any woman he wanted?

Pressing her cheek against the toilet lid, she felt the bile rising in her throat again. She silently willed herself not to get sick again. Then Aidan appeared in the doorway. Emma peered up to see a glass of water and a bag of saltine crackers in his hands. When she stared at him in shock, he gave her a sheepish grin. "I thought this might help."

He hadn't run away. Instead, he had tried to find something to make her better. The gesture sent Emma's emotions reeling like an out of control Merry-Go-Round. "Thank you," she whispered.

Instead of leaving them on the counter and running out the door, he grabbed the hand towel and ran it under the cold water. He then eased down beside her, taking Emma's face in his hands. "Aidan, you don't--" she protested.

"Shh, just let me take care of you." Tenderly, he swiped the rag across her cheeks and her forehead. The gesture tugged at her heart, and overwhelming love for him radiated in her chest. If there had ever been a doubt to the depth of her feelings, it was cemented at that moment. She closed her eyes so he wouldn't see her tears. "Does that feel nice?"

Unable to speak, she bobbed her head.

"I'm so sorry about the puking," he said.

Her eyes flew open. "It's not your fault."

He grinned. "Well, it kind of is considering I knocked you up."

She gave him a weak smile. "But I asked you to. If it's anyone's fault, it's mine."

"Has it been bad so far?"

She nodded. "Every morning…some afternoons." She shuddered. "And then certain smells."

Aidan twisted the rag in his hands. "I wish I could do something to help. I feel so helpless having to watch you suffer."

Her chest constricted again at his words. "It's enough you just being here—comforting me like this." She reached out to touch his cheek. "You have such a good heart and so much love to give. You're going to be a wonderful father."

He stared at her in almost disbelief—his chest rising and falling harshly. She could see him emotionally shutting down right in front of her. He shook his head. "I think you give me too much credit. Besides, I'd be a real jackass if I left you alone when you were sick." He rose off of the floor and tossed the rag on the counter.

Chewing her lip, Emma realized this was probably the best she was ever going to get from him—just enough care and concern to keep his conscience from eating at him. It wasn't ever going to be enough to make him love her or commit. She just needed to accept that fact so she could guard her heart. She could only give herself to him physically—even though she desperately hoped that physical intimacy would lead to a stronger emotional one for Aidan.

So she drew in a deep breath and pulled herself off the floor. "I'm going to take a shower."

He whirled back around in surprise. "You think you're up to it?"

"The nausea and the puking never last long. I'm feeling better now." She smiled. "You want to join me?"

"Are you sure?"

"I'm not making any promises." She pulled back the shower curtain and turned on the water. "Besides, we both need to be ready to go out in a little while because I'm going to expect you to buy me some breakfast. You know, for knocking me up and all."

He grinned. "I think I can do that."

CHAPTER NINETEEN

An hour later, Emma buckled herself in while Aidan let the top down on his convertible. "What sounds good?" he asked as he pulled out of the driveway.

"Hmm, IHOP? I keep craving pancakes."

"Then IHOP it is."

While flipping through the radio stations, Aidan's phone rang. He glanced at the caller ID and grimaced. "It's my dad."

"Haven't you talked to him since you got back?"

"No."

Emma shook her head. "I can't believe you didn't let him know you're home safe and sound. I bet he's worried out of his mind."

"Thanks for the guilt trip," Aidan mused.

She stuck her tongue out at him playfully as he answered the phone. "Hey Pop…yeah, I got in last night. Sorry I didn't call you. I was a little tired."

Emma snorted at his lie. He hadn't been too tired to go a round with her. When she met Aidan's gaze, he stuck his tongue out at her, and she giggled.

"I'm planning on coming by to see you." He paused. "I know you've really been working hard on your rose garden, but now isn't actually the best time."

Emma cleared her throat, and Aidan glanced over at her. "Take me back home and go see your dad," she murmured.

He shook his head.

"Yes, he misses you and –"

"Dad, I'll be happy to come over as long as you don't mind I have a friend with me."

Wait, what? He was actually going to take her to meet his father? That was a whole level of commitment she never imagined from him.

Aidan must've registered her surprise because he whispered, "You don't mind?"

She shook her head, and he smiled. "All right. We'll be over in ten minutes." After he hung up the phone, he turned to Emma. "Are you sure you're all right with this?"

"Why would I mind?"

Aidan shrugged. "I don't know. My dad is…well, he's a blue collar, Irish Catholic ex-Marine who loves puttering around his rose garden and playing with his grandkids."

Emma grinned at his summation. "Considering most of my mom's family is blue-collar, I think I'll be fine. Besides, he's my child's grandfather."

"I just didn't want to waste your Saturday listening to my dad drone on and on about his different species of roses or his war stories."

"I think it sounds like fun."

"You need to get out more, babe."

Emma experienced the familiar tightening in her chest at his flippant attitude. Her smile faded. "I think deep down you really don't want to introduce me to him."

Aidan glanced away from the road to stare at her. "What? Why?"

"You don't want to have to explain anything to him about what we are or what we aren't. Not to mention you don't want to have to pretend I'm your girlfriend."

"Well, I hadn't actually planned on introducing you as my girlfriend. I was going to lie and say we were working on a project together for work."

"Oh," Emma murmured.

"You didn't think I was going to waltz in there and drop the bomb on him about the baby, did you? I think that would freak him out a little."

"Are you ever planning on telling him?"

"And what would I say? 'Hey dad, this is the girl who asked me to knock her up because her biological clock was ticking. Maybe once and awhile, she'll let you see the kid if you want, but I signed a contract where I don't have to have any parental or financial obligations.'"

Emma shook her head. "You know I had that part of the contract edited. Besides I would never keep the baby away from its grandfather...or its father."

Aidan glanced over at her in surprise. "You mean you wouldn't object to me having a bigger part in the baby's life?"

Emma's heart thumped so loudly in her chest she was sure Aidan could hear it. She fought to find her voice. "Of course, I wouldn't mind. I want you to do whatever you feel comfortable with."

Aidan remained quiet for a few seconds. Then he sighed. "I want to make one thing clear. Having a bigger part doesn't mean I'm going to be a typical father and help you raise it. And I'm sure as hell not changing diapers or getting up in the middle of the night to feed it or anything."

Emma bit her lip to keep from grinning. She continued chipping away at his hardened veneer little by little. It was a small step, but she would take what she could get.

"That's okay. I didn't expect you to do any of that. I just wanted him or her to at least know who their father was."

"Then we're good to go."

Aidan pulled into the driveway of a modest brick home. Just like at his house, the yard was breathtaking. "You weren't kidding when you said your dad had a green thumb," she mused as they got out of the car.

Aidan grinned. "Wait until he shows you his rose garden."

"He has an entire rose garden?"

"Yes, with several different breeds."

"That's amazing. Maybe he would be willing to give me some gardening tips. I'd love to have more flowers growing around the window of the baby's room."

"I'm sure he would be more than happy to help."

As Emma made her way up the driveway, she stumbled. Aidan snaked an arm around her waist to steady her. "Are you all right?"

"I've just been a little dizzy lately. Another wonderful side effect of early pregnancy."

"Glad to hear it wasn't our exertions last night making you lightheaded," he replied with a smirk.

She smacked his arm playfully. "You're terrible."

"Well, hello, there!" a silver headed man called from the side of the house.

Surprise flooded Emma when Aidan didn't drop his arm from her waist. "Hey, Pop."

"Good to see you, son," Aidan's father replied with a smile. He shielded his eyes from the sun and gazed at Emma. "And who is this pretty lady?"

"This is Emma Harrison. She and I work together."

Emma extended her hand and smiled. "It's a pleasure to meet you Mr. Fitzgerald."

"Please call me Patrick," he replied, shaking her hand. "Do you like roses, Emma?"

"Yes, I do. I was just admiring all your beautiful flowers."

"Come then. Let me show you my rose garden." He held out his arm like a gentleman of the past, and Emma slipped hers through it. They strolled across the front yard with Aidan trailing behind them.

When they turned the corner, Emma gasped at the rainbow of colors. "Oh it's breathtaking!"

"Thank you. I've just worked on integrating several new breeds."

Aidan's phone rang. After he grabbed it out of his pocket, he groaned. Patrick and Emma glanced over at him. "It's work. I better take this."

"Go ahead, son. The roses will still be here when you finish," Patrick replied, good-naturedly.

Aidan walked around to the corner of the house. Emma delicately fingered a red rose before bending over to smell it. The intoxicating fragrance perfumed her senses, and she sighed with pleasure. "These are so beautiful."

Patrick beamed with pride. "Those are Don Juan's or Sweetheart Roses. They're also known as climbing roses because they grow well on arbors and sides of buildings. The nice thing about them is they're so resilient they don't need a lot of pruning to come back year after year." Patrick traced his finger over one of the thorns. "My late wife actually planted these."

Emma's heart ached at his sad expression. She reached over and rubbed Patrick's arm tenderly. "Aidan told me about her passing away. I'm very sorry for your loss. In a way, I know what it feels like to lose someone who is your whole world."

"You do?" Patrick asked softly.

"My mother died of cancer two years ago. She was everything to me, especially after my father was killed when I was six." She gave him a sad smile. "Sometimes it feels like I'll never get over it—like I'll just have this gaping hole in my heart for the rest of my life."

Patrick nodded. "Yes, that's exactly how it feels." He took her hand in his and squeezed it tight. "Thank you for sharing that with me."

"You're welcome."

Silence hung around them as Emma kept admiring Patrick's garden. She had just inhaled what she imagined was a Yellow Rose of Texas when Patrick's voice startled her. "So you and my son work together?"

"We're both at the same company, but he actually works a few floors above me."

"I see."

Emma glanced up from the rose she was admiring to find Patrick giving her a knowing look. "And you two expect me to believe there's nothing between you but that you *work* together?" he asked, with a smile.

Emma flushed. "Well, no, I mean, it's complicated."

"Isn't love always complicated?"

"I-I guess so. But we've only known each other for a couple of months, so he's not in love—I mean, *we're* not in love."

Patrick pinched his lips together. "Do you see this rose?"

Emma nodded.

"It doesn't look like it's going to bloom, does it?"

Tilting her head, Emma eyed the closed bud. "No, it doesn't."

"Ah, but that's where appearances are deceiving. Sometimes the ones that bloom fastest fade quickly. It's these that are the toughest to coax out that make some of the most gorgeous flowers." He snipped a long stemmed Don Juan and handed it to Emma. "You can tell me that you and Aidan aren't in love, but looks can be deceiving."

She gasped and almost dropped the rose. She opened her mouth to argue with Patrick, but Aidan came strolling up. "Sorry about that."

"It's all right, son. I was enjoying getting to know Emma better," Patrick replied. Emma ducked her head to avoid his intense stare. "Won't you two join me for lunch?"

"I was actually in the process of taking Em out to brunch when you called."

"Psh, who wants brunch when you can have a home cooked meal? It's your mother's Shepherd's Pie."

Emma watched as Aidan's eyes lit up, and she knew she could forgo her craving for pancakes. "That sounds delicious," she said.

Aidan raised his eyebrows questioningly, and she nodded. "Okay, then, we'll stay."

"Wonderful!" Patrick exclaimed, motioning them to the backdoor.

Emma smiled. "I have to admit I'm very impressed with the culinary skills of the Fitzgerald men."

Patrick glanced at Aidan over his shoulder. "Oh, you've cooked for Emma?"

She fought the urge to giggle at what looked like a red flush creeping across Aidan's tanned cheeks. "Yeah, just some scampi. Nothing exciting."

"He's just being modest. It was delicious."

Patrick held the door open for them. "I guess us Fitzgerald men have become forced into learning to cook—mine because of being a widower and Aidan for being a confirmed bachelor."

"I'm sure whatever you have prepared will be delicious," Emma said.

Patrick picked up an oven mitt. "Aidan, why don't you take Emma on to the dining room and set another plate at the table while I get the food together?"

"Why don't you let me help?" Emma offered.

He smiled. "That would be wonderful."

Once everything was finished, they all sat down. Patrick reached out his hands. "Aidan, would you return grace?"

Emma's mouth gaped open in shock. Never in a million years would she have pegged Aidan anything remotely close to religious, least of all being entrusted with saying the blessing.

As he reached out for her hand, Aidan winked. "Close your mouth, Em. You'll catch a fly like that."

She pinched her lips together and shot him a murderous glance. But when he took his hand in hers and grazed his fingers tenderly over her knuckles, her anger evaporated. "Dear Lord for what we are about to receive make us truly thankful. Amen."

As they lifted their heads, Patrick repeated, "Amen." Emma gave Aidan a coy smile and murmured, "Short and sweet." He merely chuckled and put his napkin in his lap.

The moment Patrick took the lid off the pot Emma's stomach clenched. *Oh no, not now. Please not now!* she silently begged. As the meaty aroma invaded her nostrils, nausea overtook her. The bile rose in her throat, and she clamped her hand over her mouth. "Sorry!" she murmured before leaping from the table, knocking her chair over in the process.

CHAPTER TWENTY

Aidan swept a nervous glance over to his father. He swallowed hard as Patrick stared at Emma's retreating form. At the sound of the bathroom door slamming, Patrick raised an expectant brow.

His mind whirled with how he was going to possibly explain Emma's behavior and keep their secret. He finally smiled apologetically. "I should have mentioned that she was a vegetarian, and that the smell of meat makes her sick."

"Don't bullshit me."

"Excuse me?" Aidan demanded, leaning forward in his seat. That was certainly not the response he expected. His lie seemed pretty plausible to him. Well except for the small fact that Emma had happily accepted a lunch invitation for meaty pie not ten minutes ago.

Patrick shook his head. "She's pregnant, isn't she?"

Aidan's own stomach churned, and he fought the urge to bolt from the table just like Emma. "What would possess you to think that?" he croaked. He sure as hell hoped Emma hadn't mentioned something to Patrick while they were looking at the roses. If anyone was going to drop the bomb about his impending fatherhood, it was going to be him.

"Because of your mother. She couldn't stand to be in the same room with meat when she was pregnant with you. Even the faintest smell would send her to the bathroom. The worst was when we were in the city and passed a hotdog stand." Patrick smiled wistfully. "I haven't seen anyone have that kind of reaction since her, not even your sisters."

Aidan cast a glance down the hall. "Emma's only about six weeks along. The morning sickness, or I guess I should say nausea, is hitting her really bad."

"I assume the child is yours?"

"Of course it is," Aidan growled.

"Surely you can see why I would question you. After all, you introduced her as a friend from work and now you're telling me she's pregnant with your child."

"I didn't quite know how to tell you."

"Are you planning on marrying her?"

"It's not that simple."

Patrick's eyebrows arched in surprise. "It isn't? I thought when you got a woman pregnant, you did the honorable thing and offered to marry her. Why the hell were you sleeping with her if you didn't love her or see a future with her? Or are you still hell bent on being the asshole who uses women for his selfish own purposes?"

Aidan narrowed his eyes and gripped the edge of the lace tablecloth. "Jesus Christ, Pop, don't hold anything back. Tell me how you really feel!"

"I'm sorry, but you're thirty-two years old. You haven't had a single long-term relationship since you broke it off with Amy." Patrick shook his head sadly. "If I'm being completely honest, I could say that Amy and Emma remind me a lot of each other. I certainly don't want to see Emma get hurt like Amy did, especially if she's carrying my grandchild."

"Look, quit playing me out as the villain. Emma wanted a baby, so I agreed to help her."

Patrick opened and closed his mouth like a fish out of water. Once he had a moment to adjust to the news, an amused smile curved on his lips. "Ah, you're like her stud horse or something?"

"Not funny."

"Sorry, son. I couldn't resist." He patted Aidan's arm. "All joking aside, I just want you to think long and hard about what you're doing. I can see you care deeply for Emma, and she does for you."

Aidan shifted in his chair and stared down at his hands. "I don't know how I feel."

"You know what your mother would say, don't you?"

Sinking fast in the quick-sand of his father's words, Aidan swept out of his chair and went to pour himself a drink. He pulled the Scotch from the cabinet. "Don't bring her into this. She badgered me enough herself. Always wondering why I broke Amy's heart, or why I wouldn't settle down, marry some nice girl from church, and punch out a bunch of kids." He conveniently left out the part about how she had made him promise on her deathbed to have children one day.

"Don't you realize son she knew that's what would really make you happy."

Aidan scowled. "But she never saw the real me—she only believed the good parts. If she had really stopped to think about it, she would have realized I never wanted to be tied down or be stuck with the same woman day in and day out."

Hurt radiated in Patrick's eyes. "Is that what you think of the forty-five years I had with your mother?"

Aidan threw his head back and stared at the water stain on the dining room ceiling. He wished he had never answered his phone or agreed to come over. Most of all, he wished he had never, *ever* thought bringing Emma with him would be a good idea. She had been right when she anticipated her presence would bring on the third degree. Aidan sighed and looked over at his father. "No, Pop, that's not what I think. But we're different people."

"Emma could be the best thing that's ever happened to you."

A snort erupted from Aidan's lips. "How the hell would you know that? You've been with her all of an hour!"

"I may be an old man, but I'm not blind. She's the total package, son. She's just as beautiful on the inside as she is on the out. How can you not be amazed by what a special young woman she is? Why if I was your age, I'd be doing everything in my power to make her mine—especially if she was carrying my child."

Aidan opened his mouth to argue, but at the sound of the bathroom door creaking, he closed it. "Not a word," he whispered to his father. When Emma appeared, her face was positively ghost-like except for the flush of embarrassment on her cheeks. She eased down in her seat and tentatively glanced across the table at Aidan.

"Are you all right?" he asked.

She gave a weak smile. "I'm fine." She then turned to Patrick. "Mr. Fitzgerald, I'm so sorry for ruining your lunch like that."

He held up his index finger to silence her. "You did no such thing." He reached across the table to squeeze her hand. "Besides, it does an old man's heart good to hear he's going to be a grandfather again."

"Shit, Pop, I said not a word!" Aidan exclaimed as Emma's eyes widened as big as saucers.

"You told him?" she demanded.

Patrick shook his head. "Now don't be getting upset with him. I'm the one who guessed it. When my late wife was pregnant with Aidan, she suffered terribly with morning sickness—well, we jokingly called it the all day sickness because it wasn't just regulated to the morning. And smells bothered her something terrible."

Emma clutched her abdomen. "It's awful."

"If I were a betting man, I'd put good money on you're carrying a boy. After all, my wife only experienced what she did with Aidan."

Emma gave a dreamy smile. "A boy would be wonderful, but I'll just as happy with a girl—as long as he or she is healthy is all that matters."

Patrick patted her hand. "Oh, but you need a boy. That way the Fitzgerald family name will go on." He turned to Aidan. "You are planning on giving the baby your last name, aren't you?"

"Jesus Christ, Pop! Lighten up."

"I'm a staunch Irish Catholic, son, I'm not going to ease up on the legitimacy of my grandchild."

Aidan felt the blood draining from his face. He immediately reached for his glass and knocked back the rest of the Scotch. At his father's continued scrutiny, he shifted in his chair. "Well, Emma and I haven't discussed it."

"Don't you want to carry on our family's name?" Patrick turned his intense gaze on Emma. "I was the only son of my parents, and I had only one son. I have five grandsons and a great-grandson, yet our name will die out with Aidan."

"Oh come on, Pop, it's not like I'll be the last Fitzgerald ever. Granddad Fitz had seven brothers!" Aidan argued.

Patrick crossed his arms over his chest in a huff. "Fine then. If you won't give the baby your name, I'll give him mine!"

When Emma squeaked across from him, Aidan knew she was upset by the overt tension between the two strong-willed men facing off. "Would you please knock it off? You're freaking Em out."

Patrick's expression immediately softened. "Emma, I'm so sorry if I offended or upset you. I'm fiercely protective of my family, and now that you're carrying my grandchild, you're a part of that."

Aidan watched as Emma's expression turned from apprehension to positively beaming. "That's very sweet of you to care so much. My baby will be very lucky to have you as a grandfather." She drew in a breath. "But before I got pregnant, Aidan and I set very clear parameters on what his role would be."

"So you object to the baby having his name?" Patrick demanded.

"Well, no…I mean, I wouldn't mind." Before Aidan could stop himself, he glowered across the table at Emma. She quickly shook her head. "But I don't want to pressure Aidan into anything. No offense, Patrick, but you're kind of putting him on the spot. I don't want Aidan to feel uncomfortable."

Patrick harrumphed and leaned back in his chair. "Fine then. I'm just an old fashioned, out of touch, old fart!"

Emma giggled. "Aw, no you're not. Actually, you remind me a lot of my mother's father. He's really been more of a father figure to me after my father died. Granddaddy is very traditional and old-fashioned. And pretty easy going until you mess with his family."

"He sounds like my kind of man."

"I think you two would get along very well. He shared your same questions and concerns when he learned I was unmarried and pregnant." Emma twisted the napkin in her lap. "Actually, he had quite a few choice words for me."

Aidan experienced a twinge of protectiveness at Emma's discomfort. "You didn't tell me that."

"Everything is okay now. In fact, he's really creative when it comes to woodworking, and he's carving the baby a rocking horse."

"That's a nice way to make amends," Patrick mused.

Emma smiled. "Yes, it is."

Patrick appeared thoughtful. Then he stood up. "Come, Emma, there's something I'd like you and the baby to have."

He held out his hand, and Emma smiled, slipping hers into his. Aidan watched as he pulled her out of the dining room chair and led her down the hall. He sat stunned, still unbelieving the effect Emma had on his father. Aidan hadn't seen him so animated in months. It was like she had brought a piece of him that was dead back to life—something not even he or his sisters had been able to do.

Curiosity caused him to rise from his chair and seek them out. He found them in his parent's bedroom. Emma stood in the middle of the room, peering intently at the walk-in closet. Shuffling noises came from within, and Aidan heard his father curse softly. Finally, Patrick appeared with a yellowed box faded with time, a beaming smile on his face. "For my grandson," he said, handing Emma the box.

She swept her free hand to her hip and challenged, "And what if it is a girl?"

"Trust me on this one." When Emma huffed in protest, Patrick laughed. "All right, all right. It will work for my granddaughter as well."

Emma opened the box's lid. Aidan leaned forward as she gently pulled away the tissue paper. A little cry escaped her lips. Gently, she pulled out a white baby's gown with intricate lace and pearls. "It's beautiful."

"It's Aidan's christening gown," Patrick said.

Aidan sucked in a breath. His father's words coupled with Emma holding a piece of past made him feel like he had been punched in the gut. If there was any doubt how his father felt about Emma and their child, it was cemented by the tiny gown in her hands. He wasn't entirely sure he was ready for this level of emotion and commitment. "Dad, Emma's not even Catholic," Aidan protested.

Without taking his eyes off Emma, Patrick shook his head. "She might humor me and have the baby Christened though."

Emma nibbled on her bottom lip. "The truth is I'm Baptist." At Patrick's sharp intake of breath, she held up her hand. "But considering you and Aidan are Catholic and the baby will be half Catholic, I suppose I could. If it meant a lot to you."

A broad smile formed on Patrick's face. "It sure would."

"Then I would be honored."

"Thank you, sweetheart," Patrick embraced Emma, squeezing her tight. "Thank you most of all for being such a beautiful light in the world...and in my son's life."

Aidan stared at his father in horror. Had he lost his mind? Emma wasn't a light in his life...was she? He tried ignoring the tears sparkling in Emma's green eyes when she pulled out of Patrick's arms. She kissed him tenderly on the cheek. "Thank you for wanting to be a part of my baby's life."

The continued exchange of emotions between his father and Emma made it feel like all the air in the room had been sucked out. Simply breathing in and out made his chest feel like a Sumo wrestler was pressing down on him. *A beautiful light in my son's life* kept replaying over and over again in his mind.

Deep down inside him, a little voice agreed with his father. Emma made him burn with desire one minute and laugh the next.

The way she interacted with Beau and his nephews tugged at his heart. She was the kind of woman if he got physically sick, she would be there to nurse him through it, and if he fell on hard times emotionally, she would be his rock.

How had he been so fucking blind?

Aidan's gaze wildly scanned the room. No, he just needed to get out of his parent's bedroom, out his father's house, and then maybe he would be able to think.

He cleared his throat. "I hate to be a party pooper, but we really need to get going. I've got a lot to take care of after being gone the last month."

Patrick nodded. "I understand, son. I'm just so glad you came by." He smiled at Emma. "That you *both* came by."

It took Aidan a moment before he was able to say, "So am I."

Emma clutched the Christening gown to her chest as she trailed Patrick out of the bedroom. Aidan followed close on their heels. "Now that we're acquainted, there's no reason for you to be a stranger. You know where I live, so you don't have to rely on Aidan to bring you by."

Jesus, two hours with the girl, and his father was already giving Emma full access to come over whenever she felt like it. For all he knew, his father would get down all the family photo albums or his old high school yearbooks to entertain Emma with. What a nightmare.

Patrick gave Emma a final hug before turning to Aidan. "Don't be a stranger."

"I'll try."

As Emma started down the porch steps, Patrick grabbed Aidan's arm. "Will you at least try to consider some of the things we talked about?" he asked, in a hushed whisper.

"I'll try, Pop. I really will."

Patrick smiled. "Good. I'm glad to hear it."

Emma slipped into the passenger seat as Aidan jogged down the front walk. When he slid inside the car, he exhaled a long, ragged breath. Emma turned and gave him a tentative smile. "That was...interesting."

"You could say that," he replied, cranking up.

After he pulled out of the driveway, he glanced over to see Emma running her fingers over the fabric of the Christening gown. "I bet you were adorable wearing this," she remarked.

"No, I've seen the pictures. I look like a chubby little pansy wearing a dress."

"You could never look like a pansy," she teased.

Aidan grunted in response. Staring ahead, he gripped the steering wheel tighter, desperately trying to keep control of the feelings raging within him. They didn't speak for a few minutes.

When Emma finally did, her voice was strained. "I'm sorry for today."

Aidan tore his gaze off the road to stare at her. "What are you talking about?"

"Meeting your father. It was too much pressure and commitment for you. I can tell."

"No, it wasn't."

"Oh please. You were about to hyperventilate under the stress when we were in your parent's bedroom." Emma shook her head. "I seriously started to worry you were going to have a stroke or something."

"It wasn't that bad."

The skin on his cheek singed from the glare Emma was giving him. "At least be honest about the situation, Aidan."

A low growl erupted from the back of his throat. "Fine. That was a total and complete mind fuck for me, okay?"

"That's better."

"Yeah, right."

"I'm serious. I always want you to be honest with me, especially about how you feel."

"Women always say that, and then the moment you tell them how things are, you get verbally or physically bitch slapped."

Silence echoed through the car for a few minutes. Finally, Emma spoke. "Look, I don't have to keep the gown. You can give it back to Patrick and explain to him you only agreed to give your DNA, not yourself."

He banged his fist into the steering wheel. "Dammit, Em, that's not what I want!"

Cutting across two lanes, he wheeled into a supermarket parking lot. After screeching to a stop, he killed the engine. When he turned to face Emma, her eyes were wide, and she had pressed herself up against the door as far away from him as possible. "When I said today was a mind-fuck, it was in more ways than one. Seeing you with my father—the way he reacted to you—it's made me come unhinged. But not in the way you think."

"Oh?"

He shook his head. "When I met you, my life was exactly like I wanted it to be. Then I was only thinking with my dick when I thought I could get you pregnant and walk away. And now…it's all so fucking complicated I don't know which way is up anymore."

"I'm sorry. I didn't mean to cause problems for you or to be a burden."

Aidan rolled his eyes. "Jesus, Em, how can you even think that?"

Her brows furrowed. "Because you said—"

With a frustrated grunt, he raked his hands through his hair. "Dammit, I'm no good at this. I'm saying and doing everything wrong."

"I don't understand," she murmured.

"Deep down, I'm still the same person I was when we first started all this—no marriage, no major commitment, no long-term relationships." He sighed. "But…I want to try to have more with you."

Emma gasped. "You do?"

He stared at her intently. "Even though I hate to admit it, I really missed you while I was gone."

"Are you sure you didn't just miss the sex?"

He scowled at her. "Yeah, I'm sure."

She gave him a tentative smile. "Then that's very flattering."

"Fuck, I didn't think you'd make me work this hard for it."

"Excuse me?"

"I thought…" He shook his head. "I thought you wanted *us* even more than I did."

"I do," she replied softly.

"You have a hell of a way of showing it."

She glared at him. "Well, you're not really playing fair. You've been kind and considerate, if not downright caring, the entire time we were trying to conceive, yet you constantly kept me at arm's length. Every time I thought you might truly be interested in me, you'd shut down. And now you wait to spring the fact you might want more when I'm a hormone fueled emotional wreck."

"What difference does that make?"

"Everything!" She pointed out the windshield to where a teenage bag boy was collecting carts. "I'm so whacked out on hormones right now that kid could ask me to marry him, and I would say yes."

"That's fucked up," Aidan mused.

"Yeah, it's called estrogen, and it's working overtime right now. If you want to know what that feels like, it's kind of like how the massive dose of testosterone pumping through you fuels the head below your waist, driving most of your decisions."

Aidan threw his head back and laughed. "Are you trying to say I only think with my dick?"

"I don't think I'd be pregnant right now if you didn't," Emma said softly.

His expression darkened. "Am I to assume that's the estrogen talking or are you just trying to cut me?"

Emma ducked her head. "Yes and no. It's just that everything is so emotionally overwhelming right now. Meeting Patrick today…" She bit down on her lip and then stared out the car window. "I know we were only together for such a short time, but it was almost like the moment I met him I felt a connection to something I haven't had in a very, very long time—a father's love. I've only felt that before with my grandfather, and he's my own blood."

Aidan's chest tightened at Emma's visible pain. He reached out and took her hand in his. "Em—"

She turned back to him with tears in her eyes. "You think you're trying to protect yourself? Well, so am I. As much as I want to say yes to you Aidan, I have to protect myself and the baby."

"The baby? Do you honestly think I'd do anything to hurt it?"

"Not intentionally. But I can't let you get invested in our lives if you might bail when some woman in a short skirt and huge breasts turns your head."

"That was fucking low," he growled.

She wiped her eyes. "I'm sorry, but you know at some fundamental level it's the truth. You've said yourself a million times that you don't do long-term relationships."

"Yeah, well, people can change you know."

"You can't imagine how much I want to believe that," she whispered.

Aidan sighed, drumming his fingers on the steering wheel. "Look, that phone call I got from work was about how I have to fly to DC on Tuesday. I'll be gone for a few days. Will you think about it while I'm gone?"

"I will if you will."

"What's that supposed to mean?"

"It means I want you to make sure you fully comprehend what you're asking of me and yourself. And I want you to have a pretty clear picture of just what 'more' means to you."

"Fine." He gave her a pointed look. "I will if you will."

The corners of her mouth quirked up in a smile. "It's a deal."

CHAPTER TWENTY-ONE

The sound of a car in the driveway caused Beau to hop off the couch and start barking madly at the window. "What is it boy?" Emma asked, abandoning her book. Beau whined and raced to the front door. Rising from the couch, Emma started over to the window. Surely Aidan's niece, Megan, hadn't changed her mind about Emma baby-sitting and come back for her four month old son, Mason. She had struck up an almost instant friendship when Emma met her at Sunday lunch at Patrick's. Even with Aidan out town, Patrick had insisted she and his future *grandson* come join them. It had been a little overwhelming being with all of Aidan's sisters and their families, but overall, she had a wonderful time being part of his family.

Since Megan had been thrilled by the prospect of Emma baby-sitting, she couldn't imagine that she would have changed her mind. When Emma peeked through the blinds, her heart leapt into her throat.

It was Aidan.

What was he doing here? When she had talked to him the night before, he had told her it would be another week before he came home. Glancing down at her faded Scooby Doo pajama bottoms and ratty tank top, she shook her head. There was no time to try and make herself more presentable. Of course, explaining Mason's presence was going to be a little more difficult.

She threw open the front door. Beau scurried out into the night, yapping and wagging his tail. He mowed into Aidan and almost knocked him down as Emma hurried out onto the porch. "Hey! What are you doing here?"

Aidan scratched a wiggling Beau. "My last few meetings got rescheduled for next week. I hopped the first plane home, so I could surprise you."

Swaying on her feet, Emma fought to catch her breath. He had actually done something spontaneously romantic? "Aw, that's sweet. It's a very nice surprise."

Abandoning Beau, he closed the gap between them. "I also wanted to come straight over here to see if you had given anymore thought to us having more."

"I have."

Aidan's brows furrowed. "And?"

"The answer is yes," she replied with a smile.

Aidan's expression turned over like a switch from apprehension to happiness. "I'm so glad to hear that. I've been thinking about it the whole time I was gone."

"So have I."

"Most of all, I wanted things resolved before I have to go back to DC."

"When do you leave again?"

"Tuesday." Emma's chest tightened at the prospect.

Aidan's hungry eyes roamed over her, and he grinned. "Barefoot and pregnant, huh? Now all I need is you to go in the kitchen and fix me some dinner."

She rolled her eyes. "I would have cooked you something if I knew you were coming. The best I've got is the left-over pizza I ordered in tonight."

He pulled her to him, crisscrossing his arms around her waist. "I'll forget all about dinner if you'll come inside and give me a real homecoming," he teased, licking a moist trail up her neck.

She shivered with her building need, but then shook her head. "Um, I don't think that's going to be possible."

"Why not?"

"I have company."

Aidan's arms tensed around her. He jerked his head back to stare at her with a puzzled expression. "You have a guy with you?"

She nodded. "A very handsome one, too."

His jaw tensed. "But you just said…you just agreed to having more with *me*."

She bit her lip to keep from grinning at his outrage. "I know. But he was here before I knew how you felt. And I have to admit, there's just something about this guy I can't resist."

Without another word, he slung out of her embrace and barreled in the doorway. "Wait, Aidan, I'm—"

He ignored her and busted through the foyer. Hot on his heels, she tried to catch him before he started yelling and screaming for the imaginary guy to get the hell out of there, least of all before he woke up Mason. She watched as he skidded to a stop and froze in front of the Pack N Play where Mason slept.

He whirled around. "*Mason.* You mean I just got all worked up over a baby?"

She giggled. "Yes."

Aidan exhaled in a wheeze, and he bent over to rest his elbows on his knees. "I can't believe you just did that to me! I was expecting to have to throw some dude out of here."

"Oh, just what every girl wants—a possessive, raging Knight in Shining Armor."

He scowled at her and swept one of his hands to his chest. "No, shit, I think I'm having a heart attack or something."

Emma walked over to him and pressed her hand over his heart. "Aw, poor baby, want me to kiss it and make it better?"

He poked out his bottom lip and gave her a puppy-dog face until she leaned in and kissed his heart over his shirt. "Thank you." He cast a glance over his shoulder at Mason. "So what exactly is he doing here?"

She wrapped her arms around his neck and pressed against him. "What can I say? I have a thing for the men of the Fitzgerald family."

The corners of Aidan's lips turned up in a slight smirk at her statement. "Is that right?"

"That and Megan's overwhelmed with exams right now, so I offered to keep him to let her get some uninterrupted work done. Plus it's good practice for me."

"Wait, so he's spending the night?"

"Yep." She leaned up to teasingly nip his lips with her tongue. "But he's sleeping in the Pack N Play, and you get to be in the bed. With me."

"Hmm, I like that scenario." He kissed her hungrily while guiding her back towards the couch.

"Whoa, wait a minute. I didn't mean for us to get started now," she murmured against his lips.

"When is there a better time?"

Emma let him push her down onto the cushions. "We really should wait until Mason goes down for the night. He's going to need a bottle and a bath."

"He's fine." He eased himself on top of her, still careful not to bear too much weight on her. While one hand delved under her tank top, the other went for the waistband of her pajama bottoms and then stopped. "Damn, are these Scooby Doo?"

She giggled. "I wasn't expecting company, and I have a slight obsession from growing up with the old cartoon."

"They almost killed my hard-on."

She slid her hand between them and then quirked her eyebrows. "Seems fine to me."

"Hmm, keep doing that, and I think it'll be more than fine."

She kept rubbing him through his pants while he licked a hot trail down her neck to her breastbone. As he lowered the straps on her tank top to bare her breasts, a shriek came from the other side of the room. For a minute it didn't register with her, but then Mason started wailing loudly. She immediately broke their kiss and jerked her hand off his cock. "Stop…baby," she panted.

"No, it feels so good," he murmured against her collarbone.

Emma rolled her eyes and smacked his chest. "Aidan, are you deaf? Mason's crying."

"Oh shit." With an agonized groan, Aidan pulled away from her. She slid out from under him and hurried over to the Pack N Play. Mason held his arms out to her as giant tears slid down his cheeks. "Aw, shh, it's okay, sweet boy," she said, scooping him up. His cries quieted a little when he was in her arms. "What's the matter angel? Are you hungry?"

Emma kissed Mason's cheek and rubbed wide circles over his back while he grinned at Aidan over her shoulder.

"What a little cock-blocker," Aidan grumbled.

Emma gasped and whirled around. "What did you just call him?"

"A cock-blocker, which is exactly what he is at the moment."

Mason screeched a cry, and Emma hugged him tighter. "Don't listen to Uncle Aidan, sweetheart. He didn't mean it."

Aidan motioned to Mason. "Look at him. He's perfectly fine as long as you're holding him."

She shook her head. "You're a complete and total asshole."

"You shouldn't cuss in front of the baby," he chided with a grin.

Emma widened her eyes. With a huff, she walked over to Aidan. "It's almost time for him to eat. Hold him while I go fix his bottle."

Surprisingly Aidan didn't protest when Emma thrust Mason into his arms. Mason immediately stopped snubbing and stared wide-eyed at Aidan. "Yeah, that's right. You're stuck with me now, and I don't have a nice rack for you to snuggle up to."

Emma smacked his arm. "Don't you dare talk to him like that! He's only a baby! Breasts are just food to him, pervert!"

"Damn, Em, when did you get so violent?" he joked.

Mason gave Aidan a toothless grin when Emma stomped off. Aidan chuckled. "I guess she's right, huh? But one day you'll understand what it's like to be left at half-mast by some chick."

"I heard that!" she called to him as she slammed the refrigerator door. After heating the formula, she returned to the living room just as Mason started to get fussy again. Aidan started to hand him back to her, but she shook her head. "Can you give it to him while I go run his bath?"

He gave her a playful smirk. "And if I refused, does that mean I wouldn't have any chance of getting back in your Scooby Doo pajamas tonight?"

"I would say the odds would be slim to none."

Aidan took the bottle from her. "Guess it wouldn't hurt for me to feed him. It's been awhile since one of my sister's forced me to do this, so I'm a little rusty. But you're on your own for the diaper changing."

Emma swept her hands to her hips. "So let me get this straight. You're basically only feeding Mason not to help me out, but to ensure you'll get laid tonight?"

"I consider it a win-win situation for both of us." He gazed down at Mason who was sucking his bottle down. "And for him, too."

"Just when I think you've moved past being a sex-crazed asshole, you act like this."

Aidan cocked his eyebrows. "All my married friends have warned me about how bad your sex life takes a dive after you have kids. I guess you're giving me an early warning, huh?"

"You're impossible!" She stalked off to her bedroom. After slipping inside the bathroom, she turned on the faucet and tested the temperature. Once it had filled up enough, she turned off the water and headed back into the living room. With Mason in the crook of one arm, Aidan flipped channels on the remote with the other.

"Did you burp him?"

He glanced away from the TV. "Huh?"

She rolled her eyes and took the empty bottle from Aidan. "I'm gathering that you never had much to do with your nephews and nieces when they were babies?"

"Not a whole lot. Why?"

"Because once you give a baby a bottle, you have to burp them, or the gas will cause them pain."

"Fine, I'll burp him." Aidan brought Mason to his chest and swatted his back.

"A little harder," Emma instructed.

After Aidan gave two quick pats, Mason burped loudly and then promptly spit-up all over his shoulder. "Jesus Christ!" Aidan cried, staring down in horror at his shirt.

"Oh, calm down. It's just a little spit-up."

"This is a hundred dollar shirt, Em."

"You act like he did it on purpose." She handed him the box of wet wipes from the table and then picked Mason up. "While I'm giving him his bath, would you do me a favor and put the Pack N Play in my bedroom?"

"Yeah, whatever."

"Thank you."

As she went down the hall, she heard Aidan grumbling to himself as he washed off his shirt. Once she got Mason bathed and into his pajamas, his eyes were heavy. Peeking out the bathroom door, she saw the Pack N Play set up and realized Aidan had done what she asked. That redeemed him a little in her eyes. She rocked Mason for a few minutes in the glider until she knew he was sound asleep.

When she started out of the bedroom, she thought about Aidan's sarcastic comment about babies and sex. She was still irritated with him for being selfish, but she didn't want to turn him totally off the idea of marriage and children when things were going so well between them. Raging a war within herself, she finally let the devil on her shoulder win out, rather than the angel. After all, she loved being right, and she was going to prove Aidan wrong if it was the last thing she did.

She tiptoed over to her dresser and opened the bottom drawer. Buried at the bottom under bras and panties was a black corset with spaghetti straps and garters that Casey made her buy for baby-making. She hadn't ended up needing it. With its frilly black panties, it was definitely the most daring piece of lingerie she owned. Fortunately, she could get away with leaving the last few snaps unbuttoned for her expanding belly.

"Yep, this will do the trick," she whispered. Grabbing it, she hurried into the bathroom and changed. When she eyed herself in the mirror, she didn't look like an expectant mother sporting a tiny baby bump. She looked like a full-fledged vixen.

She padded down the hall. When she got into the kitchen, she could hear the high energy voice of a sports reporter echoing through the living room.

"Mason's asleep," she announced.

"He didn't give you much trouble?" Aidan asked, never taking his eyes off the television.

"No, he went to sleep like an angel."

"That's good."

"Want a beer?"

"Yeah. That'd be nice."

She got one out the fridge and walked slowly over to the couch. He didn't even look her way when she handed it to him. He popped the top and took a swig.

"What are you watching?"

"The Braves game."

"You wanna play a game instead?" she asked coyly.

He took another sip of beer before turning to look at her. As his gaze swept over her body, he spewed the liquid out of his mouth. "Jesus, Em, what the hell are you wearing?"

She glanced down at her ensemble like it was the most normal thing she owned. "Just a surprise for you. Don't you like it?"

"Oh I like it." Aidan licked his lips, his eyes lingering on the cleavage spilling out of the bustier. "It's just I thought after I had acted like such a freaking prick, I was striking out in the sex department tonight."

"Well, I should give you a good spanking for being so bad earlier."

Aidan laughed. "I think I might enjoy that."

With a suggestive smile, she rose off of the couch. Aidan's gaze widened at the sight of her garters and lacy thigh highs. She took a pillow off the couch and dropped it on the floor. Bending over him, her fingers went to the button of his pants. "I wanted to finish what we started earlier before we got interrupted, if that's okay."

"That's fine with me."

She slid his zipper down, and Aidan lifted his hips to allow her to pull his pants off. His erection strained against his underwear. Kneeling between his legs on the pillow, she ran her hands up and down the inside of his thighs, her fingernails scraping against his sensitive skin. "Please, Em," Aidan murmured.

Emma smiled sweetly at him as she pulled down the waistband of his underwear and freed his erection. Taking him in one hand, she licked a slow trail from root to tip. Her tongue flicked and swirled around the head. She suctioned just the head in her mouth and then released it. Aidan groaned. "Babe, don't tease me. It's been too long."

She continued her slow assault on him, feeling him grow larger with her ministrations. She blew air on his glistening tip, which caused a low growl from Aidan. When he started to protest again, she slid him into her mouth. Aidan gasped and bucked his hips, causing her to take him deeper. She slid him in and out, sucking hard on the rim of his head, while gripping him with her hand. Each time she did, he moaned in pleasure. "Oh Em, oh fuck!"

She sped up the pace as his fingers tangled into her hair. "I'm going to come if you don't stop," he warned.

But she wanted all of him so she just kept working her mouth over his cock, taking him deeper and deeper each time along with suctioning more pressure around him. Finally, he cried out, lifting his hips and bathing the inside of her mouth with him. She licked and sucked until he was dry, and when she gazed up at him, his eyes burned down on her. "God, that was good!"

"I'm glad you liked it."

He bent over and pulled her onto his lap. Emma felt herself grow wetter as she straddled him. Aidan's hands found their way to her breasts, lifting them out of her bustier. As he cupped them, he glanced up at her with a smirk. "I think I get the meaning of your little game now."

"My game?" she asked innocently.

He nodded. "You wanted to prove to me that you can have a baby and still have a hot sex life."

She arched her eyebrows. "Oh, do you think that what I just did was really that hot?"

Aidan rolled her nipples between his fingers, causing them to harden. "You wearing something this sexy and then sucking me off? Hell yes, that's incredibly hot."

"I just wanted to welcome you home." She rubbed herself over his slackened cock, bringing it back to life with several determined thrusts of her hips.

"Em, you're driving me wild," Aidan murmured, his lips brushing against her breasts.

"Take me to bed then," she commanded.

"With pleasure." He gripped her by the hips and pushed her onto her feet. As he stood up, he dropped his underwear.

"And hurry up and take off your shirt. It smells," Emma instructed as she started to the bedroom. She swayed her hips provocatively to get his attention. She snickered when she heard the buttons popping on Aidan's shirt and them scattering across the hardwood floor. Only he would ruin an expensive shirt for sex.

She barely made it down the hall before he reached her side. He wrapped his arms around her waist, pulling her into his arms. His breath scorched against her cheek. "I'm going to make you come so hard you'll scream my name."

Emma shivered in anticipation as she pressed herself against Aidan. "Shh, we'll have to be quiet, or we'll wake Mason," she replied.

Aidan snickered. "I didn't expect an audience."

"Well, what do you suggest?"

He glanced across the hall and then pulled her into the guest bedroom. He started to shut the door, but Emma shook her head. "I won't be able to hear Mason."

Aidan grunted in frustration and then pushed her towards the bed. His fingers deftly unhooked the clasps on her bustier. When her breasts were freed, his mouth immediately closed over one nipple.

His erection pressed against her belly, and she felt herself growing more and more aroused. His hands went to her panties, shimming them down her legs.

He spun her around and bent her over the edge of the bed, her elbows resting on the mattress. He spread her legs further apart. His cock nudged her entrance from behind, and he asked, "Is this okay?"

"Umm, hmm," she murmured.

On the first thrust, Emma cried out. Aidan leaned over her back, his voice ringing in her ear. "Don't wake Mason up," he warned.

She glanced over her shoulder at him. "What happened to making me scream?" she panted.

"Oh, I can still do that." His hand reached around and found her throbbing clit. He stroked it as he pounded in and out of her. "Is it too much, babe?" he asked, in a hoarse voice. She knew he was still afraid of doing anything to hurt the baby.

She shook her head. "No, it's good. *So* good." Aidan's other hand snaked around to cup her breast, pinching the nipple between his fingers. "Yes, oh yes!" Emma cried, almost reaching her first orgasm.

When Aidan removed his hand, she mewled in frustration. Once her high started unraveling, he brought his fingers back, deftly stroking and caressing her, building her back up again. "Yes! Oh, Aidan, oh please! Aidan!" she cried.

"Please what?"

"Please keep touching me! Please make me come!"

He stroked her faster and faster until she pressed her face against the mattress, fisting the sheets in her hands, and screamed.

Feeling himself close, Aidan gripped Emma's hips tighter and buried his face in her neck. He came so hard but didn't bother masking his throaty cries. When he was finished, he pulled her up and turned her around to face him. "If you keep giving me homecomings like this, I think I'll request to travel even more."

"Aw, that would be nice, but then I would miss you too much during the week."

Aidan grinned. "Miss me or the sex?" he asked, throwing back her usual question.

She cocked her head. "Why the sex of course!"

He grunted and smacked her playfully on the ass. "I've said it once, and I'll say it again. That mouth of yours is trouble."

She wiggled out of his embrace. "I'm going to go take a shower. Want to join me?"

"You don't even need to ask."

CHAPTER TWENTY-TWO

A little after three, the sound of Mason's cries woke Emma. She pushed against Aidan who was sprawled on top of her. "Wake up, Aidan."

"Hmm?"

"Mason's crying."

He groaned and rolled off of her. As Emma threw on her robe, Mason let out a high pitched squeal. "Jesus, that kid has a set of lungs on him," Aidan said before pulling a pillow over his head.

She hurried over to the Pack N Play. "Shh, it's okay, sweetheart," she murmured, picking Mason up. His wailing eased a little, but he still continued crying.

Aidan's voice came muffled from under the pillow. "Em, would you mind taking him and the screaming somewhere else?"

Rage burned through Emma. How dare he treat her that way? Shifting Mason onto her shoulder, she used her free hand to smack Aidan's naked back. Hard.

He flung back the pillow and glared up at her. "What the hell was that for?"

"Why are you being such an insensitive asshole?"

"Because I'm overworked, jet-lagged, and just want to sleep," he growled.

Emma shook her head. "Your behavior tonight is seriously giving me something to think about."

Aidan rose up in the bed and rubbed his eyes. "What are you bitching about now?"

"Is this how it's going to be with our baby? You only thinking of your own selfish needs, resenting the baby when it comes between us and sex, and most of all, making it seem like I'm a single parent when you're in the same room with me?"

With a roll of his eyes, Aidan jerked off the sheet. "Fine. I'll go fix his fucking bottle. Will that make you happy?"

"Maybe," she replied. Even though he stomped bare-assed out of the room, Emma grinned that her speech had affected him enough to react. Every little battle was a victory in her favor. She eased down in the glider, rubbing Mason's back. "Hang on sweetheart. Uncle Aidan's going to get your bottle."

Her words had little effect on him, and by the time Aidan came back, he was red-faced, snorting with hungry anger, and flailing his arms and legs.

"Damn, Little Man, take a chill," Aidan said, shoving the bottle at Emma.

"Thank you," she said, with a smile. "Looks like temper tantrums run in the Fitzgerald family," she mused, as Mason latched onto the bottle.

"I have no idea what you're talking about," Aidan replied with a grin. He collapsed back onto the bed. "He obviously gets that from his father—the dickhead who knocked Megan up and ran off."

"What a jerk. Who could even think of leaving an angel like Mason or a sweetheart like Megan," Emma replied. She eased the glider to and fro as Mason sucked the milk down greedily. "You were hungry, weren't you?" she asked, as she placed him on her shoulder and burped him.

Cradling him to her chest, she gave him his pacifier. After she began humming softly, she saw the calming effect it had on him. When she started singing softly, Mason's eyes grew heavier and heavier. Then he was fast asleep.

When she stood up to put him back to bed, she did a double take at the sight of Aidan propped up on one elbow, staring at her. With only the light from the hallway, she couldn't quite tell if it was lust or love that burned in his eyes.

"What?" she whispered, easing Mason down onto the mattress.

"I've never heard you sing before."

"Oh that." She ducked her head, trying to fight the embarrassment pricking her skin. She pulled the blanket over Mason.

"You're really good."

She jerked her gaze up to stare over at Aidan in surprise. "Seriously?"

"Like an angel." He took her hand and pulled her back into the bed. "I mean, you told me you sang and all at church and at the bar, but I had no idea you were that good."

"You're just being nice."

"And when have I ever done that?" Aidan mused, with a sly smile.

Emma giggled. "Okay, I guess you're right about that one."

His lips grazed along her collarbone before he glanced up at her. "I'm serious, Em. Your voice is absolutely amazing."

"Thank you." She pressed her lips to his. "Anytime you want me to sing you to sleep, I will."

"I'd like that."

Emma scooted closer to Aidan, burying her face in the crook of his arm. "I really hate you have to leave again."

"So do I," he murmured.

She fought with herself before asking the next question. "I know we agreed that we both wanted 'more', but did you ever figure out what that meant to you?"

His fingers, which had been rubbing lazy circles over her skin, froze on her shoulder blade. "Not exactly. Did you?"

Propping her chin on his chest, she brought her gaze to his. "I would hope it meant at the very least monogamy."

"Of course it would." He creased his brows at her. "You know I haven't been with anyone else since I propositioned you that night at O'Malley's."

"I know. It's just—"

"You're afraid because of my past I might not be able to stay monogamous?"

"Yes," she whispered.

He sighed. "I can understand why you feel that way, Em. But I was serious when I told you I wanted to try for more with you. I can't make any sweeping guarantees, but I at least want to try. I like you. I like spending time with you, even outside the bedroom."

Emma knew that what Aidan was offering was huge for him. It felt like nothing to her, but after all, she wasn't a commitment phobic womanizer. The fact he hadn't gone on some exotic sex tour of India or hooked up with someone in the Delhi office meant he was honestly trying. She stared into his eyes. "I can accept that."

"And I would assume you aren't on the look-out either, right?"

Emma couldn't help the contemptuous snort that escaped her lips. "Do you even have to ask? Besides, the last time I checked being pregnant didn't put you on Maxim's Hot 100 list."

He rolled his eyes. "There you go putting yourself down again about your sex appeal. You always so oblivious to the effect you have on other men."

"Yeah right."

"You didn't even realize the night I got in from India and met you at O'Malley's, I almost got in a bar fight with all the men who were ogling you."

"Seriously?" Emma asked.

"How can I get it through your head how fucking sexy you are?"

She pointed at her expanding bump. "This is sexy to you?"

"I could care less if you have a belly or not, Em. *You* are the one who makes yourself sexy, not a body. It's not even the way you looked in that luscious lingerie you had on earlier. It's the way you swayed your hips and shook your ass in front of me, knowing it would drive me insane, or the way you sucked me off with total abandon."

Heat filled Emma's cheeks at his words while warmth pulsed through her veins at the sincerity in which he spoke them. "So you're still going to be rampant for me when I'm nine months pregnant, maybe thirty pounds overweight, and swollen up like a Goodyear blimp?"

Aidan chuckled. "Yes, I will."

"Hmm, we'll see about that one."

Just as Emma was settling down to go to sleep, Aidan asked, "So our definition of more is merely not dating anyone else?"

"I think that's a pretty good start. Don't you?" Even though she wanted *everything* and more with Aidan, she didn't want to scare him off. She thought it best to continue with relationship baby-steps and work her way up to the really big ones like moving in together or dare she even hope and dream, marriage.

"I suppose so. I mean, we're already spending all our time together. No need to work on that."

"I agree."

"So we're good with our 'more'?" Aidan asked.

Even though she wanted to cry, scream, and rail that she hated their definition of more, she merely smiled. "Yeah, we're good."

CHAPTER TWENTY-THREE

Two Months Later

Soaking in the oversized tub, Emma eyed her swollen feet with disgust. She had thought she wouldn't have to face the particularly unattractive side effect of pregnancy until she was much farther along. But as she moved out of her first trimester into her second, her feet had started going under daily transformations. Since she had spent most of the day on them doing back to back advertising presentations, they were worse than usual.

Beau lounged on the tile in front of the tub, snoring slightly. With Aidan traveling out of town every other week with his Vice President status, Beau had become as much her dog as his. She picked him up from Doggy Daycare, and he helped pass the lonely nights without Aidan by sleeping by her side.

Emma had just rewarmed the water for a longer soak when Beau raised his head up. After giving a yip, he ran to the bathroom door. "Oh, I bet Daddy's home from New York," she said. As Beau wiggled all over and swung his tail to and fro, Emma couldn't help sharing his excitement.

"Em?" Aidan's voice bellowed from the hallway.

"In the bathtub," she called.

He threw the door open and grinned broadly at her. "Hey baby!" Beau yapped at Aidan's heels as he started over to the tub. He gave her lingering kiss before turning his attention to Beau.

"How was your trip?" she asked, as he scratched Beau's ears.

Aidan groaned. "The same ol' shit."

She wrinkled her nose. "Which means the same ol' shit of leaving back out of here next week, right?"

"Unfortunately yes. I guess that's what they pay me the big bucks for." He eyed her bubble bath covered form. "Isn't it a little early for that?"

She giggled and pulled one of her legs out of the water. "I suppose it is, but I thought I would soak awhile to make my swollen pregnancy clown feet go down."

Kneeling down, he took her foot in one of his hands and kissed the instep. "I'll massage them for you when you get out."

Emma cocked her eyebrows at him. "Uh-huh, and what do you want in return for such treatment?"

Aidan chuckled. "Who said I wanted something in return? My Baby Mama's feet are swollen, so I feel a responsibility to make things better."

She grinned. "Water's still warm. You could join me."

His fingers immediately went to his shirt buttons. "You don't have to ask me twice."

Emma gazed appreciatively at him while he stripped. Each time he was gone, it made her miss and crave him all the more. After stepping into the tub, he wrapped his arms around her, pulling her onto his lap. He surprised her when he kissed her tenderly, rather than with his usual hungry passion. Of course, when he ran his fingers up her spine, it caused her to shiver with anticipation.

"Are you going to tell me what's on your mind?" Aidan asked.

"Huh?"

He chuckled. "You feel a little tense, that's all."

"Just a stressful day at work," she lied.

"And what else?" he prompted.

"Fine. There's something I've been waiting to ask you."

"Okay. Shoot."

"So about this next business trip?" she asked.

"Hmm?" he murmured, tangling his fingers through her damp hair.

"Do you have plans for the weekend after you get back?"

"Not that I know of. Why?"

Emma knew it was now or never to approach him with this potential bomb. Sure two months had rolled by where they had been spending more and more time together. He kept his devotion to monogamy, even going so far as to skype and call her late nights when he was away. Most nights he was in town, she slept over or he slept at her house. But they still hadn't quite breached the level of commitment she wanted, nor had they said the "l" word that she so craved to hear.

"Well, it's my family's annual Barn Dance up in the mountains. My mom's family that is."

Aidan snickered. "And what exactly is a Barn Dance?"

"Exactly what it sounds like. My cousins' band plays music, people dance, there's usually homemade BBQ…and moonshine." Emma grinned at Aidan's wide eyes. "Mainly it's a family reunion of sorts. I planned on going up on Saturday afternoon and coming back Sunday evening. I would really like it if you joined me. My grandparents are especially interested in meeting you."

Aidan smiled. "Sure."

"Really?" Emma squeaked, unable to hold back her shock.

Aidan nodded. "You've suffered through meeting most of my family. I should repay the favor. Besides, I always love getting out of the city for the mountains. We could even take Beau with us."

Emma laughed. "Oh, he'll be in doggie heaven at my grandparents. They have about thirty acres of land along with a pond."

"That sounds amazing for more than just Beau."

Emma couldn't still the fluttering of her heart at his excitement about meeting her family. "So I can tell Grammy we're coming?"

"Of course. I wouldn't miss it for the world."

CHAPTER TWENTY-FOUR

Aidan threw the last of his clothes in the suitcase and then zipped it up. He grunted in frustration when his cell went off in his pocket. Since he was already running late to pick up Emma, he didn't need any more interruptions. Luckily, he knew it wasn't her demanding to know where he was because it wasn't her familiar ring tone. "Hello?"

A slightly inebriated voice boomed on the other line. "Fitzy, where the hell are ya man? The entire gang is down at O'Malley's waiting on your sorry ass!"

It was his buddy Blake. Aidan had conveniently forgotten to tell him and the other guys from work he wouldn't be making their usual Saturday meet-up. "Sorry dude, I'm about to head out of town with Em."

"You're with Emma *again*?" he whined, over the roar of the boisterous crowd in the background.

"Yeah, we're going to visit her family up in the mountains. A Barn Dance or some shit."

"Fuck that, man. You spend all your time with her now. Not to mention you've got a kid on the way. You might as well have grown a vagina."

"Yeah, spending lots of sexy time with a beautiful, fiery redhead really makes me a pussy!" Aidan replied, with a chuckle.

Blake snorted. "You have no idea the fucking quicksand you're treading on. Sure, it seems like easy fun now, but just wait. Emma's no fool. She's tightening her noose, and you're too mind fucked to see it."

"Don't be saying shit like that about Emma," Aidan snarled.

"I'm not the only one saying it, Fitzy. The whole gang is worried about you. And don't say we don't know what we're talking about. Three of us have been through divorces, remember?"

Aidan shifted the phone to his other ear. He wasn't enjoying the turn the conversation had taken. He didn't like Blake's tone or the potential truth in his words either. "Nice groups of friends I've got running their mouths behind my back."

"Yeah, well, just mark my words. If you don't get out fast, you'll wish you had listened to us one day."

"Go fuck yourself, Blake!" Aidan shouted before hanging up. He shoved his phone back in his pocket. Who the hell did Blake think he was? Emma wasn't forcing him to do anything. No woman ever *had* and no woman ever *would.* He was with her because he was enjoying what they had. There was nothing wrong with that. He was giving just as much as he wanted to, and she wasn't forcing his hand at anything else.

At the thought of his friends drinking and giving him shit about Emma, he couldn't help muttering, "Douchebags." He grabbed his suitcase and whistled for Beau. "Come on, boy. Let's get the hell out of here."

Beau happily complied and went into full wiggling mode when he saw he was getting in the car. Knowing he was running late, he sped along the interstate and then zipped along the familiar streets over to Emma's house. He pulled in her driveway at a little after three. He ignored the text buzzing in his pocket because he was sure it was her. Instead, he hopped out. Beau started to nudge forward, but he shook his head. "Stay boy."

After jogging up the front walk, he smacked the doorbell. "It's open!" she called.

As he pushed through the door, he saw her suitcase and purse sitting on the foyer floor. He heard rustling around in the kitchen. "Sorry, I'm a little late. Beau took forever to pee," he lied. He didn't feel the need to tell her one of his asshat friends had made him later than Beau's bladder.

"You didn't leave him at home, did you?"

Aidan laughed. "No, he's having a fit in the car. I swear he recognizes your house."

Emma's girlish giggle floated back to him. "Poor baby. It's been his off and on again home the last few months. I put him a rawhide bone in my purse to help make the trip. But we'll probably need to stop off once to let him pee." She gave a frustrated sigh. "Who am I kidding? *I'll* probably have to stop more to pee than Beau will!"

She came around the corner, and his heart shuddered to a stop. Every time he saw her after being out of town, she took his breath away. She wore an emerald green sundress with thin spaghetti straps. The hemline fell just below her knees. Her enhanced pregnancy cleavage strained against the cups on the bodice. But it was the brown cowboy boots that made him do a double take.

Emma started to rush past him to throw something in her suitcase when Aidan reached out and pulled her to him. "Damn, you look sexy as hell."

Her brows furrowed as she glanced down at herself. "Seriously?"

He licked his lips and nodded.

"This is one of the few dresses I can still get into. I think it might be time to cave in and buy some more maternity clothes."

His fingers splayed over her baby bump, touching her tenderly over the thin material. "To be four and a half months pregnant, you're barely even showing."

She blew a stray strand of hair out of her face. "Tell that to my zippers."

"And the boots?"

"Oh, these help me stay true to my country roots. I wear them all the time when I'm in the mountains."

He grinned. "I like them…a *lot*." Cocking his head, he gave her his best 'I want to devour you' smile.

Emma wagged her finger at him. "Oh no. Don't *even* go there."

"Baby, I've hardly seen you, least of all touched you, in the last week. I'm about to explode!"

"We need to get on the road. It's already after three," she protested.

"What's wrong with taking a little detour?" Before she could argue anymore, Aidan crushed his lips against hers, his warm tongue sweeping into her mouth. He snaked one arm around her waist, drawing her against him. She started to squirm away when he pressed his erection into her. "Don't make me meet your grandparents with a hard on."

She smirked at him and started wiggling out of his embrace. "It's a long drive. I'm sure you will cool off by then."

With a frustrated grunt, Aidan tightened one of his arms around her waist. He then brought his other hand to slip one of her tiny straps off her shoulder, pushing the material down to bare her breast. As he kneaded her flesh, his thumb brushed back and forth across her hardened nipple. When he heard her suck in a breath, he teasingly pinched the bud. It appeared to do the trick because a surge of passion overtook Emma. She brought her lips to Aidan's while arching herself against him.

He licked from her chin up to her ear. "I want you so bad, Emma," he murmured. When he took her chin between his fingers and tilted her head back, Emma stared at him with hooded eyes.

"Then take me," she murmured.

Kissing her again, his hand slid under her dress. Emma moaned into his mouth when his fingers found the heat between her legs. He stroked her over her panties until he could feel her moist desire through the fabric. Then he delved his fingers inside her — keeping the same rhythm with his tongue as with his fingers. She tore her lips from his, her breath coming in heavy pants. "Mmm, Aidan…yes, God! Aidan! Yes!" she cried, pinching shut her eyes as he brought her to the brink.

She whimpered when his fingers slid out of her. His hand then went to jerk her panties down to her knees. He brought Emma's hand to his crotch. She reached out to fumble with the button and then the zipper on his jeans. Once she freed his erection, she stroked him hard and fast, using the drops of pre come for friction.

Aidan sucked in a ragged breath and then removed her hand. "That's enough of that," he muttered in a strained voice.

He backed up to the couch, pushing his pants and underwear over his hips. He tugged Emma's hand, jerking her to him. They collapsed onto the couch with Emma's heat straddling him. After guiding himself into her, he started moving her hips against him. Frantically, he thrust himself in and out of her as Emma leaned over to kiss him. She didn't last very long before going over the edge again.

Even though he was close, Aidan didn't want to come. Nothing felt as good as being buried deep inside Emma. He kept raising his hips and bringing her hard down on his cock. He threw his head back and closed his eyes as the intense sensations rolled over him. Finally, when he thought he couldn't stand it anymore, he gave in to the release and came flooding into her.

***

As Aidan cradled her to his chest, Emma covered her eyes with her hands and groaned. "What's the matter?" he asked.

"I can't believe I just let you screw my brains out right before I'm going to my grandparents."

Laughter rolled through Aidan. "I'm sorry I'm a horny bastard and couldn't help myself. But if we're really honest, it's more your fault than mine."

Emma gasped. "And just how the hell is it my fault?"

Aidan winked at her. "You just had to look so damn sexy in that dress and those cowboy boots."

"You're impossible," she huffed. Secretly, she was more than pleased to hear him calling her sexy and not being able to keep his hands off of her. The bigger she got, the less desirable she felt. But then Aidan made her feel as beautiful as the day he first propositioned her at O'Malley's.

He kissed her neck while running his hands up and down her back. "Damn, I missed you," he murmured against her throat.

"Me or the sex?" she asked, repeating her familiar question.

"After all this time, are we still playing that game?" he growled. "You. I fucking missed *you*, okay?"

She pulled away to grin at him. "Oh, Aidan, you're so romantic. Whisper more sweet words to me!"

His eyes widened, but then he laughed. "Sorry, guess that wasn't really romantic, huh?"

"I appreciate the sentiment. I've missed you, too." She ran her fingers through his hair and smiled. "Even though it brought us together, I really loathe your job sometimes."

"Tell me about," Aidan grumbled.

"You think you're still going to be traveling like this when the baby gets here?"

"I hope things will calm down by then." He feathered kisses along her jaw-line. "They think they can use and abuse me because I'm a bachelor. Maybe I should tell them I'm going to be a father, and they'll go easy on me."

Emma stiffened. "You mean you haven't told anyone in your department about the baby?"

"Not exactly…I mean, my friends and work buddies know." He grinned. "Spending time with you has kinda cut into our beer binges down at O'Malley's, and they're not really happy about it."

A grunt of frustration erupted from Emma's lips. Jerking herself off of Aidan lap, she worked at wriggling her panties back up her thighs and readjusting her dress.

"What's wrong?"

"You seriously have to ask that question?"

He grimaced. "You're pissed because I haven't told my boss about the baby."

"Of course I am!" she huffed, stalking across the room for her suitcase.

Aidan rose off the couch and adjusted his pants. "Em, wait, would you listen to me?"

She whirled around. "Is this when you tell me you're sorry and that you just didn't think about mentioning it? That somehow the fact you were going to be a father in less than five months just slipped your mind?"

He held up his hands defensively. "Look, I really am sorry. It's been crazy at work the past two months that we've been working on being more of a couple. I've barely been in the home office a week straight. I promise you that I'm not being intentionally deceptive about you or the baby. I swear."

When she realized the sincerity in Aidan's voice, Emma sighed. "I'm sorry. I shouldn't have freaked out like that. These stupid hormones make me totally irrational sometimes."

"No, you were right to get pissed. It's not like I've gone out of my way to introduce you to my friends or tell them we're official."

Emma felt the electricity in the room shift. Was Aidan really talking about making things more official between them? Did that mean maybe living together? It seemed like a quantum leap considering they hadn't even spoken the "l" word yet. It wasn't for the fact that Emma wasn't deeply in love with Aidan. She was just too afraid of scaring him away. Their entire relationship was such a fragile balloon that she was afraid would pop at any moment.

Aidan raised his eyebrows questioningly at her. "So are we okay?"

She smiled. "We're fine."

"Good then. Let's get the hell out of town then!" Aidan said, grabbing Emma's suitcase.

She drew in a deep breath and tried to mentally and emotionally prepare herself for what was to come.

CHAPTER TWENTY-FIVE

When Beau saw her coming down the driveway, he started barking and wagging his tail. His head was out the backseat window as she came around the car.

"Did you miss me sweet boy?" He pressed against the door and gave an appreciative whine. "Aw, I missed you, too!" She shot Aidan a disgusted look over her shoulder. "You shouldn't have left him in the car this long!"

"All the windows are down." He gestured to Beau's wiggling body. "Look at him. He's perfectly fine."

"I guess so," Emma murmured, scratching behind Beau's ears.

"You spoil him too much," Aidan mused, tossing her suitcase in the backseat.

"I do not."

"Oh really? Every time I come in the door, he starts looking for you. He could give a shit less about me now. Not to mention, he expects to lie around on the couch and eat my table scraps."

She blushed. "Oops." As soon as she slid across the seat, Beau leaned over the headrest to lick her cheek. "Are you ready to get the city grit out of your fur?" Emma asked, patting the Lab's head. He wagged his tail and licked her again. "Yep, I think he's ready."

Aidan snorted as he pulled out of the driveway. "Once he sees all those wide open spaces, he may never want to come back."

After he took the 75 North exit, they started their pilgrimage out of the city. The urban backdrop melted away into an emerald blur of trees and pastureland. The closer they got to the mountains the cooler the swirling air around them became.

A pang of homesickness reverberated through Emma as they drove along the familiar roads. She had spent her whole childhood in the mountains until she had gone to college in Atlanta. There was a very large part of her that longed to move back, especially when it came to raising the baby.

When they neared her grandparents' property, she leaned forward in her seat. "Okay, you're going to turn right at the black mailbox."

Aidan turned to her in surprise. "Onto that gravel road?"

"Yep."

After they wound around a couple of curves, they came to an open field. Up the hillside was her grandparent's house and barn. Aidan turned to her with widened eyes at the sight of the multitude of cars and people milling around. "This is all your family?"

She nodded. "There are usually about fifty people or more. By the time the barn dance starts tonight, it'll be around a hundred." She eyed the skeptical expression on his face. "You sure you're up to this?"

"Sure, it'll be fine as long as no one wants to kick my ass for knocking you up."

Emma laughed. "Most of my family is okay with my pregnancy. My grandfather and some of my uncles might give you a hard time though." She hesitated before dropping a bomb on him. "Um, since we aren't married, don't plan on us sharing a bedroom tonight."

"Excuse me?"

Emma grimaced. "My grandparents are very old-fashioned. They won't condone us sleeping in the same bed if we aren't married."

"Even though you're pregnant with my child?"

"Yes."

He exhaled noisily. "Good thing I got some before we left. It would have been a long, long weekend." He laughed when she smacked his arm playfully in outrage.

"Come on. Let's go face the firing squad," Emma said, with a grin.

"Fabulous," Aidan groaned as he climbed out of the car. He clipped the leash to Beau's collar and let the squirming lab out of the backseat.

Delicious aromas filled Emma's nostrils, and her stomach growled. She was so thankful her nausea had passed because she wanted nothing more than some of her grandmother's Brunswick stew.

"Is that homemade BBQ I smell?" Aidan asked.

"Yes, it is. Everything will be homemade from the apple pie to the moonshine."

"Damn, I think I've died and gone to heaven. Well, not exactly at the part about the moonshine."

Emma giggled. "Good luck not having my uncles force some homebrew on you. They'll want you to prove your manhood."

Aidan opened his mouth to protest, but a woman's voice cut him off. "Emma!" she shrieked, clapping her hands. Emma didn't even have to turn to recognize the voice. Just the sound of it echoing around her coated her body with a thick blanket of love. Spinning around, she saw her grandmother striding towards her.

From her teased silver bouffant hairdo to the worn red and white gingham apron she wore tied firmly over her dress, Grammy never seemed to age or change. She was the one constant beacon in the storm Emma had been able to count on her entire life for love, support, and strength.

Grammy's face lit up like a Fourth of July sparkler. "There's my beautiful baby!" she exclaimed, drawing Emma into her strong embrace. Squeezing her tight, she said, "I've missed you so much, darlin'."

"I missed you, too, Grammy."

She pulled away and smiled. "You're going to have to start coming up here more than twice a month. Your granddaddy and I get mighty lonesome for you."

Emma giggled. "We talk every other day. Do I really need to come up that much more?"

"Yes, you do. Especially when the baby gets here." She reached out to gently touch Emma's swollen belly. "Look how big you've gotten!"

"Tell me about it. None of my clothes fit."

"Well, consider yourself lucky you didn't start showing right off the bat. Your mama had to have maternity clothes the second month she was pregnant with you!"

Emma smiled at the memory of her mother laughing about how she practically showed from conception.

"So how are you feeling?" Grammy asked, her brow creasing with worry.

"Better. Thank God the morning sickness stopped now that I'm out of the first trimester. I'll get to find out what I'm having next week. I'm doing the early gender sonogram."

Grammy's beaming face grew even brighter. "Wonderful. Of course, I still say you're carrying it like a boy."

Emma glanced over at Aidan and grinned. "That would make Aidan's father happy to hear you say that. He's sworn since the moment I met him, it's a boy."

Grammy turned her intense green eyes on Aidan. "So this incredibly handsome and dashing man you've brought with you must be Mr. Fitzgerald?"

Heat rose in Emma's cheeks both at her grandmother's compliments and how she was to make the introduction. "Yes, this is Aidan. He's…"

"The sperm donor?" Grammy questioned.

Aidan chuckled. "Yes, but in more ways than one."

Grammy clutched her stomach and doubled over with laughter. When she recovered, she held out her arms for Aidan. "Well, come here and give me a hug, Mr. Sperm Donor."

Emma watched in amazement as Aidan willingly hugged Grammy. She couldn't believe how effortlessly he already seemed to be interacting with her family, considering how he had freaked out so much when she met his nephews and Patrick.

Patting Aidan's back, Grammy said, "We're so very happy to have you here with us for the weekend. I hope you'll enjoy yourself."

He gave her a dazzling smile. "Thank you, ma'am. It's a pleasure to be here."

Grammy wagged a finger at him. "As for fathering Em's baby, there's something I need to say about that."

Emma chewed her bottom lip and threw a worried glance between her grandmother and Aidan. Her chest tightened in apprehension at what Grammy might say to him. If it was anything like the early phone calls and first visit she had with her grandparents about her unmarried pregnancy, Aidan was in for a severe tongue-lashing.

"Yes, ma'am?" Aidan asked pleasantly, but Emma couldn't help noticing how he flicked Beau's leash back and forth with nervous energy.

"Having a child on her own is certainly not what my husband or I wanted for Emma. We'd rather she had found a husband and then had children." She shook her head sadly. "At one time, she had that. But then life hasn't exactly been fair to Em. She deserves all the happiness in the world, and I know that nothing will make her happier than finally having her dream of motherhood come true."

Tears filled Emma's eyes at the overwhelming love and truth in her grandmother's words. When she dared to look over at Aidan, he was smiling. "I couldn't agree with you more, Mrs. Anderson. I'm just very grateful I got to help make Emma's dreams come true."

Grammy cupped Emma's chin and smiled. "You're positively glowing, sweetheart. I don't think I've seen that look in your eyes since before your mother passed away."

"Oh, thank you," Emma replied, wiping away a tear.

Grammy patted Aidan's arm. "So after all of that, I just want to thank you for making Emma so happy and in turn, her family as well."

"You're more than welcome, Mrs. Anderson."

"Please call me Virginia." She then made a tsking noise at the sight of some women carrying pans of food to the barn. "Oh dear, you're gone for one minute, and people take it upon themselves to do everything. I better go make sure dinner isn't a total disaster!"

Once she was out of earshot, Aidan exhaled noisily. "Well, that was certainly unexpected."

"The warm welcome?"

Shaking his head, he slipped an arm around Emma's waist. "No, I didn't realize I'd be such a hero for knocking you up. Don't they usually get the shotguns after you in these parts?"

Emma giggled. "Let's just say it would be a whole lot different if we were teenagers." She titled her head to gaze up at him. "Of course, I highly doubt the teenage Aidan would have given me the time of day."

"You never know. I would have been very interested in corrupting you and stealing your virtue."

Emma nudged him playfully. "Then Granddaddy and my uncles would have shot your most prized possession off."

Aidan chuckled. "That would have been a tragedy."

"Oh yes, you wouldn't have been able to get me pregnant later on," she mused.

He pressed his lips against her ear, causing her to shiver. "Or give you mind blowing multiple orgasms."

"Aidan!" she squealed, shoving him away.

He laughed at her outrage. "You know I'm right though."

A booming voice interrupted them. "Emmie Lou, get on over here and give me a hug!"

She rolled her eyes but smiled in spite of herself. "While Grammy might have been a piece of cake, Granddaddy is probably going to be a real pain in the ass about all this," she said to Aidan. She felt him tense a little as he followed her over to where a silver headed man stood in faded jeans. "Granddaddy, when are you going to learn I'm a little too old for that nickname?"

He grinned. "Nonsense. You'll always be my baby girl and my little Emmie Lou!"

Emma hugged him tight, closing her eyes in contentment as his familiar scent of peppermint and Old Spice filled her nose. "I've missed you."

He pushed her shoulders back and cocked a bushy, silver eyebrow at her. "It's been two whole weeks, Baby Girl! I's about to send the boys down to the city to check up on you."

"I'm sorry, but things have been a little crazy lately." She noticed her grandfather's gaze was no longer focused on her. Instead, he stared quizzically at Aidan. "Oh, Granddaddy, I want you to meet someone." Grabbing Aidan's hand, she pulled him forward. At the sight of their fingers intertwined, the congenial expression on Granddaddy's face evaporated, much to her dismay, and was replaced by one of veiled anger. Emma couldn't help noticing that Aidan's forehead had broken out in beads of sweat not from the heat, but from Granddaddy's intense glare. "This is Aidan

Fitzgerald. He's my baby's father." She smiled at Aidan. "And this is my grandfather, Earl."

"Nice to meet you, sir," Aidan said, his voice cracking slightly.

Earl shifted his chaw of tobacco and eyed Aidan's hand. He reluctantly pumped it up and down. "Nice meetin' ya."

"Emma!" someone called. When she threw a glance over her shoulder, her cousin Dave waved.

"One second. I'll be right back."

CHAPTER TWENTY-SIX

Aidan reluctantly let go of Emma's hand. Frankly, he wanted to be a downright pansy and run after her. The last thing in the world he wanted was to be left with the old man. He shifted uncomfortably on his feet, wiping the sheen of sweat off his face with the back of his hand.

Earl spit out a stream of tobacco juice. "So you plannin' on stickin' around after the baby is born?"

"Yes, sir."

"You gonna help out with raisin' it?"

"Well, we haven't really worked all that out yet." As Earl's expression darkened even more, Aidan quickly replied, "But I'm going to try. Honest, I am."

Earl's eyes narrowed. "What about marryin' her?"

Aidan felt like he'd been kicked in the balls. He fought to catch his breath. *Shit, if I answer this question wrong, this dude is seriously going to kill me.* His mouth ran dry, and he licked his lips. *Is it getting darker out here, or am I'm going to pass out?*

"Son, you didn't answer my question. Are you gonna marry my Emmie Lou or not?"

"Granddaddy!" Emma cried, her eyes wide with horror. Aidan wheezed in relief that he was momentarily off the hook.

"What darlin'? It's an honest question."

Emma flushed red from her cheeks down to her neck. Even her bare shoulders were tinged. "No, it isn't. Aidan and I are comfortable with the arrangement we have. If we get ready to change anything, we'll let you know, but until then, we don't want to feel any pressure, okay?" When her gaze flickered over to Aidan's to see if he was okay with her answer, he nodded.

Earl kissed the top of Emma's head. "Fine, Baby Girl. I won't mention it again." He gave Aidan one last smoldering look of disgust before strolling away.

"He's just messing with you," Emma said. When he didn't reply, Emma reached over and rubbed his arm. "You aren't really afraid of him, are you?"

He glanced back at Earl. Surrounded by four of his grandsons, he sat whittling on a stick. The long blade of his knife gleamed in the sunlight causing Aidan to shudder. "Hell yes, I am! I know he seems like your sweet little grandfather, but the man could *end* me if he wanted, probably with his bare hands. And I'm sure your uncles and cousins wouldn't mind helping him bury me in a shallow grave."

The corners of Emma's lips turned up. "You aren't serious?"

He snorted. "Frankly, I'm a little scared to go to sleep tonight for fear he'll sneak in my room and whittle my dick off for getting you pregnant."

"That would be a tragic loss now wouldn't it?"

"Oh yes, it would."

Emma giggled. "It's not just about me being his only daughter's child or his baby granddaughter or the typical grandfatherly/fatherly protecting me from the Big Bad Wolf aka men stealing my virtue." Her amused expression turned dark. "He's taking my pregnancy a little harder than Grammy because he's old-fashioned. Being a deacon at his church, he's never going to be able to accept that I'm bringing a 'bastard', so to speak, into the world."

Aidan sucked in a sharp breath and narrowed his eyes. "He actually said that to you?"

"Not in those exact terms, but yes."

"That's a hell of a way to think about his great-grandchild."

"Yeah, well, your father felt the same way. Remember how he wanted to give the baby his name?"

"That's true," Aidan relented.

The clanging of a bell interrupted them. Aidan whirled around to see Virginia holding an old cowbell. She grinned. "All right everybody! Dinner time!" she shouted, motioning towards the barn.

"Hungry?" Emma asked.

"Famished." He grinned and draped his arm over her shoulder. "I worked up quite an appetite this afternoon."

Her mouth dropped open before she elbowed him in the gut. "You're terrible!"

"You know you love me," he teased.

When she stiffened slightly, he knew he had said the wrong thing. His loaded words had a different connotation than what he intended. Quickly, he tried recovering. "I mean, what's there not to love about a foul mouthed pervert who is always looking for the sexual innuendo in life, right?"

"Exactly," she replied, with a grin.

Aidan's couldn't stop his jaw from dropping when they reached the barn. The outside rustic appearance was quite deceiving when it came to the inside. All the stalls had been cleared out to leave one giant room. There were ten to twenty round tables set up with folding chairs. In the center of the room, a small, wooden stage rose from the ground where several guys were tuning their instruments.

"Pretty cool, huh?" Emma asked.

"I had no idea you guys took it this serious."

"Yep. There's even a small kitchen in the back, too." She giggled at what he assumed was his bewildered expressions. "With as much extended family as I have, we needed a place where we can all get together."

"Jesus, I don't think I even know this many people, least of all be related to them," he mused, as she steered him toward the food table.

"Trust me, by the end of the night, they'll consider you family. I like to think of us as the family in *My Big Fat Greek Wedding*, except we're Southern."

Aidan wasn't sure if that was really such a bad thing. Everyone had been so welcoming and friendly to him—even with him technically being the asshole who had knocked Emma up and not married her.

After fixing teeming plates of BBQ along with mouthwatering sides, Emma led him to an empty table. When he bit into his sandwich, he moaned. "Oh.My.God. This is delicious!"

Emma smiled. "The sauce is Grammy's own recipe."

"Really? She could seriously sell bottle and sell it. It's ten times better than most of the BBQ joints in Atlanta."

"You'll have to tell her that. It'll make her day."

"I'll be happy to."

An elderly man shuffled up to the table. "This seat taken, Em?"

"No, Uncle Pete. We were saving it just for you and Aunt Ella."

Pete smiled broadly at Emma before giving her a hug. Aidan couldn't help reveling in the effect she seemed to have on everyone up here. She was always charming to everyone back in Atlanta, but there was something almost angelic about her up here.

More people crowded inside the barn, and the band started playing. Aidan had just polished off his second plate of BBQ and was debating a third when Earl sauntered up to him. Aidan warily eyed the Mason jar in Earl's hand that was filled with clear liquid.

"Ever had any homebrew, City Boy?" he asked.

"Granddaddy, his name is Aidan," Emma hissed.

"Excuse me. You ever had any homebrew, *Aidan*?"

"No sir, I don't believe I have."

Earl thrust out the Mason jar. "Why don't you try a little?"

"Is that a trick question, sir?"

"Whaddya mean?"

Aidan sucked in a ragged breath before he spoke. "Well, it's just Emma told me about you being a very religious man, so I wouldn't imagine you do a lot of drinking. If I accept, you'll think me a drunkard who doesn't deserve to date your granddaughter. On the other hand, if you do enjoy a drink once in awhile and I refuse, then you're going to consider me a sissified city boy. Right?"

Earl stared Aidan down. Finally, a wide grin broke on his face. He thumped Aidan heartily on the back. "I like your way of thinking." Without breaking Aidan's gaze, he brought the Mason jar to his lips and took a long gulp. "A little sip of spirits never hurt anyone."

Aidan laughed as he took the moonshine from Earl. The moment the liquid entered his mouth it burned a fiery stream of torment down his throat and into his stomach. With Earl watching him expectantly, he did his best to fight his watering eyes and the urge to choke and hack. "Good stuff," he replied, mustering the manliest voice he could. He quickly passed the jar back before he could be expected to drink anymore.

With a chuckle, Earl turned to Emma. "Maybe he's a keeper after all, Emmie Lou."

She widened her eyes as Earl walked off. "I can't believe you've managed to win him over, especially so fast. It took Travis ages not to get a death glare 24/7, and we'd known each other our whole lives."

Aidan smirked at her. "After everything we've been through, I can't believe you doubted my ability to charm the pants off your grandfather." He leaned over and whispered in her ear. "Let's not forget all the times I've managed to charm the panties off of you."

Playfully, she pushed him back. "You seem to forget the first time you tried to play Marketing McDreamy with me at the Christmas Party, and I said absolutely and totally not."

Aidan chuckled. "That's the truth. Worst rejection of my life."

"I doubt that."

"Trust me, babe. It was."

She couldn't hide the surprise on her face. To change the subject, she said, "Would you go get us some dessert?"

He raised his eyebrows. "Still hungry?"

She laughed. "Asks the man who ate two plates of BBQ to my one."

"All right. I'll go get you something sweet."

She kissed his cheek. "The baby and I thank you for it."

"Yeah, yeah. You're going to milk this pregnancy thing for everything it's worth, aren't you?"

"Damn straight," she replied.

Chuckling, he rose out of his chair. "Anything specific you'd like?"

"Maybe a little sampling of everything?"

He gave her a mini-salute. "Yes, ma'am."

After hitting up the desserts in a major way, Aidan started back to the table with two plates filled to the brim. When he got there, Emma held a tiny infant in her arms while chatting up a young couple. "Oh, Aidan, these are my cousins Stacy and Mark." She glanced down at the baby in her arms and a broad grin stretched on her face. "And this is my namesake, Emma Kate."

"You're kidding."

Stacy smiled. "Well, Emma Katherine was our great-grandmother's name, but I couldn't imagine a sweeter person to name my baby after than Em."

"Neither could I," Aidan replied, winking at Emma.

"Come on, hon, we better go get a plate before all the food is gone," Mark suggested.

When Stacy reached for the baby, Emma shook her head. "I can watch her while you guys eat."

"Really?"

"Of course. It'll be good practice."

Mark chuckled. "Wow, I don't think we've had a baby-free meal in the six weeks since Emma Kate was born.";

"Thanks, Em," Stacy replied.

Aidan eased down beside Emma as Mark and Stacy walked off. Her appetite seemed to have evaporated with the baby's appearance. So he started working his way through his plate of sweets as Emma cooed at the baby. "Isn't she beautiful?" she asked.

Aidan cut his eyes over to the infant swathed in pink from head to toe. "She's almost as beautiful as her namesake."

Emma laughed. "Aren't you the charmer?"

When he had overloaded himself with sugar, he pushed his plate away. Emma leaned over, holding the baby out to him. "Want to take her for awhile?"

"So you can eat?"

"No, I just thought you might like to be around a little girl for once. You only have younger nephews."

Aidan eyed Emma Kate warily. She was so tiny and fragile compared to Mason's bulk. He was afraid he might break her somehow. "Seriously, Em, I don't know anything about little girls."

"And we could just as easily be having a girl." She then handed Emma Kate over to him. Reluctantly, he nestled her in the crook of his arm. Her eyes fluttered open, and she stared up at him. Her face began to crumple, and she looked like at any minute she was going to scream.

"Shit! I've pissed her off!" Aidan moaned.

Emma laughed. "No, you haven't. Just rock her a little and put her pacifier in."

Aidan fumbled for the bib where the pacifier was attached. When Emma Kate opened her mouth to cry, he popped it in. Immediately, she started sucking on it and calmed down. He swayed his arms back and forth, and within a few minutes, her eyes grew heavy. When she was asleep, Aidan glanced over at Emma. He couldn't fight the proud grin that stretched on his face.

"You're a natural," Emma replied.

"I don't know about that."

Mark and Stacy came back to the table with their food. "Good for you, bud. You know, preparing for the future," Mark said, motioning to Emma Kate in Aidan's arms. "I'd barely been around a kid before I had mine."

"Well, I'm lucky to have lots of nieces and nephews." He shifted Emma Kate in his arms. "And from them, I know enough about dirty diapers that I'm pretty sure she's soaked through."

Mark groaned. "Fabulous."

Emma rose out of her chair. "No, no. I'll go change her." Aidan happily gave her the baby before glancing down to see if he was wet as well.

Stacy handed Emma the diaper bag with a grin. "You're the best, cuz."

"No problem."

As Aidan watched Emma's retreating form, a piercing giggle erupted in his ear. "Hey, handsome, I'm Mary. You wanna dance?"

Aidan turned around to see a girl—a very gorgeous girl, but a teenage one at that, beaming at him. "Um, I don't think so."

Her ruby red lips puckered in a pout. "Why not?"

"First of all, I'm here with Emma, and second, I think I'm a little too old for you."

"I'm nineteen. Besides, Emma is my cousin. She won't mind."

Aidan fought the urge to say *Like hell she wouldn't*! Even pregnant, Emma had enough hellcat in her to knock Mary into next Tuesday for flirting with him. With an exasperated sigh, he held his hands up. "Look, it's really nice of you to ask, but really, I have to say no."

Emma picked that moment to come back with the baby. She surveyed the two of them before speaking. "What's going on?"

"I wanted to dance with Aidan, and he won't," Mary admitted.

Aidan gritted his teeth. "And I clearly explained to her that I was here with you."

"One little dance wouldn't hurt." Emma then titled her head up at him—giving him a sickeningly sweet smile. "I don't mind, if you don't."

Oh no, she had not just sold him out to her horny cousin. He knew she must have some motive for doing this. It was some way of getting a dig at him for not making them more of an official couple—to illustrate he was more available or something. That or he was just way too paranoid about her motives.

"Fine," he muttered, as Mary jerked him by the hand and dragged him to the dance floor. Thankfully, it was an upbeat song, so he wouldn't be forced to press up against her. He had no idea how to dance like the music called for, and by the look of pure amusement radiating on Emma's face, he knew he was making a fool of himself. He was going to get her back for this if it was the last thing he ever did.

When the dance ended, he forced a smile. "Thank you, Mary."

"Anytime, hot stuff," she replied, smacking his ass. She gave him a wink before hurrying off to join a gaggle of girls in the corner.

"What the fuck?" he muttered under his breath.

"Still up for a dance, stud?" Emma asked.

"Considering your cousin just mauled my ass, I'm not really feeling it."

Emma giggled. "Oh please? I wanna dance with my man."

The music turned over from a fast breakdown to a sweet ballad. Aidan reluctantly let Emma wrap her arms around him. "I'm sorry you got molested," she said, gazing up at him.

Aidan snorted. "Whatever. I just can't believe you pawned me out like that to her. I thought there would be a catfight when you saw us talking."

Emma rolled her eyes. "I'm not that jealous."

"Oh really?"

She grinned. "Besides, when I was changing Emma Kate, I heard some of the girls saying they had bet Mary she wouldn't have the balls to dance with you. I figured I should let her win big tonight."

Aidan threw his head back and chuckled. "I cannot believe they were doing that."

"You're a good-looking older man, why wouldn't they?" She wrapped her arms tighter around him. "Back in the day, I might have even put a little money on getting to dance with you."

His lips nuzzled her neck. "Babe, I'm yours for free anytime, anywhere."

"Hmm, I just might have to take you up on that," she replied.

After swaying to another slow song, they returned to their seats as the band appeared to be taking break. The lead singer, who Emma had introduced as Dave, took the microphone. "I just want to take a moment while all my friends and family are here to make a big announcement. Yesterday, I asked Laurel, the love of my life, to marry me, and she said yes!" Dave said.

While the crowd erupted in bellowing cheers and whistles, Aidan felt Emma tense beside him. Although she plastered a beaming smile to her face, he could tell her cousin's engagement bothered her. It didn't take much for him to understand why. He knew that even though she was thrilled to be having the baby, she still wanted what Laurel had—love, commitment, and a sparkling diamond on her finger. Aidan wondered if he was the man who could give Emma that or if she was just wasting her time believing he could.

"Now, I'd like to take a break for a few minutes and dance with my lovely fiancée." His gaze searched through the crowd until it honed in on their table. "Em, would you come up and do the honors?"

If Emma had tensed before, she went absolutely rigid at the prospect of singing. "No, no, no! I haven't sung in so long."

"That's not true. You regaled Mason and me with your vocal stylings a few months ago," Aidan argued.

Emma shot him a death glare. "I think there's a hell of a lot of difference singing a baby to sleep in the privacy of my own bedroom than in a barn full of people!" she hissed under her breath. She then shook her head at Dave. "Really, I couldn't."

A tall, leggy blonde came bounding up behind them. It didn't take Aidan long to deduce she was Laurel. "Oh please, Emma, sing *Cowboy Take Me Away*! You were singing that the night Dave and I met!"

Aidan brought his lips closer to Emma's ear. "Go on. You know you could knock their socks off singing in the shower."

She jerked away to stare at him, her mouth a perfect o of surprise. "Really?"

He nodded.

"Okay, okay, I'll do it."

Another cheer went through the crowd when Emma rose out of her seat. As she climbed onto the stage, Aidan leaned forward in his chair. He couldn't wait to actually see her perform.

Emma's shaking hand took the microphone off the stand. She cleared her throat a few times before speaking. "I think you all know I haven't sung professionally in two years, so you have to believe me when I say that only pure and true love could get me on this stage. It's the love I feel for Dave, who over the years has been like a brother to me, and it's the love between him and his sweet, beautiful fiancée that makes me able to sing this song for you." Her gaze went to Dave and Laurel who were already wrapped in each other's arms, waiting expectantly on their song. "This one is for you."

The twang of the rosin coming across a fiddle's bow coupled with two guitars echoed through the barn. Aidan watched as Emma's nervousness faded away the moment she heard the familiar chords. With complete confidence, she brought the microphone to her lips and began singing. The room filled with people melted away, and for Aidan, it became only the two of them. Pinching his eyes shut, he let her velvety voice wash over him. He didn't care if the lyrics were about a cowboy sweeping a woman away from the big city into the wide-open spaces of the country. He just focused on the immense pride that filled him at her performance.

When she finished, applause and cheers roared through the room so loud they stung Aidan's ears. Emma flushed a deep crimson, but a beaming smile filled her face. She curtsied prettily. "Thank you," she murmured.

"Now sing *Sweet Dreams*, Emmie Lou!" Earl shouted.

Emma shook her head furiously as she started to put the microphone back on the stand. "No, Granddaddy, I've sung enough for one night."

Earl stomped his foot on the sawdust floor. "Emma Katherine Harrison, your granddaddy wants to hear some Patsy Cline, so sing *Sweet Dreams*!"

Aidan couldn't help chuckling at the stalemate between Emma and her grandfather. "Uh-oh, Em, he's calling you by your full name. Better do what the man says," he called.

She shot him a murderous look before turning back to her cousins. "I assume you guys remember *Sweet Dreams*?"

Dave, who had rejoined the stage, held up his hands. "Oh no, this one is all a cappella, little cuz."

Pointing a finger at them, Emma said, "I just want you to know I'm going to hurt each and every one of you for this!"

The boys laughed heartily as they shuffled off the stage. Emma turned back to the crowd and pointed her finger then at Aidan. "That goes for you, too."

He grinned. "I'll happily take whatever you want to dish out. Now make your granddaddy happy and sing."

When Aidan glanced over at Earl, he nodded and smiled at him. Maybe he was really off the hook…or at least his dick was. He settled back in his chair and focused his attention on Emma.

The moment Emma began singing the old country song a hush fell over the barn. If she had been good on *Cowboy Take Me Away*, she was hitting this one out of the park like a grand slam. Closing her eyes, she belted out the lyrics with such feeling and emotion that Aidan noticed tears sparkling in several people's eyes.

Aidan's enjoyment began to fade when Emma got to the second verse. A haunting, aching quality entered her voice as she sang Patsy's lyrics about never wearing the ring of her lover or having him reciprocate her love. His chest tightened at how so much of the song could relate to him and Emma. He wondered if she often had sweet dreams of a life together with him—one that might never come true.

Thundering applause jolted him out of his thoughts. Emma had finished singing and now half the room were on their feet cheering for her. She flushed and grinned. "Thank you," she murmured into the microphone.

Dave and her other cousins joined Emma back on stage. Each one hugged and kissed her before picking up their instruments. They started up a song as she came back to join him. "So what did you think?" she asked breathlessly.

"Absolutely amazing."

Emma beamed at his compliments. "Really?"

He nodded. "You were spectacular singing to Mason, but damn…you were like American Idol good up there."

She giggled and kissed his cheek. "Thanks." After eyeing the couples on the dance floor, she turned back to him with a pleading look. "Want to dance again?"

He groaned. "If we must."

***

It was after eleven by the time the last guest left. Pleasantly exhausted, Aidan dragged himself up the hillside to the house. After grabbing their suitcases out of the car, he joined Emma as they trailed behind Earl and Virginia. "Now Aidan, you're going to be sleeping here," Virginia said, pointing to a bedroom.

He dropped his suitcase in the doorway. It didn't take him long to surmise his bedroom just happened to be next door to Earl and Virginia's. It was a nice way for them to keep tabs on him. He smiled back at them. "Looks cozy. Thank you."

"Emma, you're going to be in your mama's old bedroom." Earl then looked pointedly at Aidan. "Way down the hallway from us."

Aidan turned a laugh into a cough. It was so absurd that he and Emma were in their thirties and being treated like teenagers. "Then I suppose I should say goodnight now," he said. Wrapping his hands around her waist, he pulled her against him. "Sweet dreams, Emma."

"Sweet dreams to you, too, Aidan," she murmured.

And even though he knew Earl wouldn't like it, he gave Emma a chaste kiss on the lips. She grinned at him before saying goodnight to her grandparents. With a final wave, she went on down the hallway.

Reluctantly, he went inside and closed his door.

CHAPTER TWENTY-SEVEN

Emma felt she was doing something truly illicit when she tip-toed past her grandparent's bedroom towards Aidan's. Her trembling hand slowly turned the knob, and she breathed a sigh of relief at finding it unlocked. Slowly, she pushed it open, trying not to let its loud creak echo through the hallway. She lamented the fact she hadn't thought to grab the WD40 from under the kitchen sink.

Emma found Aidan propped up in bed with multi-colored paperwork strewn over the handmade quilt. Beau lay next to him. At the sight of her, Aidan's eyebrows shot up so far they disappeared into his hairline. "What the hell are you doing?" he hissed.

Holding up a finger, she closed the door behind her before responding. When she turned back around, she grinned. "I wanted to see you."

Aidan rolled his eyes. "Jesus, Em, just when I think my dick is safe from your grandfather's wrath, you sneak in here."

She giggled as she made her way over to the bed. "Oh come on. You know he's not going to do anything like that."

"I'm not holding my breath." His eyes roamed over her practically sheer nightgown. "What do you really want?"

"Can't you tell? I want that hot bod of yours…*bad*!" she teased.

He grunted. "Don't torture me by saying things like that."

"Actually, I thought you might like to go for a midnight swim."

"Really?"

Emma nodded. "The pond is just below the house."

"Is it safe?"

"Sure, that's where I learned to swim." Nudging his knee with her elbow, she said, "Of course, I wasn't an All State Swim Champion, so what do I know?"

Aidan shook his head as he threw off the quilt. "There goes that mouth of yours again."

Emma giggled. "So I guess that means you're up for it?"

"Yeah, yeah. I'm in," Aidan replied, stepping into his tennis shoes.

They crept out into the hallway. Aidan stepped on one of the creaky floorboards, and they both froze. When Earl didn't come streaking out into the hallway with his shotgun, they continued tip-toeing on into the living room. Emma grabbed a flashlight out of the table by the door while Aidan unlocked the deadbolt.

Once they got out onto the porch, they hurried down the steps and onto the gravel path that wound behind the house. They barely needed the flashlight with the glowing full moon illuminating the way. When they reached the long dock, they were both winded.

Aidan bent over, propping his elbows on his knees. Once he had caught his breath, he raised his head and took in the surroundings. "Damn, it's beautiful out here."

"This whole area is like the most magical place in the world," Emma replied, breathlessly. Stepping closer to him, she gave him her best coy smile. "You know I haven't been skinny dipping with a boy in a long, long time."

He grinned. "Have you not?"

Emma shook her head. She brought her nightgown over her head, leaving her completely naked in the moonlight.

A pained noise erupted from Aidan's throat. "Fuck, this whole time you weren't wearing *any* underwear?"

"Nope."

"I should have ravished you in the bedroom then!"

She giggled as Aidan proceeded to tear off his shirt and boxers at record speed. When he reached for her, she backed away. "I said skinny-dipping, not defiling my grandparent's pond by having sex."

His hands swept to his naked hips, drawing her attention to his erection. "Did you really think I hauled my ass out here just for a midnight swim?"

"I don't know what you might have thought, but that's *not* what is happening."

"Yeah, we'll just see about that one."

"Guess you'll have to catch me first," she teased before diving off the dock.

As she plunged into the depths, the icy water pricked over her body like tiny needles. She had no idea that it would be so cold this late in the summer. Usually, it was like tepid bath water.

When Emma broke the surface, she fought the chattering of her teeth. She whirled around at the sound of splashing behind her. Even in the dim light, she could see the gleam in Aidan's eyes. "I do believe I'm going to catch you." She giggled as he closed the gap between them in two fluid breaststrokes.

Instead of fighting him, she gleefully let Aidan pull her against his chest. "Gotcha!" he said.

She poked her lip out. "Not a fair fight, considering I'm pregnant and you're a good swimmer."

"True, very true. What kind of man would I be to take advantage of my Baby Mama? I'll behave now, and we'll have a nice swim."

She arched her eyebrows in surprise. "Seriously?"

He gave her a wolfish grin. "Well, there's also the fact this cold water is doing nothing for my hard on!"

"Then I guess after our swim, we'll just have to make it to land for any action."

CHAPTER TWENTY-EIGHT

Later, as they remained intertwined on the sandy shoreline, a tangle of arms and legs, Aidan's brows furrowed. "What's wrong?" Emma asked.

"I'm just surprised you haven't blown my horndog ass to the curb yet."

"Huh?"

"You know, the constant sex stuff. I would have thought you wouldn't be up for it being pregnant."

Emma burst out laughing both at his statement and the serious expression on his face. She rubbed the stubble on his chin. "So I guess this is when I know you didn't read the pregnancy book I gave you."

Aidan grunted. "Yeah, the moment I pulled that one out on a plane or in public someone would have come to revoke my balls."

Emma rolled her eyes. "Reading a pregnancy book would not emasculate you in the least bit. Besides, you could have bought it for your iPad." At his doubtful look, she tweaked his nose with her fingers. "If you had read it, you would have known that a woman's sex drive often increases during pregnancy so much that husbands and boyfriends just can't keep up."

"You're shitting me?" he asked, his dark blue eyes wide.

"Nope. I'm not."

Aidan grinned. "That's fanfuckingtastic."

Emma laughed. "Yeah and who knows what else might be lurking under the cover of that book. I suggest you read it."

"Fine. I will."

Inwardly, she did a victory dance even though she had to be a little deceptive to get him to read about pregnancy. The more he knew and understood about the coming months the better. At times, pregnancy wasn't entirely attractive, and she wanted him to be prepared.

Aidan pulled himself off of her and got to his feet. Emma stayed motionless, admiring his naked form in the moonlight. He turned back to her and offered her his hand. All inappropriate thoughts of him vanished at his gentlemanly behavior. When he helped her up, she gave him a chaste kiss on the lips in thanks.

"Damn, I wish we had thought about a towel," Aidan said.

Emma grinned. "Ask and you shall receive." She walked over to the edge of the dock where a worn, wooden box the size of a steamer truck sat. It was something Granddaddy had made a long time ago for his grandchildren to house their swimming gear. She pulled out two checkered picnic blankets. "Not exactly towels and they're a little musty, but they'll do the trick."

Aidan appreciatively took one from her. "Sounds good to me."

As he dried off, Emma wrapped herself in the faded blanket. When she shivered, he reached over and started rubbing her arms to warm her. "Ready to go back inside?"

"Let's stay out here awhile."

"Are you serious?"

Emma nodded and motioned towards a hammock drawn between two massive oak trees. "It's a beautiful night, and we can do some stargazing."

Aidan snorted. "Stargazing in a hammock? That sounds like a bad romance novel cliché."

"Oh, I didn't realize you enjoyed reading bodice ripper novels with their throbbing and pulsing members."

"Ha, ha," he replied, playfully smacking her ass.

After Emma threw on her gown and Aidan put on his boxers, she took his hand and led him over to the hammock. After she lay down, she pulled him down beside her. Once she wrapped her arms around him, she titled her head up at him. "So is this really so bad?"

He grinned. "Nope. It's quite nice, actually."

"Good. I'm glad you think so."

"I can't believe how much brighter the stars are once you get out of the city. Being up in the mountains makes you feel like you could reach out and touch them," Aidan mused.

"Everything is more beautiful out here."

"Do I detect a hint of homesickness in your voice?"

Stalling, Emma's gaze followed a droplet of water as it trailed down Aidan's bare chest. "Em?" he prompted.

She sighed. "Sometimes I think I'd really like to move back up here—especially to raise the baby."

Aidan tensed beneath her. "Are you serious?"

"This is where I grew up—the place I hold most dear in the world. All my family is here. If something happened to me or with the baby and I needed her, Grammy's almost an hour away."

"Are you trying to say you feel alone back in Atlanta?"

"Well, no, I mean, Casey has always been there…and you're there."

Aidan grunted. "Wow, I rate after Casey, huh?"

"I didn't mean it like that." She raised her head to meet his intense gaze. "You know how much you mean to me, and how much I…care for you."

Relief filled her when Aidan's expression lightened. "But I don't know anything about babies, nor am I a certainty, right?"

"Exactly." She then held her breath waiting for him to say that she had nothing to worry about in the certainty department. That he wanted even more with her. That he would be there always—in the middle of the night if the baby got sick and she was scared to death or if she was exhausted from a long day at work and needed a few minutes to decompress.

"If you're worried about being all alone, you've got my dad, my sisters, and Megan. I promise you'll have a support system in them."

"That's good to know," she murmured, fighting the tears. Her chest clenched in agony with Aidan's response. He didn't mention anything about being more of an official couple or him being there for her. So how could she truly count on him? Instead, he had skirted responsibility and commitment once again. When was she going to learn? Or more importantly, when was she going to give up on him?

***

The sharp jolt of the hammock's sway woke Emma up. Fluttering her eyelids, she looked up at the sky. Early morning sunlight streaked across it, making it a swirling mixture of blues, pinks, and oranges. Somehow she and Aidan had managed to fall asleep under the stars. At the sound of someone clearing his throat, Emma tried scrambling out of the hammock, but Aidan wrapped his arms tighter around her. "Where do you think you're going?" he asked sleepily.

Emma swept her gaze from Aidan over to where Granddaddy stood, arms folded over his chest. "We have company," she whispered.

Aidan's blue eyes flew open, and a look of horror crossed his face when his drowsy eyes focused on Earl. He immediately jerked away from Emma and held up his hands in mock surrender. "I'm really sorry about this, sir. I never meant to go against your wishes by sleeping with Emma under your roof," he said, sounding more like a pleading teenager than a man.

Earl peered around the woods and then up at the sky. "Don't quite look like you're under my roof, does it?" he asked, the corners of his lips turning up.

Emma exchanged a glance with Aidan. Was her grandfather really going to let them off the hook so easily? "I'm sorry, Granddaddy."

Earl shrugged. "Guess there ain't much I can say about it. You're both grown adults. What you do is your business, even if I don't agree with it."

"But I still don't want you to be disappointed in me," she replied.

"I could never be disappointed in you, Emmie Lou." He patted her leg. "I love ya too much, even when you drag a poor feller out of his bed to go skinny dipping."

Emma's hand flew to her mouth while Aidan burst out laughing. "But how...?"

"That don't matter. I's not comin' out here to give you two a hard time. Your grandmother just wanted me to tell the two of you that breakfast was ready. Then we're going to church." He gave them a knowing look. "*All* of us."

After Earl shuffled off, Aidan threw his arm over his eyes. "I cannot believe he caught us."

She giggled. "I can't believe you're complaining about that, rather than having to go to church."

"Trust me, I'm not thrilled by the prospect, but I'll go, especially if it makes him and Grammy happy."

"It will."

"Then come on. Let's go get ready to be holy!"

CHAPTER TWENTY-NINE

Aidan fought his suspension of disbelief as he sat in the backseat of a car bound for Earl and Virginia's church. The last time he had been to Mass was Mason's baptism, and he couldn't even remember a time before that. So much for keeping the promise he made to his mother about attending once a week. At least she would be proud he was getting some kind of moral guidance.

Sitting beside him, Emma remained quiet. Aidan cut his gaze over to her. She looked beautiful in an ice blue dress that was far less daring than the sundress she had worn the day before. With her hands folded in her lap, she appeared demure and innocent except for the swell of her stomach. Before he could stop himself, he reached out and took her hand and his.

A smile curved on her lips before she turned to look at him. "You sure you're okay with this?" she whispered.

"Fine."

As they pulled into the crowded parking lot, Emma shook her head. "Famous last words."

He didn't get a chance to question her. Instead, they were ambushed the moment they got out of the car. Emma coming back home to the mountains and to church seemed to have an almost celebrity status. It took him totally off guard.

Women were oohing and aahing over her while she was given countless hugs. Hands were thrust at him and introductions made. He gathered she hadn't brought a man, boyfriend, or male piece of flesh with her to church since Travis.

Finally, the throng of people cleared, and they were able to walk into the building. "So," he said, opening the door for her.

She grimaced. "So?"

"Can I get your autograph later?" he teased.

Emma giggled. "You're so bad!"

"I didn't realize I was dating the town sweetheart."

"Sorry. I forgot to mention it," she grumbled.

"Next you'll tell me you were Homecoming Queen or something."

When she pinched her lips tight, he widened his eyes. "Seriously?"

She nodded. "But it was a really small high school."

Aidan draped his arm over her shoulder. "What else have you been holding out on me, Queenie?"

"Emma? Is that you?"

Aidan felt her tense beside him. He surveyed the attractive and well-dressed woman who appeared to be in her fifties. Her beaming smile faded when her eyes honed in on Emma's swollen belly. An expression of agony flickered across her face, and Aidan thought she might burst into tears.

"Hello, Jane. It's good to see you again," Emma said, pleasantly.

Jane momentarily recovered, dragging her gaze off of Emma's stomach and back up to them. Without hesitation, she drew Emma into her arms. "You're absolutely glowing, sweetheart. I'm very proud and happy for you. I'm so glad your dreams of motherhood are finally coming true."

Emma's body trembled in Jane's embrace, and a sob rolled through her. Aidan fought the urge to drag her away from this woman who was obviously causing her so much pain. He cleared his throat. "I'm Aidan Fitzgerald. It's nice to meet you," he said, thrusting out his hand.

Jane warily eyed it over Emma's shoulder before slowly pulling away. "Where are my manners? It's nice to meet you, Aidan. I'm Jane Lewis." She took his hand in hers. "Congratulations on the baby. I'm so very, very fond of Emma." Her chin trembled. "She was once going to be my daughter-in-law."

Aidan's chest constricted. Jane was Travis's mother. Now it all made sense. Seeing Emma pregnant only made her think of Travis's child that would never be. He squeezed her hand. "I've heard lots about your son, ma'am. I'm very sorry for your loss."

She smiled. "Thank you. I appreciate that." She released his hand and stepped back. "Now you take good care of our, Emma, okay?"

"Yes ma'am," he said. Although the moment the words left his lips, he waited to be struck down. It wasn't as if he was lying in the house of God. It's just he didn't know if he could ever live up to the expectations Jane and everyone else in church and in town might have for him where Emma was concerned.

Jane gave Emma a final hug before joining her husband. As Emma wiped the tears from her eyes, Aidan exhaled noisily.

Emma gave him a sheepish grin. "Sorry about that. I should have warned you we might see them."

"No, it's okay. It was just intense. At first, I thought she was just some holy roller pissed off that you were unmarried and pregnant. But then when I found out who she was…" He shuddered. "Please tell me Travis wasn't an only child," he said as they eased on their bench.

"No, he had two sisters."

"But her only son."

Emma nodded.

"Damn." Aidan's eyes widened when he realized he had just cursed in church. "Sorry," he mumbled under his breath. He glanced over at Virginia to see if she had heard him, but luckily, she was chatting up one of her friends.

Then the service got underway. Aidan listened appreciatively as Emma belted out the hymns. His mind began to wander during the sermon, and he was never more thankful when church ended.

When he shot out of his seat, Emma laughed. "Guess you've had your fill, huh?"

"You could say that."

Earl came up behind them and thumped Aidan on the shoulder. "Come on, son, I'd like to introduce you to a few people."

Aidan reluctantly nodded. He wasn't quite sure he wanted to hear the introductions Earl might make for him. After all, he was just Emma's boyfriend...or the sperm donor...or the asshole who knocked up the sweet angel of the community.

Surprisingly everyone was very friendly and welcoming. Of course, one guy continued staring daggers at him, and Aidan wasn't too surprised to learn it was Steve—another blast from Emma's past. Even though he had a beautiful wife beside him, Aidan could tell Steve was very protective of Emma.

He was nevermore thankful when Earl ushered him out the door and into the yard. After Earl finished introducing him to just about everyone outside as well, Aidan craned his neck through the crowd for Emma. A hand patted his arm. He glanced down to see Virginia. His expression must have spoken volumes because she pointed over his shoulder. Turning his head, he saw Emma standing at the far side of the church cemetery. He then nodded at Virginia, and she gave him an encouraging smile.

Drawing in a deep breath, he started weaving his way through the maze of different shaped and colored tombstones. Finally, he reached Emma. She stood stoic and silent in front of a pink granite monument that read "Harrison". Underneath it were names "Noah and Katherine" along with their birth and death dates. A large silk flower arrangement sat at the base of the monument.

"Em," he said softly, putting his arm around her waist.

Tilting her head, she gave him a sad smile. "I'm fine. Really. I always come out here when I visit."

Aidan gazed at Emma's father's death date. "Your mom never remarried?"

"For a little while. It was about five years after my dad died. I was in middle school then. It only lasted a couple of years. Not that Paul was a bad guy or anything. I still talk to him from time to time. Mama just said there wasn't anyone in the world for her but my dad."

Aidan nodded. "Sounds like Pop."

They stood in silence for a few moments, the wind rippling their hair and clothes. Aidan's heartbeat accelerated when Emma reached out and took his hand in hers. "I don't remember much about my father, but I know my mother would have loved you," she whispered.

He squeezed her hand. "I'm glad to hear that. Considering how much Pop adores you, there should be no doubt how my mother would feel."

Emma smiled at him. "It's good our baby will have lots of guardian angels to watch over him or her."

Thinking of his mother made Aidan's throat close up. He could barely croak, "Yes, it is."

"Come on. We better get back. Grammy's got a feast waiting on us at the house."

Aidan bobbed his head and let Emma lead him back across the cemetery.

CHAPTER THIRTY

After making their goodbyes, they all piled into the car to head back to Earl and Virginia's. The moment they entered the house, the wonderful aroma of a roast wafted back to Emma. Grammy had risen early not only to prepare breakfast, but lunch as well. Even after the insanely large breakfast she had devoured, Emma's stomach still rumbled. Inhaling sharply, Aidan moaned in appreciation. "God, that smells like Heaven."

Grammy smiled at him. "Thank you, son." She then wagged a finger at Emma. "You're going to have to start cooking more for your man."

While it was silly, Emma still felt her cheeks flushing at the mention of Aidan being *her* man. He raised his eyebrows. "You mean you know how to cook like *that*," he said, jerking his thumb towards the kitchen.

She giggled. "Of course I do." She nodded her head at Grammy. "I had the best culinary teacher anyone could have."

"Hmm, I'm in for a treat then."

"Yeah, don't hold your breath on that one. Between work and the pregnancy exhaustion, I don't have a lot of time or energy for cooking."

Grammy tsked as she wrapped her red gingham apron around her waist. "You better start making time, sweet girl. After

~ 302 ~

all, the way to a man's heart is through his stomach." She then winked at Aidan before heading into the kitchen.

When Aidan snickered at Grammy's admonishment, Emma nudged him in the stomach with her elbow. "Don't make me tell her the way to your heart is through your dick," she whispered.

Aidan's eyes widened, and he made a strangled noise. He glanced left and right before hissing, "I cannot believe you just said *dick* in your grandparent's house!"

Emma laughed. "And I love how you're not even trying to argue that it isn't the truth!"

He scowled before easing down into one of the dining room chairs. On her way into the kitchen to help Grammy, she ruffled his hair playfully. He glanced at her over his shoulder and grinned.

Two of her uncles along with their wives and families sauntered in, filling the massive antique table to its capacity. Emma edged Mary out of the way before she could plop down next to Aidan. Even though she had won the bet, Mary seemed hell-bent on continuing to see how far she could get with Aidan, and Emma was happy to draw the line. Mary scowled at her before stalking down to the "kids" table.

At the scuffle between the two, Aidan chuckled. Emma responded by rolling her eyes. "Wipe the sexy little smirk off your face, or you'll keep encouraging her."

"Nothing wrong with her stopping by to say hello."

"Oh really? Last night you didn't seem too taken with her attention."

"And last night, *you* were encouraging her, not *me*." Leaning over, he nuzzled her neck before she shoved him away. "Besides, I'm still not taken with her. It's just hilarious seeing you get your panties in a twist over a fawning nineteen year old girl."

"My panties are not in a twist," Emma huffed, smacking her linen napkin down in her lap.

He took her hand in his and brought it to his lips. Kissing her knuckles, he gave her his best puppy dog expression. "You know you're the only one I want, right?"

Emma struggled to breathe. Even though he was joking around with her, his words hit straight home. "Yes, I know."

Her heart melted when he winked at her. They were interrupted by Earl taking his seat at the head of the table. "All right everyone. Let's return thanks."

After Granddaddy gave the blessing, they started passing the bowls and plates of food around. Filling hers to the brim, Emma let the familiar portions melt on her tongue. Glancing over at Aidan, he seemed to be enjoying the meal and conversation just as much as she was. For a moment, she tried to imagine what it would be like if this were every Sunday. Even if she didn't move back to the mountains, it was comforting to think of Aidan being by her side for future Sunday dinners or family events. She just didn't know if that was getting her hopes up too high.

When the main course and dessert were finished, Grammy and her aunts started gathering up some of the dishes. Emma rose out of her chair. "Here, I'll help you clean up," she said.

"Thanks, honey," Virginia replied.

While the rest of the men started vacating the table to duck-out of cleanup duty, Earl nodded at Aidan. "Come on out on the porch with me and the boys, son," he suggested.

"Are you sure?" he asked.

Earl nodded. "We can leave the women folk to the dishes while you tell me a little more about yourself."

Emma couldn't fight the smile spreading across her cheeks. She knew if Granddaddy wanted to know more about Aidan, then he had really made an impression. At his momentary hesitation, she gave him a gentle nudge. Aidan finally put one foot in front of the other to follow Granddaddy outside.

Once the dishes were done and the kitchen cleaned, Emma hurried to check on Aidan. She skidded to a stop at the sight of him lounging in the porch swing with a pocketknife in one hand and a piece of wood in the other. Her mouth gaped open. Before she could ask what the hell a city boy like himself was doing whittling, he grinned. "Your granddaddy is teaching me."

She laughed. "I see." She motioned towards the gleaming knife. "Just be careful, okay?"

"Aw, he'll be fine. He's not quite the sissified city boy I originally thought he was," Earl replied.

"High praise indeed," Emma mused, easing down next to Aidan. In a hushed voice, she murmured, "Don't even think about taking up chewing tobacco to impress Granddaddy. I won't let you anywhere near my mouth with a chaw of nastiness."

He chuckled. "You have nothing to worry about."

As the afternoon wore on, Aidan put aside his whittling and wrapped her in his arms. A happy sigh escaped her lips as she snuggled against his chest. She tried ignoring the flashback that assaulted her of sitting the same way with Travis after Sunday lunch many years before.

While Grammy filled her in on some of the local gossip she had missed in the last two weeks, Emma watched as Aidan's eyes grew heavy. It wasn't long before the heave and sigh of the porch swing caused him to nod off. She kissed his cheek and rose out of his embrace. There was somewhere she wanted to return to before they had to leave.

CHAPTER THIRTY-ONE

Aidan woke up to Beau's tongue slurping across his face. Rubbing his eyes, he peered around the front porch. The rest of Emma's extended family had left. Only Virginia sat in one of the rockers, working on a quilt for the baby while Earl read a newspaper. Aidan fought the urge to shake himself at how he felt like he was in a scene straight out of a Norman Rockwell painting.

"Well, hello there, sleepyhead. Decide to finally wake up?" Virginia asked.

"Yes, ma'am. I apologize for nodding off."

She waved her hand dismissively at him. "Why naps are the best parts of lazy Sunday afternoons."

Aidan gazed around the porch. "Where's Emma?"

"Down at the dock."

He nodded and motioned for Beau. After pounding down the porch steps, he followed the winding path around the house to the pond. When he got to the shoreline, he froze.

Emma sat on the end of the dock, dangling her legs over the edge. Her sundress was hiked up to her thighs, and she swirled her feet and calves around in the water. She leaned back with one hand while the other rubbed wide circles around her belly. A serene smile curved on her lips.

The mere sight of her sent a stabbing pain ripping through his chest. It was a pang of true and pure emotion. In that single instant, it was like the Earth shifted on its axis, and every molecule in his body shuddered to a stop.

He was in love.

A suffocating panic crippled him, causing his lungs to burn. He had never felt like this before. Not even what he had with Amy could compare. The feelings flickering within him the last few months had grown from a tiny ember into a raging fire. And now that inferno of emotions threatened to consume him.

He loved Emma.

Fuck. He absolutely and completely loved her with every fiber of his being. And that very fact scared the hell out of him.

Aidan raked a trembling hand through his hair. God, how had he let this happen? They had just been having fun spending time together, enjoying each other's company, not to mention having great sex. He had done it dozens of other times with assorted women. Of course, he had never gotten to this level of emotion for them either. He always ended it way before that could happen.

His foolish offer to *give* Emma more had ended up *taking* more from him than he could have ever bargained for. It felt like he was submerged in an undertow of his feelings and was drowning hard and fast.

He needed desperately to get away from her. If he could just put some distance between them, then his feelings could change. He might be able to go back to the way he had felt about her the weeks before or even the day before. But in reality, he knew the depth of his lie. Every time he had been away on business, he had missed her—sometimes even ached for her in his heart, not his dick.

In the end, maybe it didn't matter if he loved her. He could not imagine giving up the entirety of his life to being all she would need. To be choked by the responsibility of being a husband and father…fuck no.

Aidan started to back away, but a twig snapped beneath his feet, causing Emma to turn her head.

"Hey," she called.

Beau raced past him and down the dock. He splashed into the water, sending a small wave crashing over Emma. "Beau, you stinker!" she shouted.

Aidan forced himself forward towards Emma. She smiled at him as he approached. "Sorry, I left you in the swing. I wanted to come down here before we had to leave, and you were sleeping so peacefully I didn't want to wake you. Especially since I dragged you out of bed last night."

"It's okay." He glanced down at his watch. "We probably need to be heading back."

Emma nodded and swung her legs out of the water. After she pulled herself to her feet, she gasped.

"What's wrong?" She stood frozen, her hand pressed against her stomach. Aidan took a step forward. "Em?"

She grabbed his hand and placed it where hers had just been. "Feel that?"

Aidan almost jerked away at the slight vibrations beneath his fingertips. His heart shuddered to a stop before restarting. The baby—*his* baby—was moving. "Yes," he croaked.

Emma beamed up at him. "It's amazing, isn't it?"

He was too overwhelmed to speak, so he bobbed his head. "I've never felt it move before. I'm so glad you were here with me when it happened."

"Me too."

When the movement stopped, Emma wrapped her arms around Aidan's neck. "I can never thank you enough for giving me this wonderful gift of life. You've made me the happiest woman in the world, and I love you for it." He widened his eyes at her words while she leaned in and kissed him. "I love you, Aidan," she murmured against his lips.

Part of him wanted to be honest with her and himself and openly admit that he loved her. But the hardened part of him refused to let go and give her those three simple words. He pulled away from her kiss. "Em, I…"

Although hurt radiated in her eyes, Emma gave him a shy smile. "It's okay. You don't have to say it back. I just wanted to tell you how I felt." She took his hand in hers. "Come on, we better get going." He let her tug him down the dock and back up the hillside.

CHAPTER THIRTY-TWO

The shrill beeping of the alarm jolted Emma awake. Knowing what a deep sleeper Aidan was, she rolled over, shaking him gently. "Babe, the alarm."

He grunted before smacking his hand on the clock repeatedly before it finally went off.

When Aidan fell back over in bed, Emma fought the urge to run her hands down his bare chest. He was always so handsome in the mornings—his face so rugged, his sandy hair disheveled. Instead, she snuggled against his side. When she draped her leg over his thigh, he stiffened. "You can have the shower first," he mumbled.

"You could always join me," she suggested.

"No, go ahead," he said, pulling away from her. "I wanna sleep in a little longer."

Stung by his words and actions, Emma jerked back. Salty tears streaked down her cheeks as she made her way into the bathroom. He had been so different, so distant since they had come back from the mountains. He had been working later and later hours the last week at the office. By the time he got home at night, she was already in bed or asleep. He hadn't touched her intimately since they had made love on the pond's shore at her grandparents.

Leaning against the shower wall, fear crippled her. Had committing the carnal mistake of telling Aidan she loved him driven him away? What happened now? Did she just pretend she had never uttered it and hope things would return to normal, or did she push things even further by demanding to know what his intentions were?

After spending the entirety of her shower crying, Emma tried to pull herself together to get ready for work. Throwing on her robe, she stepped out of the bathroom. Aidan still hadn't stirred from the bed. Maybe she was making something out of nothing, and he was truly just tired.

She eased down on the mattress and rubbed his bare back. "Wake up, sleepyhead, or you'll be late for work."

He grunted as he rolled over to face her. "Fucking job from hell."

"You haven't forgotten what today is?"

"No, it's the baby's gender sonogram."

Emma smiled that he remembered. "It's at four. You'll still be able to make it, right?"

He fisted the sleep out of his eyes. "Sure. I had Marilyn cancel all my afternoon appointments."

Leaning over, Emma gave him a quick kiss. "I'm glad to hear that." A contented sigh escaped her lips. "I can't wait to see if your dad and Grammy are right about it being a boy."

"Yeah, that'll be something," he said, his voice devoid of emotion. From his tone, she might as well have been discussing whether it was going to rain outside, not what his first born child would be. Instinctively, her hand went to her abdomen as if to protect the baby from Aidan's callous attitude. When he swept his gaze to hers, she ducked her head so he couldn't read the hurt in her eyes.

"So I'll see you this afternoon," he said, flinging the sheet back.

Unable to speak for fear of sobbing, she merely nodded.

Without another word to her or a goodbye kiss, he hopped out of bed and stalked into the bathroom.

When Aidan glanced at himself in the bathroom mirror, he shook his head in disgust. "Yeah, that's right, drive the stake into her heart even deeper, you fucking asshole," he muttered under his breath.

Defeated, he turned on the shower. Standing under the scorching water, he let it pound and singe his skin. He rolled his shoulders from the burden that hung heavy around him. The one he felt cloaked and suffocated by since the day on the dock. Damn that day—the one that had completely fucked up his life. At times, his lips burned from Emma's declaration of love against his mouth after their kiss. Even his fingers tingled, and he could almost feel the baby's movement under them.

Love like he had never known entered him that day, and instead of embracing it, he kept railing against it.

~ 313 ~

Closing his eyes, all he could see was Emma's rejected form in the bedroom, the silent sobs she tried to hide from him. Would it really have killed him to show her a little more attention and kindness on today of all days? He groaned and banged his head against the shower wall. No, he'd gone full on bastard by refusing her advances and acting like a total douchebag about the ultrasound.

Damn, he was just exhausted. The constant traveling and the late hours were wrecking him physically. Then everything with Emma was tearing him apart emotionally. He couldn't sleep without taking something, and he usually had to chase that with alcohol to even get it to work. The more he was in Emma's presence, the more he felt like he was drowning. Like a true coward, he tried avoiding her as much as possible. Some nights he debated sleeping on the couch in his office.

He didn't know what he was going to do. But something had to give.

CHAPTER THIRTY-THREE

For the rest of the day, Emma felt overcome with giddiness. She refused to let Aidan's morning attitude ruin her excitement. Casey lifted her spirits by taking her out for a pre-celebratory lunch. Then at a little after four, she pushed through the doors of her OB/GYN's office and tried to fight her out of control nerves.

When she started to sign in, the receptionist gave her an apologetic smile. "It's probably going to be awhile. Our technician got held up at the Sandy Springs office."

Emma's heart momentarily sank. "You're kidding? You mean I'm going to have to wait even longer? I'm already about to bust!"

"I can only imagine! She's trying to get over here as fast as she can."

Emma grinned. "I understand. I'm just glad I can find out now. I don't know how women waited nine months in the past."

The receptionist laughed. "I know, right? But I promise we'll call you back the minute she walks through the door."

"Thanks." Emma then plopped down in one of the comfy chairs and took her iPad out of her purse. She thought she might as well read until Aidan or the technician showed up. She got so lost in her romance novel she barely realized her phone was ringing.

Grabbing for it, she saw it was Aidan calling. "Hey, where are you?"

When he spoke, his voice was hushed, and she knew he must've been in a meeting or right outside of one. "The fucking CEO showed up out of nowhere two hours ago wanting to go over all the reports we've been working on. I don't know if I'm going to be able to make it."

"It's okay. The sonogram technician is running late from one of their other offices. Just try to come whenever you can, okay?"

"Okay. I'll try."

"Love you," she said.

The only response she got was the click of the line going dead. At first, she tried reasoning with herself that he had to go because of his job. But arguing with herself didn't help. She fought the overwhelming urge to burst out in tears. Not only was she facing the sonogram alone, but Aidan hadn't even bothered to say good-bye. And he still refused to say he loved her back.

Digging a tissue out of her purse to dab her moist eyes, she glanced up at the commotion coming in the doctor's office door. "At least let me go in first and see if it's okay," a familiar voice said.

A man snorted in response. "Screw that! Big Papa can just kiss my ass if he doesn't want me here!"

Emma's heart surged at the sound of Casey and Connor bickering. At the sight of her, they shut up. "Hey, what are you two doing here?"

Connor gazed around the practically empty waiting room. "I think the better question is where's Big Papa?"

Emma rolled her eyes. "Would you stop calling him that? And he got stuck in a meeting."

"Oh," Casey murmured.

They were interrupted by a nurse poking her head into the waiting room. "Ms. Harrison? We're ready for you now."

"Oh, okay, thanks," Emma replied, popping out of her seat. She had hoped for a longer delay to give Aidan more time, but it didn't look like she was in luck.

Out of the corner of her eye, Emma saw Casey throw a hesitant glance at Connor before she stepped forward. "Want us to come back with you?"

Emma nodded. "I'd love that."

Casey beamed while Connor cleared his throat. "We'll just stay until Big Papa, erm, I mean, Aidan gets here. Then we'll let you guys have your moment."

His sincerity and thoughtfulness touched Emma, and she reached out and ruffled his hair—a sign of her affection since their teenage days. She smiled. "Thanks."

The nurse held the door open for them. When they stopped in front of a set of scales, Emma groaned. "Do we really have to do this part?"

The nurse laughed. "Sorry honey. We need to know how much weight you're gaining and how you're measuring."

"Fabulous," Emma replied, stepping on the scales.

Casey and Connor peered over her shoulder to see the number. "Do you guys mind!" Emma exclaimed.

"You've only gained fifteen pounds. That's very good," the nurse said, marking it in Emma's chart.

"Guess you and Big Papa have really been burning the calories when he's in town, huh?" Connor joked. While he and Casey dissolved in giggles, Emma shot them a murderous glance.

They followed the nurse into the ultrasound room, which was muted with light. Emma recognized the technician, Janine, from her previous ultrasounds.

"Big day, huh?" Janine asked.

"Yes, a really big one."

Janine's gaze honed in on Connor. "This must be the proud father, huh?"

Connor widened his eyes, and he held up his hands. "No, no, just a friend."

"The father is caught in a business meeting. I hope he can make it before we're done," Emma explained.

"No problem. I'll be sure to make you photocopies and a DVD of the ultrasound just in case he doesn't."

"Thanks, Janine."

She patted the examining table. "You know the drill by now."

Emma nodded. After climbing up, she laid back and got comfortable. When she started to unbutton her pants, a strangled cry came from Connor's throat. "Wait, you're not going to be naked are you?"

At his apprehension, both Emma and Casey snickered. "No, silly. You're just lucky this is an abdominal one and not a transvaginal," Emma replied.

Connor's brow creased. "What's the difference?"

Janine swiveled in her chair and picked up the transvaginal wand. She waved it at Connor, and he paled when he realized what all it entailed. "Oh shit."

Casey thumped him on the back. "See, nothing to worry about. You're not going to be scarred by having to see Em's vagina."

"Ha, fucking ha," he grumbled. But when he eased down into his chair, he pushed it as far against the wall as possible, so there wouldn't even be the possibility of seeing anything.

Janine squirted the jelly-like substance onto Emma's belly. The coolness caused her to shiver. "Sorry about that. I would have had it warmed for you, but I didn't have time," Janine apologized.

Emma smiled. "It's okay."

Janine then began running the wand over Emma's abdomen. Craning her neck, Emma stared at the grainy image forming on the screen. She sucked in an apprehensive breath until the sound of her baby's heartbeat filled the room.

"For you first timers, there's the heartbeat," Janine said to Connor and Casey before pointing on the screen at the tiny billowing in and out of the heart.

"Oh wow," Casey said.

Janine smiled down at Emma. "It looks *and* sounds very strong, too."

"That's good to hear."

Pressing the wand harder on Emma's stomach, Janine peered at the screen. "Well, you're in luck. Your baby is giving us a pretty good shot between the legs."

"Really?"

Janine nodded. "Sometimes they're lying at angles which block the gender, or they'll just be stubborn and turn where we can't see. But yours must want us to know without a shadow of a doubt."

Emma's chest tightened. Her mouth ran dry, and she licked her lips. Glancing over her shoulder, she eyed Casey and Connor. They both leaned forward so far in their chairs that Emma feared they would fall in the floor.

"So what it is?" Emma croaked.

Janine smiled. "It's a strong, healthy….boy."

A sob erupted from Emma's throat as happy tears stung her eyes. Patrick and Grammy had been right. It was a boy. She was going to give Aidan a son to carry on his family name. She closed her eyes and gave a silent prayer of thanks to God that her son was strong and healthy.

When she opened her eyes, Connor and Casey were at her side. Both leaned over to hug her. "Congratulations, Mama!" Casey said, kissing Em's cheek.

"A boy, huh? Hope he's as handsome and smart as his Gunkle Connor."

"Gunkle?" Emma questioned.

"You know, 'gay uncle'."

Casey snickered. "I'm not sure how Big Papa Fitzgerald is going to feel about that one."

Emma laughed. "I think he'll be okay with it. I mean, who doesn't appreciate people to love their child?"

"Hell yeah, I'm going to love him! He's part of you, so that makes him all the more loveable," Conner said, with a wink.

Janine handed Emma a DVD along with several print-outs of the ultrasound. "Congratulations again."

"Thanks," Emma murmured, her gaze honing in on the grainy images in her hand.

"So when are you going to tell Big Papa?" Casey asked.

"Oh, um, I guess when he gets in tonight. I don't want to tell him over the phone or by text or something."

"You should go surprise him at work," Connor suggested.

Emma ran her fingers over the ultrasound picture. At any moment, she expected it to evaporate and for it all to have been just a dream. After Casey cleared her throat, Emma bobbed her head. "That sounds like a good idea. From the way he sounded, it could be pretty late."

Casey pulled Emma into her embrace and then kissed her cheek. "I'm so proud and happy for you."

Emma grinned. "Thank you." She squeezed Casey tight. "Most of all, thank you for being my rock through all of this, especially today." She smiled at Connor. "And you, too."

"We wouldn't have it any other way," Casey replied as Connor nodded. She kissed Emma's cheek. "Now go on and tell Big Papa the happy news."

"I sure will!"

CHAPTER THIRTY-FOUR

"I want to thank you all for staying late. I'm thrilled at how everything has panned out, and I look forward to a successful merger."

As soon as the CEO exited the boardroom, Aidan dug his phone out of his jacket pocket. Glancing down at the time, he grimaced. There was no way in hell he could get across town to Emma's appointment. Shame echoed through him when he felt relieved at missing the ultrasound. Confirming the baby's sex made its impending arrival all the more real. Loosening his tie, he fought the choking feeling that continued to plague him. His hand tingled again, and he was right back on the dock feeling the baby move with Emma.

He was rubbing his fingers under his collar when someone cleared her throat. He glanced up to find the boardroom empty except for a stacked brunette who was new to his department.

"I don't think we've been formerly introduced," the brunette said with an inviting smile. "I'm Heather Donnovan."

He extended his hand. "Aidan Fitzgerald."

"Oh, I know who you are," Heather replied, letting her hand linger on his a little longer than it should have. "You have quite a reputation here."

Aidan's eyebrows arched. "Do I?"

She nodded. "Both in and out of the boardroom."

For the first time in his whole life, Aidan was completely inept at how to handle a woman's advances. Normally, he would have taken the initiative from the moment she stayed back to be alone with him. But now he was at a total loss for words.

She tilted her head to the right and grinned coyly. "You know I'm new here in Atlanta, so I don't know a lot of people. Would you like to have a drink with me?"

Aidan's heartbeat accelerated as the weight of Heather's question crashed over him. His mind and heart battled against each other. It sent his blood pumping harder and harder through his veins until it pounded like a brass band in his ears. He had been down this road many, many times before. He knew exactly what Heather was insinuating, and it wasn't just a harmless drink after work.

He could almost taste the need radiating off of her. If he made the move, she probably wouldn't object to him fucking her right on the boardroom table. The very thought of pushing up her skirt, tearing off her panties and devouring her sent heat stirring below his waist.

And then the image of Emma lounging on her grandparent's dock, her hand tenderly stroking the belly that carried his child, flashed before his eyes. She loved him, and deep down, he loved her. He shouldn't take Heather's offer. No, he *couldn't* take her offer.

But then the suffocating weight of a relationship and impending fatherhood once again bore down on him. He had never asked for any of it. All he wanted was to finally get Emma into bed and then move on like he always did. He clenched his teeth. Damn, Emma, for making him want more with her...for making him *love* her.

No, he would not drown himself in his feelings for Emma. He would get out now while he still could.

"There's O'Malley's across the street," he croaked.

"That sounds wonderful," Heather replied, her voice a throaty purr.

When he started to walk around the side of the desk, Aidan found himself rooted to the floor. His brain screamed at his feet and legs to pick themselves up, but they refused. It was as if they owed some strange allegiance to his heart and to Emma. At Heather's puzzled expression, he forced a smile to his face. "Sorry, sitting in meetings like that always makes me a little stiff."

"In some places that isn't a problem," she replied, with a giggle.

He laughed at her innuendo while his legs and feet finally worked. He grabbed his briefcase and started out the boardroom door with her.

Even though Heather chatted non-stop the entire elevator ride down, Aidan didn't hear her. He bobbed his head at certain points or smiled, and that seemed to be enough to pacify her. All he could do was focus on what he was trying to accomplish. He had to purge Emma from his system, and if it took fucking Heather to do it, then he was going to do it.

He held the door open for her as they swept into O'Malley's. He cringed at the sight of Jenny behind the hostess booth. At the sight of him, her eyes lit up. Her face started to break into a wide grin, but then she noticed Heather. Her expression immediately darkened, and anger flashed in her usually cool blue eyes.

Aidan cleared his throat. "We need a booth, Jenny."

She shook her head furiously, causing her blonde ponytail to swish back in forth. "I'm sorry, but we seem to be full tonight."

Staring past her, Aidan eyed the half empty bar and turned his pointed gaze back on her. "Looks to me like you've got plenty of room."

"No, I'm sorry we don't. I guess you and your *friend* will have to go somewhere else."

Heather clicked towards Jenny on her high-end heels that Aidan wagered probably cost more than Jenny made in a week. He held his breath as Heather surmised Jenny. Then her plump red lips curved into a cat-like smile. "Looks like someone is a little jealous that we're here together, Aidan. What's the matter, honey? Are you one of Aidan's spurned lovers or former one night stands?" Heather ran her acrylic nails up his back, causing him to shudder. "I'm glad to see you live up to your bad boy reputation. I'm pretty much guaranteed an interesting evening now."

Jenny sputtered something under her breath that Aidan didn't catch. Heather cast one last superior glance at Jenny before saying, "I'll wait for you outside. I'm sure you've got a well-stocked liquor cabinet at your house. No need to waste our time here."

At Heather's departure, Jenny's eyebrows shot up so high they disappeared into her hairline. "Where is Emma? Better yet, what the hell are you doing with *her*?"

Aidan narrowed his eyes. "Frankly, it's none of your damn business!"

"Well, I'm sorry, but when one of my friend's is about to fuck up his life royally, I make it my business!" Jenny countered.

A growl erupted deep in his throat. "I don't need this bullshit from you."

Sadness washed over Jenny's expression. "I'm begging you, Aidan. Don't do this. I've never seen you as happy since you've been coming in here with Emma. She's so good for you, don't you see that?" When he started to walk away, she grabbed his arm. "Before you go home with that skank for a night of mindless and meaningless sex, think long and hard about what you have with Emma, and don't break her heart…and yours."

Aidan stared into Jenny's pleading eyes before slinging her arm away. Without another word, he stormed through the door and out to Heather's side.

***

After Heather followed him home, Aidan got out of the car. He had barely closed the door when Heather launched herself at him, pinning him to the car. His mind instantly flashed back to his and Emma's first kiss in the dingy parking deck. An ache rolled through his chest.

Grabbing Heather to him, he tried to make himself forget. Her tongue swept into his mouth as her fingers went to his hair. Her lips were harsh, and it lacked the tenderness he had with Emma. He shook his head, trying to rid any thoughts of her.

At his reaction, Heather broke their kiss, tugging his bottom lip between her teeth. "Take me inside and fuck me until I scream!"

He chuckled at her directness. "I think I can do that."

It had been so long since he had been with a demanding female. Aidan could barely get up the front walk with Heather running her hands over him as well as rubbing her hips against his. "I have nosy neighbors, you know," he said, when her hand caressed his buttocks.

"Ooh, an audience, huh? That's kinky."

He gazed down at her. "You're a naughty girl, aren't you?"

She giggled. "Oh yeah."

When they got inside, Aidan kicked the front door closed behind him. Heather wrapped her arms around his neck, grinding her pelvis against his groin. Normally, he would have been at half-mast already, but there was nothing stirring below his waist. "Show me your tits," he said, in a voice he couldn't believe was his own. He tried ignoring the churning of his stomach.

With an obliging smile, Heather ripped her shirt over her head. Aidan's hands immediately went to her breasts. After kneading them through her bra, Heather's Double D implants didn't turn him on or feel the same way in his hands that Emma's natural breasts did. He pinched his eyes shut. *Quit fucking thinking about Emma!*

Grabbing Heather by the waist, he dragged them over to the couch. He plopped down and jerked her to straddle his lap. He brought his mouth to hers, desperate to feel anything for Heather and not Emma. After unbuttoning his shirt, Heather raked her nails down his chest. Rocking against him, she moaned against his lips. She was close to getting off just from writing against him, and he felt nothing.

No, that wasn't entirely true. Everything he had ever felt for Emma pulsed through him. Her laugh, her shy smile, her giggle— they flooded his mind. She might as well have been in the room with them. He could feel her all around him. His nose stung with the smell of her perfume while his body ached for the feel of her delicate curves beneath him.

When he dared himself to look at Heather again, he finally felt something. Revulsion. How in the hell had he gotten to this point? What could have possibly possessed him to think bringing

Heather home was a good idea? Fighting the rising bile in his throat, he started to push Heather off his lap.

At the same moment, her hand went to his crotch. When she found his lack of arousal, she jerked her lips off of his. "Um, what's going on?"

Raking a shaky hand through his hair, he sighed. "I can't do this."

She cocked her head at him. "Do you have some impotence problem or something?"

"I wish."

"What the hell does that mean?"

It means you have to leave right now. It means I'm making the biggest mistake of my life. I love Emma, and I cannot do this to her. He shook his head. "I'm really sorry, Heather."

"Aw, don't get embarrassed, babe. We can work this out." She gave him a seductive smile. "*I* can work this out."

CHAPTER THIRTY-FIVE

Halfway to Aidan's office, Emma thought of Beau stuck at Doggy Daycare. "Shit!" She whipped across two lanes to the symphony of honking horns. Her mind had been so occupied with her new baby, she had forgotten all about her old one.

She screeched into a parking space and hurried out of the car. The moment Beau saw her through the fence his entire body started wiggling all over, bringing a grin to Emma's face. "Hiya boy, did you think I'd forgotten you?"

He gave an appreciative bark and ran over to the entrance door to wait for her. Sandy, the owner, greeted Emma with a smile. "I was just beginning to think Beau might end up spending the night with us."

"No, I'm so sorry. I had my ultrasound this afternoon, and it got delayed."

"And what are we having?" Sandy asked.

"A boy."

"Oh that's wonderful!" She opened the door and clipped on Beau's leash. "Did you hear that? You're going to be a big brother."

Beau ignored her and headed straight for Emma. He nudged her belly with his wet nose as if saying hello to the baby. Sandy's eyes widened. "That is so sweet!"

Emma laughed. "He's just started doing that in the last few days. Ironically, after I felt the baby move for the first time." Emma shook her head. "It's like he's finally sensing something is different, and it's not just fat inside this belly!"

Sandy chuckled. "He probably didn't notice anything because you're barely showing!"

"Aw, I appreciate that. I feel like I'm ballooning up."

Beau jerked on his leash. "All right, boy, we'll go home and see Daddy." His ears perked up at the mention of Aidan. "Night, Sandy."

"Night!" she replied, waving.

Emma wrestled Beau to the car and got him inside. "There's no way I'm taking you to Daddy's office. I guess I better drop you off at home before I go see him."

Beau whined at the prospect as they pulled out of the parking lot. Since Aidan's house was closer, she figured she would take him there.

At the sight of Aidan's car in the driveway, Emma's heart shuddered to a stop. The fact a silver Audi sat next to it caused her lungs to constrict. She fought to breathe. Thoughts flashed through her mind like a lightning storm. *He said his meeting was running late. He's supposed to still be at work. He's at home.*

With shaky hands, she killed the engine and opened the car door. Beau lunged out, but Emma didn't even bother holding his leash. Instead she focused on trying to put one foot in front of the other up the sidewalk.

Using the key he'd given her, she pushed open the front door. The living room was bathed in darkness except for the muted lights from the chandelier. Aidan lounged on the couch while a leggy brunette straddled his lap. He was still fully clothed except his shirt was unbuttoned and untucked. The woman, on the other hand, had stripped off her shirt, and her short skirt had ridden up her thighs. Aidan's hands were on her forearms as if he was about to push her off of him.

For a few agonizing seconds, Emma could only stare in disbelief. Blinking, she tried waking herself up from the nightmare in front of her, but no matter how hard she tried, she couldn't. It was all too real. The man she loved and the father of her child had stood her up on one of the most important days of her life to screw another woman. A strangled cry erupted from her lips.

At the noise behind them, Aidan startled. When he saw Emma standing there, his eyes widened in horror, and he sucked in a breath. "What are you doing here?" he demanded.

Tears pricked and stung her eyes, but Emma gave a maniacal laugh. "What am *I* doing here? I think the better question is what the hell are *you* doing?"

The sound of another voice caused the brunette to whirl around. Her gaze trailed from Emma's face down to her swollen belly. A hiss erupted from her lips before she shook her head. "I don't fucking believe this." She turned her head and then her wrath on Aidan. "No wonder you couldn't get it up! The guilt of cheating on your pregnant wife must've really been eating at you!"

"She's not my wife…yet," Aidan replied, his voice hushed.

The brunette sent a stinging slap across Aidan's cheek, and Emma had to bite her lip not to thank her for doing it. At that moment, she would have loved to have done far worse physical harm to him. "I don't care what she is! You're a fucking bastard!" She jerked herself off Aidan's lap and snatched up her shirt. After throwing it over her head, she grabbed her heels and stalked towards Emma. The fury in her face melted a little. "I'm really sorry. I heard at work he was a player, and I wanted a play. I had no idea…" her voice trailed off as she glanced at Emma's stomach.

"Thank you," Emma whispered as the woman started on by. She jumped at the slamming of the front door. On wobbly legs, she took a few step forwards, closing the gap between her and Aidan. He rose up on the couch, fumbling with the buttons on his shirt.

When she stood there, just staring, he exhaled a ragged breath. "Say something."

Emma raised her eyebrows at him. "And what would you like me to say?"

"I don't know…just anything to keep you from looking at me like that."

"Well, frankly, I think your female friend said it best. You're a fucking bastard!"

"I agree."

"And that's all you have to say for yourself? Not that you're sorry you valued the importance of today so little you skipped out on the ultrasound to cheat on me?"

Aidan shook his head. "I didn't sleep with her."

She threw her hands up in exasperation. "You were going to before I interrupted you!"

"I swear to you I was not going to screw her. I had just told her I couldn't, and that she should leave. Jesus, you heard her yourself say I couldn't get it up!"

"And that's supposed to make me feel better about the fact you had some skank riding you when I walked in here?"

"Look, I admit I fucked up. But I *am* sorry."

"Oh, I guess you're also sorry you lied to me when you said you would change. God, I was so stupid to believe you would treat me any different than Amy or the other women. I should have realized this is who you are and what you do."

"Emma, please, I am sorry!"

"Really? Do you honestly feel that or are those just some words you think you can say to make things right between us?" Her voice choked off with the sobs rising in her throat. "Are you really and truly sorry you broke my heart?"

Aidan winced. "You have no idea what I've been going through lately. I'm never going to be all that you need me to be, Emma. And the pressure from trying just broke me."

She didn't bother wiping away the tears streaming down her cheeks. "So what you're saying is trying to have a relationship with me drove you into the arms of another woman?"

His expression became anguished. "No, that's not what I mean." He shook his head wildly. "I'm fucking up what I need to say and do. And you're making this harder on me. I feel bad enough for what I've done."

"Harder on *you*?" she questioned, her voice raising an octave. "How could this possibly be hard on you? I'm the one who opened myself up to all this pain despite my better judgment." She ground the tears out of her eyes with her fist.

He took a step towards her, but she backed away from him. "Don't you dare touch me after your hands have been all over that whore!"

"Emma, please don't do this. I told you I was sorry. I'll do whatever it takes to make it up to you."

Without even thinking, Emma blurted, "Tell me you love me."

He stared at her, unblinking and unmoving. "What?"

"You've been emotionally shut off from me since the day I told you I loved you. So if you really mean it when you say you're sorry and you really don't want me to go, then say the words. Tell me you love me."

At his hesitation, stabbing pain crisscrossed through her chest. The silence echoed through her as loud as a freight train. She shook her head. "That's what I thought," she murmured.

Her hands went to the purse at her side, and she fumbled for the DVD of the sonogram. Using all the hurt and anger welling inside her, she chucked it at him. It smacked hard against his chest, causing Aidan to wince. "Not that you're even interested, but that's a video of your *son*. I can only hope and pray he grows up to be nothing like his father!"

Sobbing, she turned and fled from the room. Beau followed her out the door, howling and crying right along with her. As she fumbled with her keys, Aidan called several times for her to come back, but she refused. Then he started calling for Beau.

"Go back, boy," Emma instructed, pointing a shaky finger to Aidan. She flung open the car door, but he still wouldn't leave her side.

"Dammit, Beau, I said come!" Aidan shouted, stepping off the porch. He stalked over to them and tried dragging Beau back by the collar.

But Beau jerked away. His nose nuzzled Emma's belly, and he whined. Emma met Aidan's horrified glance. "Yeah, that's right. Your dog is even more loyal to me and your son than you are!"

With a defeated look, Aidan hung his head and released Beau's collar. "Fine, take him."

"Come on, boy. Get in the car," Emma instructed. Beau wagged his tail and eagerly hopped inside. Without another look at Aidan, she slammed the door. Squealing out of the driveway, she tried to keep her emotions in check. But it was no use. She got half a block down the road before she had to pull over. Tears blinded her eyes to where she couldn't see in front of her, and she couldn't breathe from the sobs raging through her chest.

A knock at her window caused her to jump. Hope ricocheted through Emma that Aidan had come after her. Glancing up, her heart fell.

Becky stood outside the car, peering curiously at her. "Emma?"

Damn. She hadn't even thought about the prospect of ending up on Becky's street. The last person she wanted to see was one of Aidan's sisters. Mortified, she wiped her eyes with the back of her hand and tried to compose herself. Finally, she pressed the button to roll down the window. "Hi," she said, meekly.

Becky sucked in a breath. "Oh God, he didn't?"

Tears once again filled Emma's eyes. Unable to speak, she merely bobbed her head.

"I'm so, so sorry. He loves you, sweetheart. I know he does. The whole family knows it. He's just being a stupid asshole."

Emma hiccupped between a sob. "Tell that to him and the woman he was about to sleep with before I walked in."

Becky's eyes widened. "I'm going to *kill* him," she muttered through gritted teeth. She shook her head. "And if I don't, one of the other girls will. God forbid this gets back to Pop." Becky opened the car door. "Get out. You're coming inside with me."

"No, I can't. I'm a mess. What would I say to the boys?"

"Tate's got them at movies tonight. It's just me."

When Emma continued to hesitate, Becky crossed her arms over her chest. "Listen, you're coming in the house with me if I have to drag you myself."

"I'm parked on the side of the street."

"It'll be fine." Becky eyed Beau in the backseat. "What are you doing with him?"

"He wouldn't let me go."

Becky snorted. "Whoever said men are dogs missed the mark. Beau's got true loyalty."

Emma gave a half-hearted smile. "Tell me about it."

Becky pulled Emma out of her seat and wrapped an arm around her waist. "Listen, we're going to order in some Chinese or pizza or whatever you and the baby want. Then I'm going to call the girls. We're going to have a strategy meeting about Aidan."

Emma threw up her hands. "And just what do you hope to achieve? Hog tie him and force him to be with me? In case you missed the memo, he doesn't want me! He's made that abundantly clear not only by almost screwing another woman, but by not being able to tell me he loves me."

"It's not like this is the first time he's done this, Em. Surely he's told you about Amy?"

"Yeah, how he wouldn't propose, and then she caught him with another woman and broke up with him."

"Did he also tell you how he spent the better part of that year drunk and in and out of therapy because he had a nervous breakdown over what he did to her?"

Emma gasped. "No, he didn't."

"Hmm, I guess he also managed to leave out the part where he tried over and over again to get her to come back to him, but she refused? He finally had to give up when she married someone else."

Emma could hardly believe her ears. Aidan had lied to her about what had happened with Amy. He had never allowed the true depth of his feelings for Amy to be known. "He never told me any of that."

"I know my brother. He did what he did to you tonight to push you away, not because he wanted to screw another woman. He self-sabotages himself every damn time!" She grunted in frustration. "By the way he acts about relationships, you would think he was raised in some dysfunctional home by crack-heads or something."

Emma leaned against the car and put her head in her hands. "I don't think I can handle all this!"

Becky pulled Emma's hands away, and then stared her in the eye. "You've got to decide right here and now if you're going to fight for him."

"Me? Why the hell do I have to do the fighting? He's the one who fucked up royally!"

"I didn't say he didn't. But fighting for him doesn't mean you're a doormat and go running back to his open arms, Em. It means you're willing to put up with whatever bullshit it takes to get him to win you back."

"You actually think he's going to try?"

Becky grinned. "Oh yes. Tomorrow morning, maybe even tonight, Aidan Fitzgerald is going to rue the day he ever let you walk out of his life, and you're going to get to enjoy every minute of it!"

CHAPTER THIRTY-SIX

Aidan sat in the pitch black living room for hours after Emma left. He would reach for his phone to call her and then stop himself. He would start to get up to go after her and then think himself a fool.

No, he wasn't what she needed. He could never live up to her expectations of what a husband and father should be. They were both better off. He had wanted a way out for the past week, and he had found it.

But instead of feeling relief, he felt misery.

Freedom from the choking and suffocating emotions hadn't come with Emma's departure. Instead, they felt tighter around him than ever before. Defeated, he rose off the couch to grab a beer. His foot accidentally kicked the DVD case across the room. He left it laying there as he headed into the kitchen.

After snatching the six pack out of the fridge, he started back into the living room. His eye caught the plastic DVD case, and he stopped to pick it up. Tossing it on the table, he turned on the TV and started flipping through the channels.

It was after his third beer that the curiosity finally got to him. He took the DVD out and put it in the machine. The sound of the latest basketball game faded, and it was replaced by a thump-thumping echoing through the room.

His son's heartbeat.

Frozen, Aidan stared at the grainy image on the television screen. The last time he had seen the baby it barely resembled anything. It was a strange tadpole looking thing. Now its features were prominent—its arms and legs flailed while its tiny mouth fluttered open and shut.

If he had been paralyzed by the emotions when he felt the baby move, they were nothing compared with actually seeing his son. A part of him was growing strong and healthy inside Emma. A child that he had promised his mother he would have.

But his son was gone. And so was Emma. He had thrown happiness away with both hands. Sinking down on the couch, he allowed the sobs to roll through him. The last time he had cried had been when he had lost his mother. Now he was experiencing another soul crushing loss.

With trembling fingers, he reached for his phone. After dialing the familiar number, he brought the phone to his ear. "Please answer, please answer," he begged.

"Hello?"

"Pop, it's me. I've fucked up, and I need your help."

To be continued in *The Proposal* out March 15, 2013

Acknowledgements

They say it takes a village to raise a child, and it certainly takes one to make a book come to fruition. The bulk of *The Proposition* came out of one of the darkest times of grief and despair in my adult life. It was a tiny ray of sunlight that broke through the dark clouds surrounding me. Spending time with Emma and Aidan and the cast of characters has been such a comfort and joy. I thank God from whom all blessings flow for giving me a gift of story-telling.

First, I have to thank Kelli Maine, Emily Snow, and Michelle Valentine for being treasured friends, writing buddies, and critique partners over the last three years. I don't know what I would have done without you ladies in both the professional and personal side of life. Thanks for talking me down from the ledge numerous times!! YOU ROCK!! GGBT FOREVER!!

Thanks also to Emily Snow for all things formatting and book trailers and questions!!!

Thanks go to my newest bestie and member of the Naughty Mafia, Kristen Proby. I feel like people are put into our lives for a purpose, and your friendship, help, support, and "ending magic" is appreciated more than I can ever say.

To my other beta readers: Rachel M, Riley G, Rachael A, Lori, and Rachel S: thanks for helping make *The Proposition* as amazing as it could be!!

To the ladies of LB for allowing me to share snips for critiques & giving me great support and feedback.

To Marilyn Medina for her unending support and pimping *The Proposition* as well as being an "eagle on" on the scene for typos. I feel like you were brought into my life as well—especially considering we are twinsies in so many ways!

I can't help but give an ENORMOUS heartfelt thanks to the writers, readers, and bloggers of the Romance community. After being held POW in the Young Adult world for two years, it has been a breath of fresh air being so warmly welcomed by you. Your support, your fangirling, your camaraderie is like nothing I have experienced before, and I am eternally grateful. You made writing enjoyable for me again.

Thanks also go to my family and friends who have always supported me in everything I do, including my writing. I love you all lots.

About the Author

Katie Ashley lives outside of Atlanta, Georgia with her two very spoiled dogs and one outnumbered cat. She is a writer of Romance and Erotic fiction. She has a slight obsession with Pintrest, *The Golden Girls*, Shakespeare, *Supernatural*, and *Scooby-Doo*. If speaking pretentiously, she has a BA in English, a BS in Secondary English Education, and a Masters in Adolescent English Education. By day, she educates the Youth of America by teaching high school English in the burbs.

She is the author of ***The Proposition*** and ***Music of My Heart***, which debuts Winter 2012

The Proposal, the sequel to ***The Proposition***, will be out March 15

Made in the USA
Charleston, SC
14 July 2014